WHAT FRESH HELL IS THIS?

DARK TALES

DEL HOWISON

FOREWORD BY CLIVE BARKER

Published by Crystal Lake Publishing
Where Stories Come Alive!

Crystal Lake Publishing
www.CrystalLakePub.com

WELCOME
TO ANOTHER

CRYSTAL LAKE PUBLISHING
CREATION

TABLE OF CONTENTS

This book is for every editor who took a chance on one of my stories and bought it for their anthologies. It is always a thrill to be included. It is also a good beginning for new writers and a chance to work out ideas in a succinct format. It also lets us old dogs know we are still productive and alive.

Most importantly, this book is dedicated to my wife, Sue, for taking a chance on me.

"The best way out is always through."
—**Robert Frost**

PREFACE

What is in the darkness? Everything.

EVERYBODY HAS A story to tell. Some of us have three or four. Some of us can't shut up. But that's the beauty of a book. The reader can shut a book. I don't happen to feel that the story must be long to be good. Some authors think a five-volume mega fantasy of a million words is better just because it is a million words and not 500,000 words. To which I reply "Pssst!" Yes, that's my tongue sticking out.

It's not that I haven't written novels, but there is something inherently stunning and gut-wrenching about a good short story. A laugh. A scream. The short sharp shock. A question that has hung with you for years. Maybe it's an unsettling feeling of dread you can't shake. It is all accomplished in about 7,000 words.

Once, when I interviewed Peter Straub, he told me, "I don't know how people write that little." That's one of the greats still puzzling over the construction of a tale so tight and easy in its succinctness that you finish reading it and just sit there pondering what the author has inserted into your brain. You wonder, *What Fresh Hell Is This?*

I've always felt an author's introduction should really be a part of the work. For me, it doesn't matter how many flowers you surround the graves with, if the writing is no good it's dead. You can't convince people that the stories are good if they ain't. Also remember that past performance is no indication of future enjoyment. Some settling of contents may have occurred during shipping. At least that's what it used to say on the side of my cereal box. The first thing I remember reading, a cereal box. The first words were "Free Prize Inside!" When you open the pages of this book, I hope you'll discover a prize or two inside.

My excuse is for the future. If you enjoy the stories, keep on the lookout for my next book. It may suck. I don't happen to think these do. I've had some practice with short stories, articles, novels, nonfiction, essays and what-not. I've been short-listed for a few awards and won a couple. Nice, but ultimately meaningless. The writer is only as good as their last story.

A final point about the stories inside. Some have appeared in anthologies, magazines, and online venues. Those have been touched up here as I'm never satisfied. I never quit writing something even if it is already written. Ray Bradbury taught me that.

I purchased a zombie drawer story from him. That's a story he had written and then put away in a drawer. He hadn't touched it since, that is, until I asked for a dark tale. He told me he'd send it over in a week or so. "Need to clean it up a bit first." A couple of these are original tales showing up for the first time anywhere, just like Ray's zombie story in the Dark Delicacies anthology. None of these have ever been collected in one volume before.

What you are about to read here are some of my strange ones. All of these were penned in 2023 and before. There will be more I can assure you of that. But in the meantime, I leave you these, along with a big heap of anticipation for my next project. I hope the darkness doesn't keep you awake tonight.

Thank you.

Del Howison
Burbank, CA
2024

FOREWORD

DURING THE SECOND World War, two quintessential Englishmen, film director David Lean and playwright Noël Coward, were together at work on a film about the Atlantic war, 'In Which We Serve'. Lean, who was the younger man, was intrigued by Coward's ability to keep his audience returning to his work, whether on stage, screen, or printed word, with fascination and delight.

"How do you do it?" Lean asked Coward.

Coward replied, "I always pop out of another hole."

With Coward's words in mind, there is proof of how well that dictum continues to work. In an age when generic loyalties can easily become smothering, it's wonderful to be able to celebrate the work of a writer who is willfully diverse. I speak of my friend Del Howison.

In 2019, Del wrote an extraordinary book that in its own way explores the labyrinth of emotions silenced by anger and grief, leading to a journey that inverts all expectations. The book is *The Survival of Margaret Thomas*. It is narrated by Margaret, and the tale it tells is both meticulously realistic while constantly offering the reader hints of a greater metaphysical pattern at work between the surface of the grim, desperate lives of its characters.

To say more would rob you of the chance to explore for yourselves the layers of meaning the book provides. Clearly this is a one-of-a-kind idea, not least because it is written so flawlessly.

Del now had to find a whole new way to surprise us.

Here's what he did.

He gave us an exceptional collection of his wildly divergent earlier fictions. They were written for a variety of anthologies and are each prefaced by a brief summary of how they came into being. There are stories here that sound almost as though Del had been cajoled into setting these tales down against his will; Del, the reluctant creator.

But Lord! I hope with all my heart that there will always be the sweetest voices surrounding him to send him back to his computer, enthusiastic editors who are aware of Del's singular visions of the world, whether historical or contemporary, and there will always be ways for Del to show his radical aesthetic.

Certainly, the great span of tones and styles Del brings to his fiction suggests there are very few forms of writing he cannot turn to his purpose.

Often, when called upon to write a forward such as this, I would take the opportunity to comment about favorite stories or tease the reader with what some of the tales will offer. Indeed, I wrote two paragraphs which did just that, and upon revising the text realized that such revelations were redundant, even damaging to the special nature of Del's skills. They are fictions which, like his novel, explore unexpected events in a voice that is uniquely his.

Therefore, *What Fresh Hell Is This* must remain uncharted by me in this foreword. I will gladly commend the journey to you, by all means, and celebrate the skills of your guide, Mr. Howison, but thereafter you must dare to tread this terrain that has neither sign, nor history, or stains to tell who has died there.

A fresh hell, indeed.

Clive Barker
Los Angeles
2024

The Lost Herd was my second published short story. Editor Jeff Gelb picked it up for book 11 in his erotic horror anthology series Hot Blood: Strange Bedfellows. *During a signing for the book at Dark Delicacies in Burbank, Ca., I asked Jeff if he might be interested in co-editing an anthology book named after the store. From that meeting three books under the Dark Delicacies banner were created featuring some of the strongest names in horror writing.*

That day truly changed my life, and I will forever be in Jeff's debt for that personal kick start. Lionsgate Entertainment bought The Lost Herd for a horror anthology television series called Fear Itself. *Show creator and director Mick Garris scripted it and then a writers' strike happened. It was sent north to Canada where the show was filming and at least two Canadian screenwriters rewrote the script. By the time the story aired (as the show's premiere and highest-rated episode) in 2008, it had been renamed "The Sacrifice" and contained only the barest bones of my tale. It was no longer a western but now a modern tale of gunrunners and a vampire had been added for good measure.*

But the check cleared, and I now had single card television credit for "Based on The Lost Herd by Del Howison". It was Mick, more than anyone, who made the story come alive on screen. I'm grateful.

THE LOST HERD

"Violence, even well intentioned, always rebounds upon oneself."
—Lao Tzu

THE RAIN MOVED like sheets across the open spaces of the landscape, flowing with the wind, like waves attacking a beach. It allowed the men to look up between breakers to see where they were riding. That would have been helpful had they known exactly where they were. The brims of their hats acted like gutters, funneling the rain to shoot off in mini-waterfalls and splash against the bodies of the horses they rode. The beasts themselves plodded, heads down, sightless in the downpour. Not wanting to stop for fear of drowning while standing up. Shelter, any shelter, against the weather would have been a welcome sight.

They had picked up the herd of cows three days south of the normal trail, but hadn't made it back to familiar surroundings. The men had lost the herd when, stupid and panic-stricken from flashes of lightening and slaps of thunder, the cows had run into the darkness, mooing and screaming. The men had tried to keep them calm, lest they lose a season's livelihood, but to no avail. The terrain was unfamiliar to them. Now they were lost, looking for somewhere to stop to save the rain from beating them into mush.

The rocks jutted and rose in angular slabs around them; the muddy trail they rode seemed to be the singular path between them. For all they knew, it could end in a boxed canyon or a cliff's edge in the darkness.

The point rider moved carefully between the jagged stones. As point man he was known for having cat's eyes, but even those served him little in the rain. Water gushed through the openings as they worked their way up the incline, nearly forcing them to turn and swim back down the river of mud and tumbling stone.

Gray light told them they had been riding all night and morning was arriving, with no relief in sight from the relentless downpour. Nobody spoke, even though the thunder had ceased some time ago. The downpour splashing against the rocks combined with the rushing of the water through the cut was too loud for conversation and they were too sullen for talk. There was nothing to say that each of them wousn't already thinking.

As the point man reached the top of the climb, the rocks seemed to open onto a plateau where all five of the riders could gather side by side. The point man turned to the big man riding just behind him and pointed into the distance. There, through the weak light of the new day, were the dark shadowy shapes of what appeared to be buildings. The other three pulled up alongside their leader.

"Could just be some more rock sides. Hard to tell from here," said the big man who'd been riding second.

"Hope not." Point turned and looked at one of the other riders. "Joplin is getting weak. We might have lost him if he hadn't been tied to his horse."

"Only one way to find out," returned the big man. "I just hope we're not riding out of Hell and into Hades."

He gave his mount a quick nudge with his heels and a cluck, riding ahead in the direction of the shapes. Point was next, and the other three, with nothing to lose at this juncture, followed suit. Joplin slumped forward more than the others. Holding tight onto his saddle horn, he tried to make the awkward ride as pain free as possible.

As they picked their way down the slope, the rain began to lighten up, along with their moods. Rounding a boulder, the trail dropped through some trees and the building shapes disappeared into the misty forest in the distance. Surrounding bushes and foliage indicated the steep drop in elevation they were taking on the trail. Even the smells changed, earthy with the greenery surrounding them on all sides, giving the feel of a living cave as the forest's throat swallowed them.

The rain, even though it was lessening, seemed harder, dripping from the leaves and branches. It was uneven, sporadic in its fall, splashing off the horses and men. The darkness of the woods seemed to close out sound as well as light, like the earth itself was guiding them deep into its bowels. The big man pulled up and waited for the others behind him to stop. He was peering straight ahead, as if somebody could squint to hear better.

Point broke the silence.

"What is it, Ray?"

"Nothing," he said, almost in awe. "Absolutely nothin'."

Point looked ahead and then glanced back at the others. Lemon shrugged his shoulders. Justin spit and his horse pawed the ground impatiently as he looked back up at Point.

"I've stopped for a lot of things in my life, Ray," said Point. "But I ain't never stopped for "nothin'". Right now, I'm telling you it's really gonna be somethin' if we don't get moving."

As if on cue, Joplin slid to one side of his saddle, his rope catching him from falling off his mount. He screamed out in pain and Lemon moved up alongside him, helping to straighten him up. Justin grabbed Joplin from the other side and pulled him up. Lemon looked over to Ray.

"We gotta get him off this horse, Ray! The bleeding is getting worse. This shirt is soaked through and it ain't rainwater."

"Well, we can't do it here." Ray looked back at the injured rider. "Let's keep moving. Maybe we'll run into those buildings up ahead. Ain't but one trail down so far as I can tell. If those were buildings, we gotta run into 'em."

"Yeah, and if they weren't buildings, we may have a dead man on our hands. We gotta get inside."

"Lemon!" Ray glared at the rider. "You have a better idea? Because if you don't then shut the hell up! Joplin ain't dead yet."

His voice softened in earnest. "It can't be too much further."

Ray kicked his horse back into action and continued on. Justin looked at Lemon who shrugged his shoulders, and then joined the single-file line down the trail. Point stood off to one side and let the line pass. He looked back into the darkness they'd come from. There was nothing. No sound. No light. No good. No good at all. He shook the reins of his horse to join the others and moved after them in the direction of the approaching dawn.

They had just broken through the tunnel of trees when Point called out, "Ho Ray!" The line of horses stopped and turned back towards Point. Joplin sat slumped forward on his horse, his arms dangling lifelessly. Point quickly unmounted and ran up to Joplin, raising his head by grabbing a handful of hair.

Ray came riding up. "Is he still with us?"

"Hard to tell," Point said, lifting Joplin's eyelids and then letting his head drop back down. "He's either out cold from the pain or he's dead."

Ray took his rope off his saddle and handed it down to Point.

"Here, tie his hands around the horse's neck. He'll stay mounted." He looked up in the direction they'd been headed. "It can't be far now. At least that will keep him mounted until we get there."

Point took Joplin's arms and wrapped them around the horse's neck. Then he coupled his hands together like a prisoner and tied them off.

"If we get there," he said.

Point walked back to his horse and took down his own rope. He tied one end to the reins of Joplin's horse, then jumped up on his horse and tied the other end to his saddle horn. He looked up at Ray.

"That's best we'll get. Let's go."

Ray swung his mount around and continued in the direction they had been going. Point followed with Joplin's horse in tow. The other two followed them in case Joplin figured out another way to drop off his saddle. They shot a look at the sky. No sun today. Overcast and rain seemed like the forecast, even though it kept getting lighter as the new day forced itself past the darkness.

Peeking through the thinning line of trees, the gray structures stood before them like washed-out monuments from another era. They were mining buildings, weathered and long since out of use. A mining camp from a dead vein.

From what must have been the workers' boarding house on the far side of the camp came the sound of a door opening. A woman in a slip and undershirt stepped out onto the wooden porch.

The shirt was slit in a long vee-shape and her breasts threatened to slip sideways into view with every movement. She held a shotgun in her hands, diagonally across her chest. It wasn't threatening, but it was available. She smiled as the group slowly rode towards her. Her teeth were so white they seemed to reflect what little daylight was available.

"Hello, boys. Kinda off the beaten path, aren't you?"

Ray pulled his horse to a stop in front of the porch and looked her over. He guessed her to be about twenty. Her undergarments, which had once been white, showed a lot of dirt up close.

It could have been her work outfit or her everyday wear considering the torn edges and frayed threads. Her arms were dirty from what Ray figured must have been digging. She was very thin but still gave off an aura of sexuality; a girl with the experience of a woman. When she smiled, the men could feel it in their groins. Her eyes took them each in individually. They shifted self-consciously in their saddles. Justin wrapped his hand around his saddle horn. Ray looked up at the smoke rising from the boarding house's chimney.

"I take it you live here?"

"Yep," she confirmed and shifted her weight onto her other foot. "If you call this living. It gets a little lonely out here."

"You live here alone?"

Point rode up beside Ray to get a better look.

"Not really!" The voice came from the far end of the porch as another girl stepped from around the corner. She also held a shotgun.

"Boys, this is my sister, Virginia. I'm Chelsea."

Virginia nodded at the men and licked her lips. She swiped the back of her hand across her mouth, wiping what appeared to be blood from her face. Her hands were wet and stained a dusty red. The nail on her index finger extended well beyond the tip of her finger but the other nails were black and broken off at different lengths, some down to the quick.

"You boys will have to excuse me. Wasn't expecting' no company. I just finished eatin' but I'm sure we could rustle up a little grub for you if you're hungry."

She carried a little more weight than her sister. Her clothes hid more curves and roundness.

She wasn't much cleaner than Chelsea, but smiled the same toothy grin. Point realized that they hadn't crossed any running water on the way in. Maybe there was none. Maybe all they had was a well for drinking. Joplin groaned and Ray shot him a look.

"I need to get my man inside. He is very ill."

"Follow me," Chelsea said with a waggle of her finger. "I like the way you talk. To the point. You can lay him down inside."

Justin and Lemon jumped down from their horses while Point held their leads steady. They untied Joplin and lowered him gently from his mount. Justin slipped his arms underneath Joplin's, while Lemon grabbed his feet. Joplin moaned again, on the edge of consciousness. It was a good sign. He was still with them. They walked him up the porch and inside.

"Go ahead Ray," Point said. "I'll tie up the horses and be right in."

"Yeah, go ahead Ray," a sultry voice behind them mimicked.

They turned and saw a third woman standing back a ways. She wore jeans, a torn long underwear shirt, and a pair of pistols slung just below her navel. Her hands rested on the pistol butts. Unlike the other two women, she seemed built for speed instead of just comfort. Ray grinned at Point.

"Don't be too long. I want to make sure Joplin's taken care of," Ray said over his shoulder as he walked up the porch and into the boarding house. Point took the reins to his horse and looped them around the hitching post. After doing the same with Ray's horse, he picked the reins of the other two back up and turned towards the girl.

"You got a stable here?"

She took a few steps toward him. Her sexuality was as palpable as heat. There was an old hunger present.

"Sure do," she purred and flashed him her pearlies. "Doesn't get used as much as it should, I mean with just our three horses. Lots of nice clean hay just waiting for somebody like you.

Some nice straw in there for bedding also. . .follow me."

"I don't see a problem with that," said Point.

He watched her turn and walk towards the outbuildings across the way. Her ass pitched from side to side as she went. It was a nice, tight ass, and it moved well in time with the rest of her body. He was beginning to feel his own heat rising. All that riding in the rain and in the dark had created an appetite growing within him, and it wasn't just for food. He clicked his tongue and led the horses after her. His eyes were glued to the earthquake movements of her body.

Virginia watched them cross the square and smiled to herself. She walked down the long porch and into the front door of the boarding house.

Someone swept off the top of a table with their hand, scattering the contents about the floor.

They laid Joplin on it and ripped his shirt open. Chelsea stood with Ray at Joplin's side. Her breasts heaved against the light material of the top she was wearing as she watched with concern. Despite the dirt and sweat that coated her chest, there was a feeling of animal yearning that swirled someplace deep in Ray's body. She kept glancing up at him and he suddenly wasn't as tired as he should have been.

"What happened to him?" She looked up at Ray in concern.

He thought about how nice it would be to touch her. He could see the shape her nipples made against the material.

"We'd become separated from the herd when it scattered in fright from the thunder and lighting," Ray started. "This is unfamiliar country to us, never been this far south. We knew we couldn't catch them all and we knew we needed shelter. We kicked our horses and started running after what we thought was the largest group of cattle, figuring they'd naturally find safe shelter from the storm. We entered the woods running at top speed. I guess the branch was low and stickin' out just right. It caught Joplin in the chest - like a spear it nearly ran through him, lifting him off his saddle."

"Oh shit," Virginia cursed and shuddered visibly while hugging her arms tight against her chest. It was like she was feeling that pain herself. She turned and walked away from the group. Chelsea shot her a look of agitation and then turned back to Ray.

"Lemon and I pulled him off," Ray continued, ". . .and Justin was lucky enough to pick up his horse, which had pulled up in the trees. We tied him to the saddle and somehow picked our way through the darkness to here."

Chelsea was breathing heavily as she bent over Joplin to examine the wound. She ran her fingers slowly along the edges where some of the blood had dried, causing him to moan in his stupor. She held up her blood-coated fingers to the light, examining them closely, her tongue sticking out slightly from between her lips. She picked some small dark pieces of bark off them.

"This wound will need to be cleaned out. If you boys can move him to the bed in that first room there, Virginia and I can see what we can do."

She turned in the direction of where Virginia had gone. "Virginia, bring in a bowl of fresh water."

Chelsea threw her leg up on a chair seat and began ripping a piece of cloth from the bottom of her filthy slip. Ray looked at her leg and began to feel the heat again. He felt an overwhelming desire to slowly run his hand up the inside of her knee and her thigh, until he felt the soft slit of skin he knew waited. His large hand could wrap itself almost entirely around the soft top of her leg. He knew how nice that would feel. She looked up at him as she tore the cloth with those magnificent teeth and smiled. He felt as if she could read his thoughts and a small pang of embarrassment flashed through him. She let the garb rise higher than needed as she worked it.

Its seam was high enough that, from his angle, he could see a tuft of hair edging its way out from under the edge of the cloth. She finished tearing and followed the two men carrying Joplin into the bedroom and promptly shooed them out.

"You send Virginia in with the water as soon as she gets here," she said.

She gave Ray one last smile and shut the door. Virginia went in a minute later, also shutting the door behind her.

Ray shook his head to clear his thoughts. He couldn't remember getting a rise that quickly before. Suddenly, it was as if the exhaustion covered him in a cloud and he plopped himself down in the nearest straight chair. The other two had already slid down the wall to sit on the bare floor. The Spartan furnishings didn't offer them much choice.

* * *

Point entered the barn with the horses. It was clean and utilitarian. No extras. She pointed to a couple of empty stalls next to what he assumed were the ladies' horses.

"Take your pick," she said. "I'll get some hay for them."

He watched her walk away and shook his head to himself about the upcoming prospect of bedding her right there in the fresh new straw.

"Thank you."

Point placed the horses in the stall and then fetched the other two and put them in the adjoining bin. By then she had returned with a wheelbarrow full of hay.

"Here, let me take that for you." Point awkwardly moved his arms around her to grab the handles. His crotch rubbed against that fabulous ass of hers and immediately he began to grow hard. She spun around inside his arms so that her breasts were pressed against his chest. She hummed a little guttural noise deep in her throat, and then ducked out from under his arms.

"Thank you for helping with the hay," she cooed. "We don't get many visitors out here, you know."

He wheeled the barrow over to the stalls and began pitching the hay to the horses. "I can imagine. How do you make it here?"

She sashayed over to him, twirling a strand of hair with her fingers as she spoke.

"Oh, we got a few head of beef and some chickens out back. We grow some of our own food and we barter with folks like yourself who may happen to come by. But that ain't often enough."

Point threw the last bunch of hay into the stall and turned to her. "You grow enough to barter with?"

Somehow, she just didn't strike him as the farmer type.

"Not really," she said.

"So, what do you trade with?" he asked.

She smiled and closed the distance between them.

———

The bedroom door finally creaked open and the two girls stepped out. There was blood splattered on both of them, and Chelsea was wiping her hands with the bloodied piece of cloth she had torn from her clothes. Virginia absentmindedly brushed a wisp of hair out of her face, leaving a trail of crimson across her cheek. Ray stood up to go into Joplin's room, but Chelsea placed a bloody hand on his chest.

"It's best you leave him alone right now. He's got a fever, but he's sleeping. I cleaned out the wound as best I could, but I don't have much to work with."

She smiled up into Ray's face and then grabbed his hand and started leading him away.

"Maybe you'd be kind enough to help me get cleaned up? Virginia, see if the other two boys there can help you out with your problem."

She led Ray down the hall to a door at the end, while Virginia stood before the two cowboys with her bloody hands on her hips. She began pulling her top off.

"How about some help boys?" she inquired. "I'm real dirty."

———

Out in the barn, Point stood pressed against a pile of straw in the corner of an unused stall. She stood before him and began unbuckling his belt. She licked her lips and looked into his eyes.

His internal temperature was rising perceptibly, as was the anticipation of what was about to happen. She reached down inside the front of his pants and grasped his enlarging member with her cool hand.

"If you loosen my pistols, I'll loosen yours," she whispered.

Back in the house, Ray grabbed both sides of Chelsea's shirt and ripped it open, revealing her soft breasts and large nipples. Her skin was cleaner where it had been under her clothes. Ray placed his mouth over her breast and tickled at the nipple with his tongue. She moaned deep in her throat like an animal and tossed her head back.

"It's been too long," she gasped. "You are in for quite a night tonight."

He looked up from his prize and smiled at her.

"I believe that goes for both of us."

He pulled her slip up over her head, leaving her naked before him. He laid her back on the bed and ran his dirt-caked hand down her belly, stopping as his fingers entwined with the top of her pubic hair. She nuzzled his neck, making small cooing noises. She began licking, almost tasting his skin. With his palm flat against her pubic bone, he reached down further and felt the damp heat of her anticipation. She had worked his pants down past the top of his legs and was cupping his balls with one hand while stroking his manhood with the other. It seemed to bob and weave with her every touch, and she worked carefully to be sure he didn't waste himself prior to her getting exactly what she wanted. Slowly he spread her vaginal lips and slid two fingers inside to meet her moist excitement. His fingers played rhythms inside her. He paid equal attention to both breasts with his mouth while he squeezed and kneaded her ass cheeks with his other hand. He paused to looked up at her.

"You know how you can tell if a cowboy's had sex?"

"No. How?" Her voice came out in little breaths.

He slid his hand out of her and held it up so that she could see. "Clean fingers," he said.

She squealed in mock anger, "Oh you're terrible!"

"I get worse."

His hand slid back down and this time slid three fingers inside of her. He looked directly into her eyes, only inches from his. "Bye-bye baby," he said.

With cat-like speed he pulled upward and out, tearing her pelvic bone completely away from her body and opening a long slab of skin and flesh all the way to her breasts. She was able to give out one quick scream and look down to see her insides spilling out on the mattress before she went silent. He buried his face in her belly and ate his fill.

Point lay on top of the girl, jabbing his cock into her with the ferocity of a beast. She clawed at his ass, digging pieces of skin away from his cheeks, ignoring the rancid smell around them.

She swung her head from side to side with the tidal rhythms of her approaching orgasm. As she hit her stride, Point opened his mouth and two canine-like fangs elongated from the roof of his mouth. They were beautifully magnificent saber teeth and he sunk them deep into her neck.

She died in the spasms of orgasm as he drank her highly agitated blood. It was his favorite kind and filled him with his own sexual completion.

Ray walked out of the bedroom, carrying Chelsea like a tray that he was being careful not to spill. He passed Lemon and Justin on the floor, feeding upon Virginia, who was still awake and staring up at him as he passed. Her vacant eyes managed to follow him. Her mouth opened and closed but no noise came out, other than the gurgle of some blood bubbles. Ray walked into the bedroom and laid the Chelsea on the bed next to Joplin. He took out a bloody piece of internal organ and ran it across Joplin's lips.

"Here, taste this," he said as he squeezed it to make some of the liquid fall into Joplin's mouth. "The ladies of the house prepared a special medicinal feast to help you get better. You'll be strong in no time. But I don't want you to get sick from gorging on these delicacies. Take your time."

It was only a moment before he had to stop forcing it upon Joplin. He was eating and drinking on his own, making the slurping sounds of a hungry dog. Ray stood up, wiping his hands on his pants.

"She's all yours, buddy."

Point walked into the bedroom. Looking like somebody had tossed a bucket of blood over him He gestured toward Joplin and asked, "So, how's he doing'?"

"Oh, he'll be fine," Ray said. "All he needed was a little nourishment. It truly beats that beef we've been having to survive on. We'll lay low tonight dend head out tomorrow night when the food's finished and the daylight has gone. His strength will be back by then and he should be mostly healed."

Ray smiled at the carnage before him. "Damn, that was easy. Too rarely is it offered to us like that."

Point sighed. "Loneliness can do that to you."

Ray slapped Point on the shoulder. "It sure can. So can horniness. It's every man's fantasy and every woman's nightmare."

"Ray, nobody wants to lose control unless they feel safe."

"Don't worry," Ray said. "I'm feeling pretty safe."

They both laughed and walked out of the room, towards the sounds of feasting.

Editor Eric Miller self-financed and published an anthology in 2012 entitled Hell Comes to Hollywood *featuring an arresting piece of cover art and a book full of horror stories about the entertainment business by people connected to the industry. The book went on to garner a Bram Stoker Award nomination from the Horror Writer's Association for Year's Best Anthology. Unfortunately, it didn't win. But it was quite an achievement.*

Two years later he decided he hadn't had enough punishment and put together Hell Comes to Hollywood 2 *with the same artist doing the cover and the same premise for the book. I was lucky enough to be asked to be part of that one and decided to do a lampooning turn on the reality shows which were all the rage at that time.*

One last note, **Shelley Cherwinski** *is a friend and, years earlier, had been my favorite bartender. Her name contained just that right sound combination of American melting pot and midwesternism to it. I asked her if I could use it for a character in the story. She was kind enough to allow me to do so. I gave her a copy of the book after it came out. She has never told me whether she liked the story. In fact, she has yet to speak with me again.*

THE LAST GREAT MONSTER

"Did you really run into a monster on your path, or just a mirror?"

—Terri Guillemets

THE LAST GREAT MONSTER

EARLY **SATURDAY MORNING** Shelley Cherwinski snuffed out the last great monster. She was on her way home from an 18-hour production day at the studio, going over the continuity from the day's script in her head, when she hit the beast. The impact sent her little white foreign sports car sliding to the left a glimpse of large teeth and wide eyes as the car crossed the road and bounced down into the ditch, the steering wheel spinning through her hands. The horn, just like in a Hollywood production, was stuck bleating out a continuous sheepish tone as steam rose from underneath the body of the car.

When the snowflakes of reality slowly fluttered back into her brain and she gradually awoke from the nightmarish accident. Her eyes began to focus, and in her headlights she thought she saw the back of some large animal lumbering into the woods. She was suffering the double blow of shock from the accident and the emotional trauma of seeing a monster for a split second before ramming into it. Shelley's thoughts drifted into wondering if she had monster coverage on her auto insurance. The constant horn began to give her a headache and, pissed off, she repeatedly slammed the palm of her hand against the steering unit until it quit making noise. The silence was deafening.

There were sounds. Things moved away from her in the brush, running, scrambling. Animals that had probably seen the accident and were trying to escape before they too became speed bumps. There were clinks and pops from the car; some were from the engine cooling and some were the car trying to unfold itself from its crinkled condition. There was dripping and hissing as liquids dropped onto something hot under the hood. She moved her body parts slowly knowing something could be broken.

Wait. . .Liquid was hissing as it hit something under the hood! She had to get out before she went up in flames with the car. She pulled the handle, but the door was jammed and wouldn't open. She leaned as far as she could towards the passenger side and then, with all the strength she could muster, slammed her shoulder into the driver's door.

"Oh, dear God that hurt!"

It popped open and she rolled out into the ditch. . .mostly.

As she dangled face down into the cattails and long grasses, her hair hanging in the muddy trough, the seatbelt held her firmly in place. Ass up and face down she had to get herself unbuckled.

Later, Shelly would remember seeing under the car from where she hung and not noticing any evidence of any fire. But just one of those drips could be gasoline and then it would be all over. She twisted her body and reached up, grabbing the steering wheel. That was when she heard something large moving through the woods.

Naughty words passed through her mind as she struggled to pull herself upright. Shelley clamped onto the steering wheel with her left hand while digging frantically at the seatbelt clasp with her right. When it finally popped, she slid out backwards dropping down into the muck.

Wasting no time, she crab-walked in reverse, away from the car, knowing it was going to blow up in her face at any moment. It was only when her back struck a large rock that she was able to climb to her feet. She scaled the bank to the asphalt and waited for somebody to come down the road. It really wasn't all that well traveled at 2:30 in the morning.

As she stood there, she remembered the large animal and the sound of something moving in the darkness. Her cell phone had been in her car where it had been sitting on one of those sticky pads on the dashboard. There was no telling if it was still there. She assumed that what she had hit and what she had heard in the woods were animals, maybe one and the same. In her mind, all animals could see in darkness. With the blinding headache she was cultivating, she wasn't even sure she could see in the daylight. There were blue and green dash lights glowing. From where she was standing spraddle-legged, the headlights lit the woods directly in front of the car.

The residual light from them helped her to see the immediate area around her.

As she began stumbling back towards her car, a sound came out of the trees that dropped Shelley to her knees. She grimaced as her bones smacked the gravel shoulder. The noise, which could only be described as a wailing moan, so frightened her that she became nauseous with a set of dry heaves that doubled her over. It was either from the noise, as she told it, or the trauma from the accident, which is what the cop who wrote up the report two hours later thought.

Nothing came out of the darkness to attack her and the car didn't blow up in her face. When Shelley was finally able to get back to her wrecked car, the phone was jammed in the joint where the windshield meets the dash. It was jammed so tightly that she had to strike at it with the handle of a plastic hairbrush to crack it loose.

She speed-dialed her director who told her to call the cops and then went promptly back to sleep after reminding her of her call time in six hours. Then, she called the cops.

***

She was being rolled into the ambulance after repeating her story three separate times, twice to the same cop and once to an insurance accident investigator. He assured her with a smirk that he would check out the monster insurance angle, but said she was probably covered even if it was a deer. Her cracked ribs were starting to hurt as the adrenaline began to wear off and she was painfully starting to discover areas of her body she'd never thought of before.

The cop stood with his hands in his pockets watching the red lights of Shelley's ambulance pull away and then turned to the insurance man next to him.

"Well?" he asked.

"She hit something alright. That something seems to have crawled off somewhere into the woods."

The cop flicked his flashlight quickly up and down the boundary of trees. He turned his head and spit a stringer into the ditch.

"It'll be light in another hour and I'm waiting until then before I look around. I already stepped in the filthy ditch water trying to take photos of her car."

He hiked up his leg to show the water line on the pants material.

"Hmm," the insurance man mumbled while looking at the wet shoe.

"Don't like it," said the cop. "I've already got some sort of foot rot and a big toenail the color of a school bus. I'm waiting until I can see."

"What do you think about her monster story?"

"Could have been a coyote," the cop said.

"Hmmm."

"Or a bear," he added.

"Has she been drinking?" the insurance man asked.

"Nah," the cop replied. "I didn't smell anything. Just tired, I think. Slow reflexes."

"Still," the insurance man sighed, "that monster story is a doozy."

"That it is," said the cop.

"First time for me," said the insurance man.

"Hmmm," the cop answered.

Daylight crept in with the arrival of the tow truck. It was all clinking chains and groaning metal while the cop stood near the road waving the occasional traffic around the scene. The insurance man walked over to where the cop was yelling at somebody slowly passing in a car to *quit gawking and drive.*

"Well, the truck's got it so I'm outta here," the insurance man said.

The cop turned back to him.

"I heard from University Hospital. She'll be alright," he told the insurance agent.

"That's one good thing."

"Maybe," the cop added.

"What do you mean?"

"She appears to be sticking with the monster story."

"Maybe she bumped her head when she fell out of the car. Maybe she's a little traumatized," the insurance man offered.

"Either way, I'm going to poke around a little in the woods. See what I can see."

The insurance man walked back towards his car.

"Thanks for your help, officer. I may be speaking with you later."

He climbed into his car, swung it around on the asphalt, and headed back to the city. The cop watched the car shrink in the distance and then turned to the woods. It was time to find out exactly what Shelly had hit. Whatever it was, it was big, and it had left the scene. There could be trouble and he might have to write a citation. He inadvertently touched his holster and then jumped the ditch and walked to the edge of the woods. Glancing back at the road he watched the tow truck driver putting his broom away after sweeping the glass and metal off the asphalt.

The cop turned back and wandered up the wood line one way and then back the other until he found where the "monster" had gone in. It seemed like a decent starting point.

THE LAST GREAT MONSTER

It was wide, or at least it cut a wide swath through the weeds and underbrush. At about twenty feet in, the beast appeared to be dragging some part of its body. One strong footmark dragging the other from what the cop could tell. Blood began to show up on the ground and vegetation.

What started as drips and drabs became smears and finally splashes. Then, there it was; matted fur crusted with dried blood and dirt, limbs bent in an odd direction, body crumpled to the ground. Its head and chest rolled towards its knees in a semi-fetal position, probably from the pain. Evidently the dead weight became too much to drag anymore, and it had to drop.

The cop knelt, noting the smell of the wild beast. He'd been next to elephants at a circus, and they smelled just about as bad. He couldn't tell if it was dead or alive but either way the carcass hadn't had time to ripen yet, so this was probably its natural smell. Black bears carried a similar odor with them.

He had no idea what he was looking at with it being curled up. Mammalian, certainly.

Outside of the smell the only things that resembled a bear were the claws. The legs were more amazing in that they had the backwards shaped knee of a chicken but without any other avian qualities. Full and thick like an ape, it was like a joke on the Bigfoot myth with an air of danger about it.

He turned away. He needed something else. He needed a camera crew. The cop smelled something along with the stench of the beast. He smelled money. In his report, Shelley had given him the name of her director. He knew the director would have access to a crew. The cop needed to document his findings.

He stood up to leave when something moved in the brush behind him. He turned slowly and could make out an eye and the end of a snout through the bushes. It was watching him. Another beast was watching him. His heart raced and he began to slowly back away from the body at his feet. His hand rested firmly on his holster. Death was close at hand, but he was sweating more from the anticipation of a living beast, a monster of the woods. The thing in the bushes pushed out a huff of air. There was a deep, rumbling sound and suddenly the cop was very afraid of not ever leaving the woods. With his other hand he took his phone from his pocket and snapped a couple of pictures of the dead creature. At least he had proof. Now, he needed to get out of there. . .alive.

He backed away from the monster's corpse, gun drawn, trying to keep an eye on where he was walking and the other on the woods where the second creature rumbled about in the underbrush. If what was in the bushes was anywhere near as big as what lay dead on the ground, he could be in big trouble. With each step backwards the cop felt better and better. Once he was out of sight of the beast on the ground he turned and ran for his squad car.

He slammed and locked the door before turning the key and getting the air conditioning cranking. He'd sweat through his uniform. The cold air helped him steady his breathing, too.

He pulled down the shoulder of the road about a quarter mile. On the passenger seat lay his notes for the accident report. He looked through them until he found the name and number of Shelley Cherwinski's director. He dialed the number and listened to the ring. It sounded like a cash register ringing up a sale.

∿∿

"They went in right along here," the cop explained.

He led the three men along the woods line looking for the spot where the weeds had been trampled down. He was off work and on his own at this point after having pulled the graveyard shift that brought him here the first time. The three men with him, (the director, the cameraman, and the soundman) were trudging behind on the uneven ground hoping he'd find the entrance soon. One of them had taco stand morning gas, but kept putting the smell off on the monster.

"I can smell the carcass from here," said the soundman.

The cameraman shook his head.

"Smells more like BIG BREAKFAST BURRITO #3 to me," he said. "Here we go," the cop beamed with a big smile, like he was the first man on the North Pole or something.

He started in when the director grabbed him and pulled him back.

"Wait. We need a shot of this."

The cop looked at him strangely.

"This ain't the monster," he said. "It's only where they headed into the woods."

The director smiled at him as if he were a young child without knowledge.

"I know. It's for dramatic effect when we put the entire piece together."

"Oh."

"Now, back out of the shot please."

The cameraman stepped up and slowly brought the shot up from the ground, ending on the dark wall of woods. He kept it there a moment so the viewers would be able to take in the denseness.

"Cut!"

The director turned back to the cop and waved him on.

"Lead on, McDuff," he said.

"Stamper," the cop said. "Kenneth Stamper, not McDuff."

"Great, but not what I was referring to."

"Oh, I thought you wanted me to lead you into. . ."

"Go! Go!" the director said, motioning Kenneth forward with a sweep of his hand.

Stamper turned and rattled his way into the woods followed by the cameraman, the soundman, and the director. The entourage threw him off a little and he would turn now and then to smile at the camera and make sure they were still with him. Each time the director would point forward like signaling a first down and the cop would turn and continue with his trek through the underbrush. After a couple of minutes, he stopped and turned back to the camera.

"What?"

The director was becoming frustrated with this ham actor.

"Just ahead is where I found the beast. I had been following the drag marks and with my head down had almost tripped over the body. It was right up there about fifty feet ahead."

He pointed towards a clearing. The cameraman followed the cop's hand with the shot and continued towards the spot in the woods. Then he zoomed in, very dramatically, on the bushes blocking the clearing.

"Cut!", yelled the director. "Now let's think this through first. I don't want us to just go barging into the spot."

"Do we have to do that first part again without the talking?" he asked.

"It's okay," the director said. "We were shooting MOS."

Stamper frowned.

"What does that mean?'

"Without sound."

Stamper chuckled to himself. Hollywood sure did throw away

its money on directors who didn't even know how to spell. He hoped he knew what he was doing directing.

The director looked around the area and then back at the cameraman.

"Speed, I want you and headphones here to go up on that rise behind and above the clearing. Once the two of you are set, wave at me. I'd like the shot of McDougall coming up on the body. Now get going. The light is bad enough as it is and I don't know how many takes we'll need."

"It's Stamper," the cop said. "You mean sort of like reenact the first time?"

The director slapped him on the shoulder.

"You're a pretty bright guy, McDonald. You may even have a future in show business."

"Stampe. . .You think so! Wow, that's great."

"Yeah, yeah, great. Now once Speed gives us the signal I'll call 'action' and you go through to the spot just like you did the first time. Don't be too sure of yourself. Remember, you're pretending you've never been here before. Not too fast."

"No problem," Stamper said and rubbed his hands together in anticipation.

He thought about how he was going to play out his upcoming *discovery scene*. Not too big, he told himself. That would look corny. He knew to keep his out-turned hand away from his forehead. Too silent movie-ish. Don't look at the camera. This was real. This is reality. Suddenly Speed's voice crackled over the radio.

"Once we give the signal and see the copper come into view we can walk and slide down this little hillside so that the camera moves toward him as he is moving toward us with the beast's body somewhere in between."

"What's the point?" the director shot back.

"We can't actually see the ground where he is going. We really need to see the beast and him at the same moment. This will work, trust me. We'll stay upright and the little slipping and sliding we do on the way down will just add tension to the scene. Alphonso, grab my belt as I balance this camera going down. I want you behind me anyways. Hot air rises."

With a crackle, the radio shut off. The director looked at Stamper. He knew he was going to need all the help he could get to make this look even remotely real.

"Alright," he conceded. "Let's try one like that. We can always change if we don't like it. Are you ready up there?"

"Let it rip," the cameraman barked and waved. He turned back to Alphonso.

"I didn't mean you."

Alphonso laughed and the director looked at Stamper.

"Get ready. When I say action start walking."

Stamper nodded and took a deep breath. *Oh brother*, the director thought.

"Camera?"

"Speed," the reply came back.

"Sound?"

"Good," the soundman answered.

"There's no slate so fake it."

He could hear somebody clap their hands and say, "Take one."

He looked at Stamper and pointed the direction he was to walk in.

"Annnnd Action!"

Stamper stared at him. The director shushed at him with his hands.

"Go! Go!"

Stamper shook his head and gave the director a wink to let him know he was an old pro at this. He straightened his uniform shirt and started walking. As Stamper rounded the trees, he could see the cameraman and sound guy starting down the hillside towards him. He knew he was on camera and suddenly didn't know what to do with his hands and forgot how to swing his arms. He smiled a big goofy smile and started walking like a little kid at an amusement park until a sudden revelation stopped him cold in his tracks. Speed slid to a stop on the hillside and was rear-ended by the sound man forcing out another round of windbreakers.

"I didn't ask for a tableau," the director shouted. "What?"

The camera panned from Stamper's face slowly down to the spot where the monster was laying in the field. Where the monster was supposed to be laying in the field. The grass was matted down like a deer bed, but there was no monster. Stamper was dumbfounded and stood frozen at the spot. The camera crew continued to move down off the slope and close in towards Stamper. The director ushered him forward.

"Go on. Get in there and investigate. We'll cut this footage later and fix it in post."

"Looks like something was dragged off over this way," Alphonso pointed out. "Maybe he was dragging himself."

Stamper shuffled towards the site of his failing fortunes until all four of them met in the middle. Reaching down he pulled up a tuft of odd-looking fur and pointed out some bloodied grass to the camera. They all stared down at the big spot of nothing when a rustling in the bushes made them turn. It grunted twice and was upon them before anybody had a chance to run.

∻

As the found footage broadcast later on the "Unexplained Questions" tabloid show revealed, there was a lot of screaming, a flash of teeth, odd growls, wide eyes, a splash of blood, and a spinning camera that dropped to the ground continuing to film. A blur that appeared to be the foot of some fur-covered animal briefly filled the frame. The show kept freezing that frame, having "experts" explain what it was the home audience was seeing. Since the program was syndicated, many people did not watch it at the odd hours it was played. Yet for those few cryptozoology lovers who did watch, the commentator earnestly and quite dramatically told the frightening and unbelievable story of how on that fateful Saturday, driving home from an 18-hour production day at the film studio, Shelley Cherwinski had killed the next to last great monster.

Before he passed away, Forrest J Ackerman (agent, collector, and original editor of Famous Monsters of Filmland Magazine*), began working on a zombie anthology. He wrote the foreword to it. Then, unfortunately, he went to the great Ackermansion in the sky. The project sat for a while, but publisher, Nicholas Grabowsky was determined not to let it die too. He still needed a couple of stories to round out the book. He nabbed a story from me and writer/director Axelle Carolyn and passed those along to editors J. Travis Grundon and L. B. Goddard. The anthology was complete. The final result was* Forrest J Ackerman Presents The Anthology of the Living Dead.

THE RESURRECTION OF FATHER

"[death]. . .the abyss from where no traveler is permitted to return."
—George Washington

WHEN I WAS YOUNG, I was never allowed to go with Father on one of those "take your child to work" days. I suppose it had to do with the fact that he didn't work in an office or a factory or even a fire station. Usually, he worked at home. In the basement. Alone. The door at the top of the stairs would shut tight behind him every afternoon as he made his way down to his workstation. There may as well have been a giant DO NOT DISTURB sign on it. We all knew better than to bother him. The house had better be burning down and your clothes on fire before you knocked on that door and hollered for him.

He went to work in the afternoon because he worked late into the night. He said he was able to be more accomplished that way.

That time of day was "inspirational" for him; no phones ringing or people coming by. Not that we had anybody coming by at any other time either. In the summer when I was on vacation from school, he would come down from his bedroom and have his breakfast while we had our lunch. He'd read the paper, rub my head playfully, kiss Mother and do any minor chores she had lined up for him, and then head down into the basement. It was only after I'd grown up that I realized that it wasn't like that for every household, just mine. I guess until they are exposed to something different all children think that every household is just like theirs.

We always had food on the table and clothes on our backs. We certainly weren't rich. Mom once said she had one hundred ways to make ground meat dishes. She was trying to make ends meet and stretching the budget as well as she could. Like I said, we always ate.

The door would shut and he'd be gone, clumping down the wooden stairs, and we got on with our lives. It was all very middle class, just like in the television shows. In fact, it was like *Leave It to Beaver*, but a little bit different. I don't think I ever knew what the father on that show did for a living either. I didn't care enough to know as long as Mom and Dad and my world were all okay, orderly, and undisturbed.

He used to say to me, "Would you like to make your old dad happy?"

I'd shake my head yes.

"Then keep your mom happy. Because when she's happy, I'm happy. That means you're happy. Got it, sport?"

It was his version of expressing love. I knew enough then to not upset my mother and if I ever did upset her, I knew enough to stay out of arm's reach from my father.

I can't say the same about not upsetting my father. I'd upset him, but it was mostly by accident. I never meant to make him mad. I was just a kid, and a kid is a goofy living thing that makes mistakes.

My father was a bit stern and disconnected from the family. His work demanded all his concentration. The older I became, the more I missed the idealized version of the family that was presented at church or on *Ozzie & Harriet*. Little did I know then that the show was as much a fallacy as the family I was living in.

One evening, I was throwing the ball against the side of the house. It got away from me and busted out one of the basement windows. My father had painted them all black so nobody would be able to see inside when he had the lights on at night. When that ball punched a big hole right in the middle of the basement window, light and sound came pouring out. First was the smashing and shattering of the glass, followed by an animalistic scream. A shaft of light poured out of the hole into the yard with dust and stuff all floating in the electrified beam.

I shouted, "I'm sorry! I'm sorry!" then ran to the window and stooped down to see if I'd hurt my father. I only saw inside for a moment, but it looked like there were people sleeping on a table or leaning up against the wall in a sitting position staring up at me, framed in the window.

I thought that maybe they were wounded, like they'd hurt themselves or maybe I'd hurt them with the ball. My father's face suddenly filled the hole about six inches in front of mine. He was so angry his veins were puffing out on his forehead.

"What did you do?!" He screamed at me. "What did you see?"

"Nothin'," I quickly answered to both questions. "Is everybody okay? Are you okay? Did I hurt you?" I pointed behind me to where I'd been standing. "The ball bounced and went-"

"Shut up!" he screamed at me. "Get in the house and go to your room now!"

I was stunned. The only things my father had ever gotten mad about were his workshop or my mother. I didn't need to think twice about what he said and turned and quickly marched myself off to my room. Once I got there, I threw myself down on the bed and stared up at the ceiling. I didn't cry. I think I was in shock. I could hear him nailing up a board to cover the hole; a board I was sure he had painted black.

My mother never interceded at times like these. She would hide and chose to ignore things.

This family was a very Christian middle-class family with real family values. You didn't cross my father, or he'd beat the bejesus out of you. My mother did whatever he said and took the burden of raising me so he could concentrate on his work. I was it; the only child. I have many guesses as to why that is, but they're all different and any one of them could be the truth.

It's so different looking back on my daily life from that age. I was so naïve back then. But hell, I was just a kid.

As a teenager, the kids in school would spread rumors and innuendos about me and my family.

I was never involved in any extracurricular activities. Father didn't like the idea that I'd be out of his home any longer than necessary. I always came straight home, even from high school.

My parents never participated in any community activities; no PTA, no garden club, no nothing. There was always talk about us, but it would eventually go away. We went to church once a week every Sunday evening. At least, we did when I was young. My family always went to the evening service so as not to upset my father's sleeping schedule. He liked things being regulated. He always said that regulation was what made the world go around. We ate at the same time every day and had the same thing to eat on the same day of each week—chopped meat Tuesday, ground meat Thursday, sliced meat Friday. It all sounds so abnormal when I tell somebody about it now; odd, and out of place. It didn't feel that strange when I was living it as a child.

I remember one night we came home from church and my father announced that we were never going back to that church and that he was going to go downstairs and work. This upset my mother with it being the Sabbath and us being a Christian family. She tried not to show her displeasure, but she couldn't help it.

"Why, Jim? You're down there every afternoon into the middle of the night. This is the Lord's Day. I expect you to keep it holy and teach your son the importance of something like that if we're going to start teaching God's word at home."

He stared into the distance like he always did when he was thinking. I never knew which way his emotions would flop. When he'd decided, he nodded his head "yes" and turned back to my mother. I could see in his face that he would rather be downstairs, but he glanced at me. He was still thinking.

"You're right, Becky," he said looking down at me from his six foot plus of frame. "It's not going to kill me to do a moment of parenting."

With that he walked into the living room, plopped down in an easy chair, and promptly went to sleep. My mother sighed and turned to the sink to wash up the day's dishes. She looked at me over her shoulder while placing a plate in the draining tray. I think she could have washed dishes blindfolded.

"Don't just stand there. Go up to your room and keep yourself busy with something constructive."

THE RESURRECTION OF FATHER

When I turned to go, she added, "And keep the noise down. Your father is trying to sleep."

From the sound of his snoring, he was already doing a pretty good job of it. I knew he'd wake up in an hour and then, seeing that I wasn't around, he would slink his way downstairs and get back to his work.

His work was an interesting topic. It was apparently a mixture of his different talents combined to create a steady income while "advancing the frontiers of science." At least, that's what he told me once. He said that Scientific American or Popular Science or one of those science magazines was going to do a cover story on him one day. He rubbed my head and said that when I was older, I would be following in his footsteps. "Standing on the shoulders of giants," he declared.

I had never fully understood what exactly he did, but I had my suspicions. I've since tried to pick up most of the pieces of what he left behind, but I haven't fully accomplished that just yet.

He did it so well for so long that I'm not sure I'll ever be that good. I have gotten better than he was with the living. He was still better with the dead. I do know that I will never be on the cover of Scientific American or Popular Science or any other magazines. My picture may end up posted someplace, but it probably won't be a magazine cover.

When I started dating it was an awkward thing, at least to me. I'm not sure whether my dates ever picked up on anything except that they were the lucky winners of a date with "Frederick the Super Jerk". I seldom got a second date. I only brought dates home twice. The first time my father stayed cordoned off in the basement and my mother made do with small talk while twisting her hands nervously so that her pale white skin turned red and irritated and smiling with that tic that meant she would have been more comfortable to be almost anyplace else. I pushed my glasses back up the bridge of my sweaty nose and took the first opportunity to get my date out of there. There were no emotional survivors in that debacle.

The second time occurred more from wishful thinking than anything else. A year or so had passed since my first feeble attempt and the bad memory of that evening had faded into a nostalgic haze. It was the last time and I don't mean the last time I tried to bring somebody home, I mean it was the last time I dated.

Even after the previous dating failures, I was a "normal" boy with normal needs. My father had sensed that, I suppose, and used this period in my life to tell me his secrets and begin to bring me into the business. He felt I was older, wiser, and more mature than I really was. He thought I could handle what he had to show me. He would have loved for it to be "Archuleta and Son". I think he was disappointed when I threw up on his worktable during my first sexual encounter, but, like being seasick and stuck at sea, I gradually got over my aversions and was able to at least stomach the business. That's kind of funny, stomach the business. My father showed me how a normal boy could meet his normal needs in an abnormal household. A lot of people come from dysfunctional households. He didn't want me to overdo it with us being Christians and all. But after my little head got a piece of the first girl, there were several others unbeknownst even to my Father. You always remember your first with a certain fondness, though. She had a great smile.

A religion is an unusual thing to want to start, but I guess when what you are offered doesn't meet your needs (something I was keenly aware of), you take matters into your own hands. But starting a religion? Well, that's a big undertaking. By this time, we had quit attending the neighborhood church because it didn't have what my Father wanted. He wanted his beliefs to be the doctrine of a church. So, he started his own.

My father was both a resurrectionist and a midnight dentist. He figured that even if he had been able to bring back the dead to life, they wouldn't need their teeth to mush through the brains and internal organs that he would feed them. So, the collection plate was always toothy.

He also found plenty of gold that way which paid our bills. There were many evenings when I would spend hours digging fillings and caps out of yellowed chompers.

My father also believed in reincarnation. He had this diagram hanging up on the basement wall that was a big circle cut into three equal pie shapes. The first pie piece was labeled *Incarnation*. The second piece was labeled *Disincarnation*. The final piece was *Reincarnation*.

He had picked up the idea in a book somewhere about Buddhism or New Age philosophy or something like that. It was the only part of the book he liked. Back then he wasn't experimenting with the bodies, making them jerk and stand and stuff; he was writing his own bible. He was becoming his own God. He was, by the time I was a young adult, at the second pie stage and disincarnating rapidly. He was dying and was in a hurry to prove the dead could come back. To me, being a zombie and being reborn were two different things, but to him, moving was moving.

I was being offered the keys to the kingdom. The more I reflect about it the more I realize that they were being forced upon me. My mother simply didn't have the stomach for it. I'm still not clear on how much she knew and how much she simply chose to ignore. Father was making me responsible for returning his life to him. If I seemed the least bit reluctant to accept this responsibility, he'd become angry. He'd reiterate how he had given me my life and now I was supposed to give him back his. I guess he thought it was better than freezing his head on a platter for later reattachment, like those crazies up in Michigan were pushing for.

His experiments weren't bad or evil; he'd say by way of excuse that the people were already dead. He was just using their empty vessels. When I pointed out that he was trying to refill those vessels he would switch to his "good for all mankind" speech. The end justifies the means. Did I mention that we were a conservative Christian family?

It wasn't wrong to keep the property we found with the dead either. If the family had wanted those things, they wouldn't have buried them with their relatives, he explained. I was to think of it as charity and tithing for his Church of the Undead. It wasn't greed and it wasn't crazy. Tell that to the judge.

"But Father," I'd asked searching for justification, ". . .what is the end? What will these things be, people, monsters, creatures with or without a soul?"

"Alive!" He'd shouted, becoming all excited and animated. "They would be alive," he said almost gleefully. Then he would look at me with those eyes, those blue headlights that cut right through me and say, "If not for mankind, what about for your father? You must believe in something. Why not believe in what I do? Believe in me."

He would try to only rob from fresh Jewish graves as they weren't embalmed, the bodies were very clean, and the meat remained edible if it was prepared or frozen quickly enough. However, there was seldom anything of value buried with the Jews, not very many gold teeth, so he'd still have to use other ethnicities too. He couldn't keep the bodies around for more than a day before the neighborhood dogs began to sniff curiously at the basement windows.

If my father couldn't get the dead to come back to life (he was still working out the kinks), we would eat them for dinner. They could live again through us. Many was the time I tried to figure out the essence of the secrets I'd consumed, but I was never any more successful at it than he'd been. I knew the dead could teach us many things, they taught Michelangelo anatomy, and our basement was filled with maggots and miracles. Death was so stubborn about revealing what it could show us about life.

Father always thought too small. He needed to open his mind. I ended up doing that for him.

As my father's health continued to fail, he clung ever so tighter to his self-proclaimed religion of reanimation using dead bodies. With my help, the bodies kept getting fresher and fresher until sometimes they wouldn't die until the moment when they were in our basement so that Father could try to capture the essence of their lives before it dissipated with their last breath. He wrote page upon page of religious doctrine based upon his findings and his searches within the myriads of other philosophical and theosophical texts that lined our home. In the end, he presented me with his masterpiece; his book, his bible.

In a labored voice he confided, "It is all here. I expect to return to help you grow our religion and complete the true cycle of life. I am putting all my trust in you, son. Do not fail me."

Then, he died. That was it. He went upstairs, sat down and began snoring, and then stopped snoring. That was all there was to it. The bottle of ginger ale that he held in his hand slipped and shattered on the floor next to his chair. Mother looked at me and burst into tears. Covering her face with her bloody kitchen apron, she ran upstairs to her bedroom to hide. I wrapped my arms under his shoulders and dragged Father downstairs to the basement. His heels thumped on each of the old wooden steps as I scooted him backwards into the cellar. I dragged him across the floor and sat him in the swivel chair next to where all my tools hung on a board.

I knew it would be more work for me, one person hefting bodies instead of two, cleaning them up and covering my deeds like a one-man Burke and Hare. I was already sweating like a pig and

THE RESURRECTION OF FATHER

I'd had gravity on my side most of the time. I had to get inventive. Maybe I could recruit a new parishioner.

But now it would be my way. It was the only way. I was the truth and the light. I would take everything I'd learned from Father and apply it with a few new ideas of my own and see if I didn't uncover some secrets and veer off in a new direction. I didn't believe Father had ever found the secret he had searched for his entire life. A brief scan of his bible revealed a lot of gibberish. I took the book from the work counter and tossed it in the trash bin. It was time for a new religion.

I pulled the needle-nose pliers down from the pegboard and opened Father's mouth. Now was not the time for him to quit supporting the family. There were new things to think of now. It was a new world and the night was young. Pink Floyd was playing on the radio and I caught myself humming along.

I finished my work on Father, having had to dig through part of his cheek to get into the large fillings. I dropped them one by one into the palm of the skeletal hand on the workbench that had served as an ashtray for all these years and then hung the pliers back up in the outline where they belonged next to the hacksaw.

I scooted the chair around with its back up against the bench. His neck was against the top of the chair and his head flopped backwards making it easy to position it between the two halves of the vise. I twisted the vise screw around and around until his head was held firmly in place and then reached for the hacksaw.

I was going to move at a faster rate than Father had done. I was going to learn quickly and accomplish the goal of a never-ending life. Unfortunately, Father needed to be sacrificed for the job. Why should I read his book of gibberish when I could obtain all the knowledge I needed by consuming the insides of the vessel that once held it?

The saw blade had not been replaced in some time. It was dulled from all the bone it had fought its way through. I could tell it was mangling the job. The front top of his head was looking more like it had been hit with an axe multiple times instead of sawn off. Part of the way into the top of the skull the blade snapped and became lodged in the bone. The broken serrated metal wiggled to and fro from his forehead like a worm trying to emerge from an apple.

I swapped out the blade and finished my work. Using both

hands, I twisted the separated scalp and heard the bone break free from itself with a wet snap. Lifting it up, I could see the beautifully colored coral of Father's thoughts. I took a thin fillet knife and worked it around the inside diameter of the skull; it felt like removing dog food from a can. I dug my fingers down each side of the interior of the skull and lifted the brain up. It was slick in my hands. I needed to work quickly and carefully so as not to drop it or have an accident. It was still connected at the base and, using a reliable pair of meat scissors, I poked down and snipped it loose.

I held it up high above my head, a winning trophy, while various thick liquids ran down my hands and up my arms toward my elbows. All Father's knowledge was now mine. I lowered it to my face and took a large bite out of the frontal lobe. It was as fresh as it comes. All his knowledge was in there and was now transferring to me with each mastication that allowed pieces to roll down my throat. With my knowledge plus his, I would be unstoppable.

I looked around for the right tools for tonight's job. Would I bring home a new donor or perhaps an accomplice? I was prepared for either. I knew the kit we kept . . .I mean I kept, in the trunk of the car should cover me. I shivered thinking about how fresh the meat could be. I bet Mother could really cook up something good with some fresh meat and a little bit of Father mixed in. I took another bite of his mind. I could feel the growth of knowledge within myself. Father would have been so proud. I set his brain on a plate and slipped it into the mini-refrigerator next to the bench to keep it fresh. If I struck out tonight, Father would make an excellent cold snack, like left over pizza or spaghetti but better.

I found myself thinking about her, my first love, and my groin tingled in remembrance. You always remember your first. She'd had a great smile. In fact, I still had it. It was on the table keeping a stack of books from falling over. I picked it up by the back of the jaws and placed it on Father's lap. He'd always liked her too. It's funny how you can remember somebody just by their smile.

I grabbed Father's shirt collar and ripped off a long piece. I wiped my face clean and then wiped my hands off using the material as a towel. "Good night," I said to Father and bound up the stairs two at a time. Back in the kitchen, I could hear my mother upstairs still crying. In between her whimpers I shouted to her, "I'm going out. I'll be back later!"

THE RESURRECTION OF FATHER

Yes, it was a new life, and it was mine. The dark air felt cool while it slipped against my face.

I inhaled the perfume of the night blooming Jasmine vines as I climbed in my car and made my way toward the night lights of town.

My brother was my second closest friend. He was six years older than me, so it was tough through the school years when the age difference was more marked between us. During the turbulent sixties and seventies, we were completely out of sync with our parents. My brother responded by running away from home several times. Like an escaped prisoner, he was always captured and brought back. When he was old enough, he joined the Navy and never lived at home again.

The desert was his place of solitude. A place where he could center himself. It was large and open. There was no feeling of confinement or having to obey rules he didn't agree with. I'm sure he felt beautiful and free during his numerous visits there.

This essay was originally a chapter of my novel Einstein's Cavern. *But I felt it didn't fit, so I pulled it. It was later published by a Canadian Horror magazine,* Dark Recesses. *I thought that if I was collecting my dark writings, I should include a piece of nonfiction, a piece of my own life. It speaks to the horror of isolation, of being left behind.*

VAST EXPANSE OF NOTHING

A Memoir

I HATE THE DESERT. My brother loved the desert; the entire dry, hot, sandy, void-of-life, what-life-there-is-sucks, waterless, plantless stretch of it. He spent a lot of hours trying to convince me that none of those things I just mentioned were true. He said the desert was like a beautiful woman who kept you at arm's length and could kick your ass if she wanted to. But those moments that the two of you got to spend alone were magic, dangerous magic, and you kept going back to her every chance you got because you'd become addicted. It was his personal space. She was his muse.

"A desert can get ten inches of rain each year."

"Deserts cover 20% of the earth and can be exceedingly cold."

"Rodents, reptiles, and plants thrive in the desert."

"There are parts of the desert that are big tourist attractions."

I never bought into the beautiful stillness and lovely sunrise/sunset versions of the desert that he tried to paint for me. Maybe I will buy into it more now that he's gone; when I look at the vast stretch of nothingness. Now when I regard the landscape, I see him. That makes it more beautiful to me. I guess it is all just point-of-view. I understand being alone and the desire to want to be alone and I understand isolation.

He would leave for months at a time into the arid nothingness. Upon resurfacing, he would claim he'd been out there writing music, chatting with friends of Carlos Castaneda, and getting in touch with himself. I never heard any of the music he'd composed or found him to be philosophically insightful, but I did get around to reading Castaneda's tales of Yaqui Indian Don Juan and his quest for spiritual enlightenment via the use of desert peyote. My brother did turn me on to acid, so I guess he was my gateway to my own inner awareness. Although I no longer use drugs, haven't for several decades, I do thank him for some of the escapades I've had in my life that would have passed without my ever experiencing them had he not taken the lead and introduced me.

When I think of him, I think of the word "desert." It had a double meaning with him. Not only was it the place he loved to spend time in, but he was a deserter, a real deserter. He ran from home and he ran away from the Navy in Jacksonville, Florida. They eventually caught him and brought him back. He did time and extra duty for it. That was over five decades ago.

He has since died and deserted all of us.

I went to his church memorial service back in Michigan where they set out the jar with his ashes and some dressed-up high school yearbook graduation type photograph he would have hated. The service talked about God and my brother being in a better place and a whole lot of other crap that had nothing to do with my brother or his life. When it was my turn to speak, I read some ridiculous poem I found in a book (because it was easier than telling the geriatric group of relatives in the audience what he was really like). I made some stupid joke about his making it back home from Texas the old-fashioned way—he urned it. I hated everything about it. He would have laughed at me, at the entire ceremony. The world becomes so insignificant when somebody you love dies. Sometimes it's that kind of pain that gives you something to live for.

His ex-wife was there. First time I'd seen her in a while. She was pretty, in a waif sort of way. Her family had money, but I don't believe she was getting any of it. Otherwise, why would she have lived in that shithole apartment with my brother in Houston while they were together?

She wanted his ashes and my mother let her have them. I wasn't asked. The drunk driver of the car my brother died in wanted to go free and be forgiven. My mom did that also and, again, I wasn't consulted.

For the first time in years, my brother and his ex were able to be together again. I think she left that same evening as the memorial, taking the urn with her. That was his final desertion. I ended up with nothing; not a photo, not a trinket, not even an old sock. I only had my memories.

That was all. You can't buy memories. The same scenario occurred when my father died years later. No matter what, they can't take my memories. I guess that's good enough.

I heard a few years later that my brother's ex-wife had died. I don't know if he was still with her or not, or if she had since poured him out in some dumpster along the way and used the urn to store smack. The only thing I knew was that I would never get to be with him again. He'd been my Wonder Bread, building strong minds and bodies twelve ways, except that he used chemical compounds to accomplish it. He was a magnificent disaster and ultimately a passing breeze in my life.

The last time I saw him was in Las Vegas. He'd flown from Houston to meet me (I'd come in from L.A.), my mom, and her sister who'd travelled from Michigan. We shared a room, ostensibly to talk old times and remembrances. He was high as fuck on heroin the entire trip and spent each night playing blackjack with a wad of money for which I could only guess at its origins. I was left to entertain the divorcee and the spinster. That trip was a complete disaster and was the last memory I would have of him. Delightful.

VAST EXPANSE OF NOTHING

He died some months later in the car accident. He, and the couple from the next-door apartment that he regularly hung out with and shot up with, all climbed into a car for a trip to some place. A telephone pole jumped out from the curb and smacked their car. The couple in the front seat were fine (as drunks and stoners usually are). My brother had been in the back seat, no seatbelt, leaning forward between the buckets, chatting with the people up front. When they smacked into the pole, his body shot forward and then flung back bashing his head on the metal bar at the top of the rear bench seat. The car was old, the seat worn, and since the seat was tattered and bare, the metal bar was exposed. I'm not sure it would have made any difference if the bar hadn't been exposed; the back of his head smacked that hard. From the accident reports, he was lucid for a bit afterwards. He climbed out of the car and was sitting on the curb talking to the emergency crew before he began screaming. They couldn't get him to stop. Eventually, they decided to give him a shot to knock him out. Poetic justice. His final waking moments were getting a shot of something pharmaceutical to stop his pain.

My parents, who were divorcing and living separately at the time, flew from Michigan to Houston to stay at some cheap shit motel near the hospital where they would be spending most of their time. They had little money and vowed to stay nonconfrontational while sharing a room for the sake of their son.

So loyal. So, loving. So full of shit. It was all about appearances with the both of them. My mother reminded me of Tammy Faye Baker being tested by the Lord. But not to worry, she would hold up under intense pressure in the presence of the Devil. When she would meet God on those fluffy clouds, he would say, "Good job fighting Beelzebub! You are my chosen one. Now fix your eyeliner."

Three or four days in and my father was forced to go back to work. No work equaled no money. Mother stayed and father flew back down on the weekends. This went on for a couple of weeks and nothing in my brother's condition had changed. Nothing would ever change except the size of the hospital bill. My parents knew they had to pull the plug at some point. I'm sure the choice was difficult. He was a giant carrot man, and they couldn't decide whether to leave him that way. Finally, my mother called me up one day and said they weren't going to decide until I came there and saw my brother.

Again, I flew out from California. When I stepped out of the terminal it felt like somebody had thrown a wet, hot blanket over me and that stinking humidity never let up until I climbed on a plane to go home. I took a cab to the motel and met my parents. My mother began a recitation of everything she'd been waiting to tell me since she'd arrived in Houston. I bet she even practiced quietly in front of the mirror in the bathroom at night just to get it sounding the way she figured would make the most impact. She was the ultimate drama queen. I was glad I was there so she could spew it all out (several times over) instead of exploding from keeping it all bottled up inside.

Father said nothing and sat in one of those quasi-stuffed motel room chairs that were at an uncomfortable height off the ground causing your knees to stick up even with your face. His hands were folded in his lap, par for the course. The more upset my father was the quieter he became. As I kid, I had learned that when Dad was quiet, stay out of sight and out of arm's reach. It must have really made his jaws tight to have to wait for my opinion concerning the son he despised.

When mother had finished, she looked at me and said, "Do you want to go to the hospital?"

She caught me off guard by stopping her litany so suddenly. I thought maybe she was referring to the headache she had given me.

"Uh yeah, sure," I said. That's what I was there for.

My Father seemed relieved to get out of that chair. We walked down the hall to the lobby and out the door into the sauna awaiting us outside.

"Where did you park?" I asked figuring they had a rental car.

Father looked at me like I had lost my mind.

"Oh, we don't have a car."

"How do you get around?" I asked.

"We don't have anywhere to go," Mom said, almost cheerily. "It's right across the street."

She pointed and, sure as shit, there was the hospital. So everyday these two people woke up, crossed the street, sat in the room of a nonresponsive (read dead here) son, and then traipse back across the street to eat motel coffee shop food and watch bad color television before going to bed and doing it all over again the following day. . .for weeks.

"We wanted to give him every chance," my mother said.

My father said nothing, but I noticed him lightly touch his chest.

What she wanted was not to be blamed for anything in life and put this decision off on me since Father wouldn't accept that responsibility himself. Usually, she put the decisions off on God, throwing Him under the bus, saying it was His will.

As we walked, I turned to her and said, "I'm confused. I thought he was talking to the paramedics at the scene of the accident?"

"He was," she answered, avoiding my eyes. "Then he started screaming from pain and they had to knock him out. He's been out ever since."

"For how long? Weeks?"

My father cleared his throat as we dodged the last bit of cross traffic to make it to the far curb. The front door of the hospital swooshed open with a gorgeous blast of air conditioning. I was getting a chill from the sweat turning cold on my skin through my damp shirt. Father gestured toward the elevators.

"When his head slammed against the metal bar of the backseat bench, it was traumatized, bruised. He was fine until the swelling in the brain from the bruise began to exceed the space inside his skull."

The elevator doors closed and we began to jerkily rise toward the higher floors. I was trying to wrap my thoughts around what it was I was going to walk in on.

"They had to take off the top of his skull to give his brain room to swell," she said. "But of course, it was swelling in all directions."

Of course. Oh god, no.

"They had to remove it and place it next to him on the pillow."

"What?"

This was starting to sound like a bad science fiction film. I thought of that old black and white film where they kept a disembodied head in a jar or a box. Its eyes were open, and the mouth would move, but no sound would ever come out.

"The doctor said it almost exploded out of his head when they cut off the top of his skull."

She said this almost giddily as if it was the most excitement she'd had for years. I just stared at her. The door slid open and we walked into the hall and down to his room.

"They've put it back in now."

I must have exhaled an audible sigh of relief. I absolutely did not want to see that.

"There was nothing going on," father said tapping his temple with his index finger. I knew it wasn't just the heat that was making me nauseous.

We were standing outside of his room door, which was shut. Probably for good reason, I thought. Mother took my hands and looked me in the eye for the first time since we'd left the motel. This was an extremely dramatic moment for her. There was a touch of Lana Turner in her facial over-acting.

"We wanted you to see your brother before we decided anything."

"Before she decided anything," my father muttered.

Mother continued holding my hands, jerking on my fingers like she was trying to milk them, not looking me in the eyes.

"We'll stay out here so you can go in and see your brother alone."

I nodded at her and pulled my hands out of her grasp. She was giving me that pitying look that I'd seen all my life, usually after a good whipping. It churned something in my stomach. I gave my father a quick glance. He was headed to the uncomfortable chair in the hallway to wait for me.

I opened the door to my brother's room.

He lay in the bed in the middle of the room like a museum exhibit; propped up somewhere between flat and sitting, bookended by machinery which was making the only noise in the room. His head was bandaged from the eyebrows up like a tight fitting knit cap. One of his fingers had a blood pressure clamp on it whose wiring worked back to one of the partner machines. A bag of some type of solution was IV fed into his arm and a clean bladder bag hung down the side of the bed. His eyes were closed and his color a ghastly grey and beige. His skin almost looked dirty, as if they had taken him directly from the scene of the accident and put him to bed with no cleanup, but it was probably bruising and not dirt. I was afraid to touch him. I closed the door behind me and walked over to him.

I spoke to him. I had nothing to say, except his name. It was all playing out like a scene from a bad movie; awkward and out of place. His chest moved up and down from his breathing, but I could trace the electronics back to the machine that was doing it for him. This was shitty. I finally touched his wrist, wrapped my hand around his arm, and it felt like cold clay.

The Reaper had come and gone. He wasn't doing anything on his own except sucking money out of my folks' pockets and putting it into the coffers of the hospital. Somewhere he was smiling about that. I wanted to leave, but I didn't know how long I should stay in the room so that it would feel proper to my parents, like I had given my brother a real assessment. I walked up to the head of the bed and leaned in towards his ear. It was the only time I cried.

"If you can come back," I whispered, with tears cascading down the contours of my face. "You be my ghost. We can talk."

I let the words lay there, looking at the bulge of his eyes behind the closed lids, hoping for movement. It was my last piece of communication with him. On top of being dead, he was probably on more drugs than just heroin at this stage. A cocktail of pharmaceuticals swirled mechanically around in his system. I wasn't afraid. If Houdini couldn't come back, I doubted my brother could. I wasn't even hopeful. I took one last look at meaningless numbers and lines moving on the machines and then walked out of the room.

My mother was right there waiting, all antsy and fidgety, to see my reaction. I detested both of them for not having the strength to take him off support on their own. I didn't need to see him. I didn't need that final impression stuck in my memory for the rest of my life.

My father was still sitting in one of the hallway chairs. He seemed to have grown used to sitting in uncomfortable upholstered furniture these last couple of weeks. He looked up at me and I had never seen him appear so tired. He wanted to leave Houston worse than I wanted to leave my brother's room.

"Pull the plug," I said and walked to the elevator.

They were still looking at each other, unspeaking, amazed that I could make that assessment in only a few minutes. It was easy, really. He would have done the same for me, even though he hated our parents and couldn't care less about the money drain on them. He might have wanted to fuck with their emotions while he had them in a headlock. I wasn't quite as cutthroat as he was, but there was no love lost between any of us. My mother liked to pretend that she and I were sympatico. We weren't. There was nothing tough about making this decision. He was dead. Pull the plug. All the emotion went to the memories not the cadaver.

My brother and I carried the same basic philosophy. Understand all the risks as best as you can before you do something. Whatever you do, do it to the fullest. Live your life like nobody is watching or gives a shit because they aren't, and they don't. You don't go on the dance floor if you aren't going to dance. You don't pull a gun if you aren't planning on pulling the trigger.

Never believe that others are talking about you; they're not, because you aren't that important. You don't hang around in the land of the living if you are dead. It seemed as if my brother had made it through the entire list. Check.

I never liked the desert; the vast emptiness was too overwhelming for me. But I can understand why he did. It wasn't for any of the reasons he tried to tell me, it was because it existed in a world of its own.

Now my brother is gone, my father is gone, and my mother is gone. The desert is still there.

I'm still here. Now, I was heading to the desert.

The idea for this story arrived when I saw a submissions call for an anthology that was being put together requesting completely new takes on the old movie monsters. The editor listed monsters that they were looking for and I felt nobody would pick a Tingler tale. I was right and it remains so, since the editor didn't buy my story. The original electronic implant in this story is real and its sexual arousal side effects are too. From there I went beyond with the story. The Tingler has never been in print prior to this book. I assume it wasn't what they were looking for. Maybe it's what you are looking for.

THE TINGLER

"Don't say the old lady screamed. Bring her on and let her scream."

—Mark Twain

SOMETIMES, WHEN THE buzzing became too loud, I had to leave the house. At times it was a high-pitched piercing sound, like walking into a quiet room with a piece of electronic equipment left on. Other times it was like being in one of those medical imaging machines with all the banging and whining. I'm the only one who can hear it. Even though I've learned to live with it, at the worst times I would grab a t-shirt from my room and run out to the garage. Stuffing the shirt against my mouth I'd scream as loud and as long as I could. That was the only thing that would make the sounds go away. Nobody could hear me screaming if I kept a shirt against my mouth and yelled until it had left or until it faded enough that I could cope with the noises. I was fighting a demon and I needed to scream to scare it off.

"My wife knew, of course, and she would support me as best

as she could. We had been told by several doctors that there was no cure for extreme tinnitus. We felt helpless. So, I would use my own treatment and scream away the pain. My lowest point was the day I was yelling into my shirt, I'm sure I was all red-faced with veins bulging out in my neck and forehead, when my ten-year-old daughter opened the door to the garage and saw me. She ran back into the house, terrified. Even though my wife tried to comfort her, she wouldn't talk to me for the rest of the day. She was scared to death. Daddy's little girl frightened of her own father."

"That's when you found me?" The doctor was leaning back behind his desk. "I'm glad you did."

"I hope so, Doc. I hope so. It was only after a lot of No's and continued searching."

"You understand this treatment is experimental? There may be risks associated with the treatment."

"I don't care," Mitchum said. "I'll sign a waiver if I need to."

The doctor leaned forward with his hands on his desk.

"Perfect," he smiled as he passed it over.

***

The feeling wasn't altogether unpleasant. Compared to what had been going on inside Mitchum's head, it was heaven sent. Working similarly to the way white noise eliminates outside interference for apnea sufferers, the electronic pulse hummed in his spine and the sacroiliac joints seemed to let go, stop cramping up, and loosen their grip. The sometimes-dull pain that ravaged the topography of his thighs, buttocks, upper back was gently settling, floating, releasing and he could tell that every nerve in his body was no longer on edge. The muscles had quit wailing.

"This must be what a sleep tank feels like," he said.

The doctor chuckled. "It will change with each treatment. After a few trials here in the office to see if the implant will be feasible, we'll go ahead with the operation, and you'll be able to treat yourself from home at that point."

"I'll miss seeing you, Doc."

"Not entirely," the doctor said. "You'll still need to drop in for a few follow-up visits and adjustments."

When the session ended Mitchum lay completely still for a few moments, letting the final waves of peace splash through him. He opened his eyes and smiled at the doctor.

"Goddamn, that was nice!"

He sat up on the edge of the table.

"How long will it last, Doc?"

"That is what we're going to find out. While you get dressed, I'll go out to the office and set up another appointment for you. Just come on out when you're ready."

⌁

Each session held the pain and the tinnitus at bay a little longer than the one previous, but it always came back eventually. He looked forward to the doctor visits, which worked better than acupuncture and massage for him. Then the day came. After he had dressed from his session he walked back into the doctor's office and sat on the couch while the doctor quickly finished some paperwork. He looked up and smiled at Mitchum.

"I think we're a go," the doctor said.

"What does that mean, exactly?"

"It means you are able to have the E-Spot Generator implanted."

"It sounds sexual."

"That's because it can be," the doctor explained. "In some cases it was discovered that an electrical pulse pad placed at the correct spot on or near the spine could relieve everything from back to hip pain, at least temporarily. As doctors continued research on electrode placement, they discovered added benefits, such as the relief of your tinnitus. When placed at a certain spot near the sacrum in women it corrected orgasmic dysfunction with the electric pulses. Hence the naming of it as the E-Spot Generator."

"Does it do the same kind of service for men?"

"Not yet anyway. But the name is kind of gender limiting. If it works better for you, psychologically speaking, we can call it by its nickname."

"Which is what?"

"The Tingler," the doctor said and smiled. "One of the technicians who worked on the original mechanism was fond of old horror movies. Back in 1959 Director/Producer William Castle released a film called The Tingler about a lobster-like monster that grabbed your spine during bouts of fear. The gimmick was that when it played in the theaters the production company would hook up little motors to the bottom of random theater seats. When the Tingler appeared on screen, the motors started buzzing giving the illusion that the Tingler was at your seat. People would scream and so forth. Very harmless fun. Thus, the non-scientific name."

The doctor laughed in dismissal.

"Silliness aside, the beauty of our device is that once it is implanted in your back, you'll control the frequency and intensity of its use. If your back pain becomes unbearable, turn it on.

If your tinnitus is screaming in your brain, turn it on. The electrical impulses will travel up your nerves in the spine and quell the tinnitus."

"Just that simple?"

The doctor nodded.

"That simple. Your visits here will become more and more infrequent. In fact, once it is implanted, I won't need to see you except for a couple of checkups a year or if there is some sort of malfunction."

A concerned look passed over Mitchum. "Malfunction?"

"Yes," the doctor explained. "It's a mechanical device. Like all mechanical devices it can break down. If it quits working, we'll fix it or adjust it. Otherwise, hopefully, you get your life back."

Mitchum thought about it.

"My God, that would be nice."

⁕

Mitchum learned the variations in the controls, how the slightest touch or harmonization could enhance the speed and efficiency of the tinnitus blocking powers. It wasn't exactly like white noise, which was a cover-up, but more like an erasure, an elimination of the sound in his brain, a complete removal. The only problem was that the sound never fully stayed away.

He kept the remote near his recliner and tried to use the Tingler sparingly, maybe once or twice a day for an hour total. His wife would keep the children away during these sessions to let him fully involve himself in the treatment. With his eyes closed, he could feel the vibrations, the tingling, traveling up his spine, above his shoulders, and into his neck. The back of his head would hum and occasionally he would find himself unconsciously humming the same low vibration, almost as a moan of pleasure. For him, there was no sexual component to the treatment, but there may as well have been, as the scream in his head dissipated, became weaker, and then vanished altogether. The quiet in his brain would envelope him in much the same way the shrill tone once had.

One day he fell asleep with the electrodes pulsing through his body. How long he had slept, he didn't know, but he jerked awake knowing something wasn't right. The gentle internal hum warmed him, held him, let him know everything was alright. But more than anything, it scared him. He pushed the off button on the remote and shoved it an arm's reach away on the side table. He felt like he needed to catch his breath. He wasn't exhausted. He was totally refreshed. His body and mind floated in a state of nirvana he had never experienced before; electrical heroin. It felt so unusual for him. He nervously looked around his room as if expecting somebody to be watching him. It was almost eight full hours before Mitchum noticed the tone in his head creeping up, trying to pick its way back into his brain. He let it happen, too nervous to pick the Tingler back up. He went to the garage with his trusty T-shirt, placed it against his face and. . .nothing. He had forgotten how to scream.

❧

"Did you notice any other effects other than not being able to vocalize? Did you have pain anywhere? You look okay," the doctor was shining a light in his eyes, scrutinizing the inside of his head.

"What are you looking for," Mitchum asked, "scar tissue?"

The doctor sat back and let out a sigh.

"Nothing in particular. I see nothing out of the ordinary. But we are in such an early stage of this experiment. If you feel fine and there is nothing physically wrong, I'd say enjoy the relief. This happened yesterday?"

Mitchum took a beat. "Or maybe the day before. I'm not sure. It's a little foggy and that worries me. It's almost as if I've been taking drugs. Can I become . . .?"

"Addicted?" The doctor finished his sentence for him. "Maybe. The elimination of a painful condition can be very addictive. That's what caused the opioid crisis."

The doctor walked his wheeled desk chair over to his computer and began typing in some notes.

"But in this case, we are not putting any chemicals or foreign substances into your body. We have known for an exceptionally long time that the activities of tissues and cells in the human body generate electricity, but the laws of physics dictate that any electrical current generates a corresponding magnetic field. If something goes a little off, it might create a condition like tinnitus. Hopefully by introducing a new electrical field back into your body they will work like corresponding magnetic fields and repel each other, ending the sounds in your brain."

"That's an interesting theory, Doc. For my sake, I hope it works."

The doctor turned back from the computer to face Mitchum.

"It should and in the limited experimentation in your case, it has. I understand your frustration. There are cases where the tinnitus or chronic pain has become so bad that the person committed suicide just to escape it. I won't let that happen to you.

"The nervous system requires electricity to send signals throughout your body, especially your brain. We are just trying to alter those signals a little; maybe change up the frequency. But electricity is cleaner than drugs, certainly than most pharmaceuticals. My main drive is the answer to the question— how do we get it to stop the tinnitus permanently?"

Mitchum laughed.

"Sort of a greener approach, eh Doc?"

The doctor stood and shook Mitchum's hand.

"You should be fine, but if something does pop up, don't hesitate to let me know. In the meantime, enjoy your newfound peace."

"What about my inability to scream?"

"I'm thinking that should come back as we alter or stop the use of the Tingler further down the line. We'll see. It's probably an electrical stimulus that merely needs an adjustment of one kind or another. It doesn't seem to have hindered your speech in any way. One thing at a time."

━━━∽∾━━━

THE TINGLER

It was two days later that Mitchum found himself in the produce aisle of the grocery store staring at lemons. One of the stockers noticed him and walked over.

"Is there anything I can help you find sir?"

Mitchum turned and looked at him blankly.

"Sir, are you alright? Can I help you?"

"Lemons," Mitchum said in a detached manner.

"Yes sir. You'll have to dig through to find the ripe ones. We just put these out and they are a little green still."

The stocker left Mitchum to stare at the lemons.

⌘

The fog that embraced his mind had become as debilitating as the tinnitus. His mood began to change. Mitchum realized the change and laid off the Tingler for as long as he could between flare ups.

"The lemons at the market, they were so important," Mitchum said. "I don't know why."

Maybe you were drawn to the color?"

"I'm seeing more color and less detail."

"Then," the doctor leaned forward, "That may have been something for you to focus in on. That's perfectly understandable. I'll arrange an eye exam."

"No!"

Mitchum stood up and began pacing.

"That's not the point. Don't know why I was there. I don't know how I got there! People were staring at me. I need some answers."

"Do you believe the Tingler is causing the fog?"

Mitchum stopped and stared at the doctor. "Yes. . .No. . .I don't know. I don't believe it is helping the blank spots any, but when I stop using it the tinnitus takes over."

The doctor shook his head.

"I'm going to tell you something that might sound dumb. I want you to go out and buy the best pair of noise cancelling headphones you can buy. Look online, look at electronic stores. Look everywhere. Get the best. Then stop using the Tingler. When the noise comes back, use the headphones. Whenever the noise is there, use the headphones. That will control the brain noise and eventually withdraw you from Tingler use. I'm hoping that will restore the blank spots in your memory and perception. Think of it as a replacement for your screaming."

51

"Do you think it will work?"

"We can only try. This is an experiment, remember? I want you to give me the remote for your Tingler. I don't want you to be tempted and interfere with the treatment plan without giving our experiment proper time to succeed."

Mitchum could feel his heartrate increasing and panic setting in at the thought of conceding his remote back to the doctor. He had developed a twitch in his left eye and the nervous tic was picking up in frequency. His lips felt dry and he wanted to lick them but was afraid the doctor might pick up on these different involuntary bodily quirks.

"I don't have it with me right now. When I come in for the next update, I'll bring it from home."

The doctor stood up and walked around his desk to Mitchum.

"Are you certain you can restrain yourself from giving in to the Tingler before our next appointment?"

He stared at the doctor as if everything in his body had stopped. Then his mind kicked back in and he pasted a smile on his face.

"Yes, yes of course."

The first part of the week went okay, at least what he could remember of it. Mitchum bought the headphones and used them several times early on until he felt comfortable with the settings.

He kept meaning to drop by the doctor's office to return the remote, but he never seemed to find the right time. It was just a mental crutch, he supposed. He would do it later this week.

The next day, Mitchum stomped his foot. There was nothing exceptional about that but for the fact he hadn't intended to. He was standing in the living room and his right leg picked up and stomped on the floor. His wife came running in, thinking he had dropped something.

"Sorry," he said. "I stomped."

"Why?"

He shrugged.

"Well, quit that." She looked at him for a moment trying to assess if he was okay. "You'll knock something off the walls."

She went back to what she had been doing in the other room

and he was left to ponder the loss of body control. Later, he noticed that his hand would jerk or he would have an uncontrollable spasm in his facial muscles.

One night, sitting in his favorite chair, he heard his wife.

"Mitch? Mitch! I've been talking to you for the last ten minutes and you haven't heard a single word I've said."

He looked at her, dazed, lost in some other world that she had managed to bring him back from. The fog in his brain slowly lifted, leaving behind no traces of wherever he had been.

"No, I didn't hear a word at all." He turned to her with eyes wide. "I'm frightened, Mary. Scared to death."

"This is too crazy. It's time to go back to the doctor."

"But he has nothing more for me. I've been cheating lately, using the Tingler when the pain gets so awful that it overpowers the highest setting on the headphones. I can't go on like this. We can't go on."

⸎

The doctor paced back and forth next to Mitchum examining, prodding, searching with a penlight. He made noises in his throat like he was coming to some sort of conclusion but said nothing. Finally, he sat down in the rolling chair and scooted it up near Mitchum.

"So, what you are experiencing are muscle spasms."

He flicked two fingers in the direction of Mitchum's face.

"Like the twitches in your face."

"You mean like Bell's Palsy?"

"In a way. Certain areas of your brain are stopping, shutting down, not connecting with the rest of the body."

The doctor frowned.

"No, that's not entirely correct. Let me try again. Certain areas of your brain are ceasing to connect with other areas of your nervous system, or, as in the case of your stomping foot or twitches, making connections without a conscious effort on your part. This is genuinely concerning."

"You think, Doc?" Mitchum stood up and began pacing. "I'm tired. I'm exasperated. My family is weirded out and, quite frankly, I'm scared. It's bad enough now but how far is this going to go? Am I going to start swearing uncontrollably or punch somebody for no reason?"

"Now relax. We have no reason to believe that."

"Maybe I'll just run face first into a wall for no reason. Should I even be driving a car? Am I safer on public transportation? I'm freaking out here, Doctor."

The doctor held his hands up.

"Now just take it easy. I'm sure that raising your blood pressure does nothing to help this situation. I have sent out preliminary reports to several of my colleagues and expect that we will be getting together soon. All that brain power is sure to come up with an answer."

"Soon? What does that mean? They need to finish their golf games first?"

Mitchum sat down on the examination table.

"Sorry, Doc, I'm just at such a loss here. I don't know where to turn or what to do."

"I understand. I'll write you a little something for a light sedative. Maybe that will help. It will at least calm you down."

"Thank you."

The doctor rolled over to the computer and began typing.

"One other thing Doctor. I've begun using the Tingler again."

The doctor whirled around, shocked. "What?"

"When the tinnitus became so strong that the headphones were no longer effective, I had no choice."

"I wish you hadn't done that."

"Do you have a better suggestion?"

◦◦◦

The knock on the glass of the kitchen window seemed to rouse Mitchum back to reality. They had connected the bird feeder to the outside sill so his daughter could watch the beautiful birds congregate around their birdie dinner table. Occasionally, they would knock against the glass in their frenzy for the best seeds. The noise was almost a doorbell for his daughter and she would come running into the kitchen whenever she heard the clacking against the glass. It may have been the best home project Mitchum had ever accomplished (he wasn't all that handy) and it was a delight for the whole family.

He focused his eyes through the sunlit glass and watched the birds flutter about and toss seeds onto the ground. He left the ground underneath the feeder just churned up dirt to see what kind of wildflowers may sprout from the furor above.

He slowly became aware that the faucet was running and reached down to turn it off. As he did, he noticed his hand was covered with blood. In the sink lay a large knife from the knife block on the counter. It too was bloody, crimson, and giving off a slightly metallic odor which rose from the sink and assaulted his senses. He took a quick step back, startled. The sun, through the window, lit up the front of his clothes which were darkened and stained.

He ripped his shirt open and checked himself for cuts, flipping his hands over, looking for wounds. When he found none, he quickly washed his hands off to better inspect them. He felt no pain from any wounds and breathed a sigh of relief. As he turned to leave the kitchen, he could see a red trail across the tiled floor and the legs of his daughter sticking out on the other side of the door jamb. The rest of her body was hidden behind the other side of the wall. What he could see was as bloody as he was.

***

Mitchum looked up from the bed when he heard the metal door of his cell rattle and pull open.

A guard stood there, staring at him as if he was the most disgusting thing on the planet. He stepped aside and let the doctor in.

"I'll call for you when I've finished," the doctor said.

The guard shut the door and walked away. The doctor turned back to Mitchum and sat down next to him on the bed.

"How are you doing my boy? It must have been a terrible shock?"

Mitchum stared at him as if he were an alien being.

"Why didn't you come to me if things had gotten that bad?"

"I did," Mitchum answered coldly.

The silence hung like a velvet curtain between the two men.

"I am going to work with your lawyer on your defense. We'll convince them it wasn't your fault."

"Whose fault was it then?"

"We may have found an answer," the doctor said. "I think we can cure you from this terrible disorder."

"Disorder?"

Mitchum began laughing uncontrollably. When he'd caught his breath, he took hold of the doctor by the shoulders. He leaned in toward his face.

"Guess what, Doc? You have cured me a little bit."

"What do you mean?"

"When I saw my family in the house that day, I learned how to scream again."

Alley Oops was the first short story of mine published. It remains my number one reprinted story. It was, also, the first complete story I ever wrote. The original draft of this piece was put down on paper in 1969 when I was in high school in South Lyon, Michigan and had a very encouraging English teacher, Nancy Hogg. She has my eternal gratitude.

The tale had been worked and reworked for years until a final version found a home in a Bram Stoker award-winning anthology Midnight Walks. For its longevity alone it holds a special place in my heart. I also feel it is indicative of the style of story I would go on to write for years to come featuring the twist or the short sharp shock.

I have always been influenced by the writings of horror master Robert Bloch. His combination of humor and horror landed a sweet spot in me. Although he set a high standard of taletelling which I'll never achieve, he isn't a bad role model to use as a bar to strive towards.

ALLEY OOPS

"It's immoral to steal, but you can take things."
—Anton Chekhov

DARKNESS HAD BEEN arriving earlier and earlier since the time change had gone into effect. The dull gray of the evening was pushed from the sky by the heavy curtain of night while the late autumn wind's piercing damp chill easily cut through thick layers of clothing worn by the people on the street. They grimaced and braced themselves against its grasp. With their hats pulled down and collars turned up they appeared to be a race of faceless alien creatures that leaned forward as they walked. Shafts of light from the department store windows created rectangular yellow pools on the sidewalks beckoning to those passing by to come into the warmth.

Inside, the customers shuffled from counter to counter in search of a final closing time bargain. The anxious clerks alternated between looking at their watches and straightening the counters, so they'd be able to leave as soon as the shop doors hit the last customer in the backside on their way out. In different areas of the stores, long sections of the overhead fluorescents were shut down as a "last call" to spendaholic patrons. A general cattle-like movement towards the exits had begun with the occasional housewife clutching her purse and looking up uneasily at the areas of darkened ceiling. The old-timers smiled to themselves with the knowledge of another fifteen minutes of shopping time still available. It was from this group of regulars that Lupita belonged.

Lupita was part of an even smaller subspecies of consumer. Lupita was a counter shopper. The difference between window-shopping and what Lupita did was that she did it from inside the store, browsing the aisles and enjoying the display counters. She was in her seventies. She needed more calcium than she would ever see again (as her teeth offered in testament) and she was having a harder time seeing since the onslaught of her cataracts. These daily shopping sprees were the highlight of her days; that and the "700 Club" on television. She would just listen to it with her eyes closed so as not to cause herself undo eye strain and to better feel the spirit of the Dove filling her entire two-room apartment with love and understanding. The hand of God also stretched out for a minimum ten percent tithe.

She rationalized that ten percent of what little she received each month was a very small price to pay for eternal life and the answers to all her prayers. The eternal life was yet to come and she was positive that before she died,she would manage to get all her prayers answered.

God didn't do it all at once. There were other people in the world to consider, after all. A good, God-fearing woman like herself couldn't be selfish about blessings and still plan on receiving her reward in heaven.

She didn't mind not being able to buy the things she pawed at and picked through in the department stores. That was just the way things were, even if she did imagine herself wearing and owning the prized goods that were on the mannequins and hanging from the racks. It was pleasure enough for her just to be able to touch them. Her blessing of new clothes would have to wait.

She had used today's prayer to ask God to let her see things a little better. Since her cataracts had stolen the deed to her sight, the colors had faded, even in the store's bright neon lights. The materials she ran through her fingers still felt lovely. There was no change in her sense of touch, but the fashions just weren't the same without color. Despite her age, she'd always felt knowledgeable when it came to fashion and fashion trends. After all, she saw the latest ones in the department store every day. But if God could only help her with a little more color sense. . .

Fifteen minutes and the time to leave this wonderland for the day had come at last. There was always a strange feeling when she left each day at closing time. That's what they say isn't it? Everybody looks good at closing. She paused for a moment to consider. It was just the opposite here. She felt like she looked good until closing and then went out into the real world, her old self.

"Lupita."

She raised her hand in "good night" at the sound of the guard's stern voice and started shuffling towards the door. Tomorrow was another day, and her daily shop routine would begin again.

He always felt he was running faster when he was running into the wind. The rush of air blasting against his face as it blew his hair back and the roar in his ears combined to make him feel like the Flash. He could only imagine what it might feel like to ride a motorcycle. That would be so cool. Right now he was just a wannabe, but someday he would have enough money to buy that motorcycle or just about anything else he wanted.

He still had the purse clutched tight to his side as he ran into the wind, a blur moving swiftly across the comic book page. He wanted to be sure he'd put enough distance between himself and the original owner of the bag before he slowed down. The woman had been in such a tizzy when he'd snatched it that he knew it would take her a few moments to recover from the shock.

Then she'd probably act like a typical female and run in circles yelling and flailing her arms. He had to laugh at the imagery. Like a chicken with its head cut off. Ha! They were all so damn pathetic, so damn useless. His father had been right.

With more distance between him and the woman he felt safe enough to finally slow down.

The alley before him offered a dark refuge from prying eyes and he headed into it to find a place to check out his prize. Except for the streetlights at each end of the alley, it remained shadow-filled and secretive. Halfway down the asphalt strip he stopped and crouched down against a building. The purse was already unzipped (another dumb move by a stupid woman), so he dumped the contents out onto the ground against the wall to block the wind. Quickly, he spread everything out in front of him so that he could see everything better. Other than the wallet and some loose change, there didn't appear to be anything of value. He scooped up the silver change from the ground and dumped it in his pockets. The wallet contained a twenty and two tens, which he also took.

Swearing silently to himself for such a small haul, he hurled the wallet over a fence into an adjoining backyard. He kicked and scattered everything on the ground in different directions.

Then he began to walk towards the opposite end of the alley carrying the empty purse with him.

After he'd gone a couple of blocks, he'd drop the purse in a trashcan or shrub. Nothing would be left together, no arrows to point towards him. He had to cover his tracks every time. He'd have to steal again. Nobody who really knew how to party could live on forty bucks a night.

As she stepped out of the building, the wind caught Lupita on the side of the face and shoved her sideways against the storefront. She side-hopped on one leg a moment trying to balance herself and turned in towards the back of a building.

"The Devil's wind," she muttered through a mouthful of stalactites.

She stuck her hand inside of her coat pocket and pulled out her babushka. The wind pulled and grabbed at the material turning it into a windsock. She held the corners tightly and yanked it down across her head. The wind continued to tear at it, this way and that, until she finally had secured it down to her satisfaction. She pulled it close against her head and tied it windstorm-tight under her chin. Her head almost felt hermetically sealed against Satan. She couldn't see very well anyway, so having it pulled so far down over her face caused her no additional problems. Once she managed to arrive home, she would have to brush her hair for hours before she could sleep on it.

Now that she had battened down the hatches, she was ready to forge ahead and find her way home. It wasn't far, only a couple of blocks. The wind was cutting through her thin summer coat. It pierced every threadbare inch of the cheap and ancient material, and she was feeling unprepared, naked against nature's blast. It was, however, the warmest coat she owned. It was the only coat she owned. There would come a time when she would be able to get one of those quilted thick coats she'd seen in the store tonight. She would be so toasty and warm in a number like that. All her friends would stop her on the street and want to touch her lovely coat. Someday.

In the meantime, she layered underneath it with newspaper store flyers as best she could for insulation.

She looked ahead at the two windy blocks before her. The traffic signals bounced on the wire and swayed in the air while flyers and newspapers scrambled past her like they were trying to shake their printing loose. She sighed. Just because you're old doesn't mean you have to fall into a routine, she thought. If she took the alley, just for tonight, she'd not only cut off some distance but maybe some of the breeze too. She slid the strap of her battered purse up her arm and headed for the entrance of the alley.

He moved quickly and light like something being buffeted about. Almost invisibly, he flashed down the alley keeping his eyes open to any opportunity that he might encounter. The wind was both a curse and a blessing. While it covered up any sounds he might make, it also caused him to jump at every scuttle of paper or clang of metal. He didn't like it. He was nervous enough without help from Mother Nature. He would have been a lot happier sitting in some quiet corner with a quart of beer and a full paper of cocaine. But he'd need much more than forty dollars to come up with enough for a good bindle and something to drink too. One more good purse snatch could complete his evening and he was anxious to get it over with as soon as possible.

He came to the mouth of the alley and stood back in the shadow of the building. He needed to plan his next move. While he stood there facing the wind, it brought the sound to him. The noise was human in origin, no doubt, and it was talking. But it was only one voice, like a radio, maybe. There was no response from a second party.

He peeked around the corner of the building trying to focus in. What he could make out was a lump of clothing; a shapeless, formless, indefinite mass of clothing. He knew it was human from the sound and he could tell it was female by the pitch. But the way it huddled inside of its clothes left its configuration up for question. High up on the part of the lump he took for an arm and a shoulder, was a purse. His ticket for fun and games had just been punched.

Lupita reached the mouth of the alley and turned down it towards home. The changing of direction as she rounded the corner stopped the wind from slamming her sideways and it became a battering ram instead. She pulled on her material cocooning her clothes about herself a bit tighter, gritted her teeth, and leaned her body forward against the tempest with determination.

She wasn't thrilled with traversing the alley, but anything that cut down on the travel time home tonight was a plus. She couldn't shrug off colds and flu like she used to, though, and her bones would ache for days after a bout with illness. If she could get home relatively quickly maybe she could avoid getting sick.

The clanging of a metal lid blowing off a trashcan and smacking down onto the asphalt made her jump. A piece of bubble wrap dancing down the alley hugged around one of her legs causing her to kick at it before she realized what it was. She reached down and peeled it away, feeling like a fool to be so nervous. After all, this was her neighborhood, her old familiar neighborhood where she'd grown up. There was no need to be frightened. But for some reason she couldn't shake her feeling of encroaching danger.

She'd finished walking the length of one alley and only had one more to go. They were only the short ends of the blocks. Then, she would round the corner and be home; warm and safe.

She would have some hot cocoa to drink and put her feet up. It was so silly to worry. She'd truly get a chuckle about this. She tried the mind trick of thinking warm toasty thoughts and actually felt a little better. She'd spent her tithe well. The Lord was watching over her.

He watched and then followed behind her into the mouth of the next alley. He'd been watching her ever since he'd heard her approach. Backing into the darkness, she had passed within no more than ten or twelve feet of him. She didn't see him because she had her babushka wrapped down so tight about her face it was like looking through a periscope. Lost in her own world and muttering to herself, she plowed as straight and narrow course as she could manage. She couldn't have been anymore wobbly had she been drunk.

He knew she couldn't hear him. Occasionally, the sound of her one-sided conversation would carry down to him on the wind. He could tell by the way she jumped when some plastic blew against her leg that she was skittish and he'd have to be quick. He laughed to himself. Maybe she thought it was a rat or something.

"No rats out tonight lady," he whispered. "Only one mean old junkyard dog come to get his bone."

He moved faster now to catch up to her, skirting the shadows in case she happened to glance back. He wanted to grab her before she reached the end of the alley so he could keep his face in the lane's darkness when he caught her. There could be no chance for her to identify him.

The way she was bent into the wind she'd never be able to stop him. Grab it and run. His heart thumped in anticipation. Stealth, baby, stealth!

Lupita stuck out her chin and allowed herself one deep cold breath of relief and a small smile of satisfaction. She could see the streetlight at the end of the alley, shadows from tree branches danced across the face of it waving at her to hurry and come home. It wouldn't be long now.

Home was just around the corner. She pulled the babushka down so tight about her face that she was afraid she might tear the material. So close.

She was knocked sideways by his assault, like being blindsided by a car. It was a move he had perfected long before tonight. The idea was to knock the victim one way while grabbing the purse and moving in the opposite direction. It almost always snapped the woman and her purse apart like a wishbone. Almost always. This time, the strap sat up so high onto her shoulder that it helped to righten her stance when he pulled on it. He was running in opposite direction when he realized he wasn't going anywhere. He turned and saw the woman with the scarf-covered face holding on to her purse strap like it was a lifeline to a rowboat. He couldn't believe it. It wasn't his night.

Holding firm onto the strap he quickly glanced around the alley for some help. There it was.

A stick the size of a cane lay not eight feet away from where they struggled. Although he couldn't get her to release the prize, he began pulling her in the general direction of the wood.

She wasn't strong enough to stop him from yanking her in that direction.

Keeping one hand grasped firmly around the purse strap, he reached out with the other for the stick. A bit more, just a step. His fingers scraped at it, bumping against it, and pushing it further from his grasp. More dammit, one more step. The only audible sound was the wind. It rushed past their ears with a locomotive moan and covered up the grunts and groans made by the two of them to any passersby. Finally, barely, his fingers were able to grab the stick. It felt good in his hand, weighty enough. He turned back and took one last look at the living clothes hamper still holding the purse strap. He swung his club for all he was worth.

The blow caught her on the upper right side of the face, snapping her head back with an audible crack. Her grip on her purse never weakened. At this point, she was probably holding on more by reflex, using the strap as a lifeline. He turned, facing her straight on and swung again. This time the blow came down from above, hitting her on the top of the head and slamming her to her knees. Still she held on, even as he jerked and wiggled the purse. He was angry. From his hip he swung his bat one-handed, putting his body behind it, imbedding the scarf in the side of her face.

She fell to the pavement, the cheap vinyl strap snapping under her weight and the purse was finally freed. The bloody side of her face thumped onto the asphalt with a sickening thud. A dark stain soaked its way quickly through the material, spreading out and forming a small slow-moving stream that ran from her head. The ends of the babushka fluttered in the wind as it tried unsuccessfully to pull itself out from under her wet cheek. Breathing hard, he held up the purse like a trophy. He had his prize, but it had been too much work. It had taken too large of a toll, too much time, too much effort. He dumped the contents carelessly on the ground and the wind scattered them quickly. There was no wallet, no money.

He was angry about the effort involved for zero payout. He was angry with her resistance.

He was angry about her strength and sheer determination. It had all been for naught. He swore and kicked the purse into the darkness of the alley. Raising the stick, he rained a series of blows to her body. The muted thuds sounded like he was beating a mattress.

"Bitch! You bitch," he screamed, working the frustration out of his system.

Smacking her one final blow on the top of the head he saw her split brains glisten and reflect the streetlight. The blood oozed out from under her mouth in a puddle on the asphalt. Finally he tossed the stick aside, breathing heavily. He spat at the form on the ground and wiped his mouth with the length of his sleeve.

Another sudden blast of frigid air shot down the alley, grabbing the end of her kerchief and finally peeling it away from her bloody face. He stood there and stared down into the face of his grandmother.

I have always been an admirer of writer/editor Jonathan Maberry, so when he told me the concept of his anthology Out of Tune *and invited me to submit a story, I jumped at the chance. To have an anthology of horror and supernatural stories which find their origins in historic folk tunes is a very interesting premise. A great majority of folksongs were already storytelling set to music, so it was difficult to find one I liked that hadn't told the complete tale in the lyrics of the song. I didn't feel like transcribing somebody else's story.*

As a teenager I first heard "Black is the Color of My True Love's Hair" in a comedy sketch by the Smothers Brothers. Later I came across a video of a live/in studio performance of the song by Nina Simone and was mesmerized. That was all I needed.

For his anthology Jonathan took that extra step and had a folklorist from a university write a page after each story giving the history of the song the story was based on. The result was an intelligent and interesting anthology worthy of any horror lover or historical aficionado's time. As I mentioned in my Preface, everybody has a story to tell.

BLACK IS THE COLOR OF MY TRUE LOVE'S HAIR

"...unstable souls...they are the children of curse"
—2 Peter 2:14, 1599 Geneva Bible

IN THE FAR CORNER of a forgotten stone garden stands a most unusual gravestone; a chiseled sandstone child, solemn and expressionless. She watches the seasons pass without comment. Dismissed in the shadowed extremity of this hallowed place by the statues of weeping angels draped over the gravesite or stone urns and granite wreaths, the lone child stands erect, arms at her side, staring straight ahead. Unnerving in its simplicity. Where other monuments were entwined by nature's vines and roots, in this neglected corner of the garden the girl stands clean.

The ground about her, wasted and brown as if Mother Earth has offered up the final rejection, allowing no peace. The original carving, although graced with great artistic emotion, is somewhat crudely set as if it was toiled upon by unskilled hands. From the direction she faces, the winds and rains have wiped away many details of her surface and the only inscription offered to the curious is hard to read and incomplete.

Mara L rr
orn 1889 – D ed 19 0
To soon was taken om hi wo
Bl k is th c l r of y tru ov s h r

Her face remains mostly intact, though softened with time and weather. Her mouth, wiped clean. If one were to walk around the girl, they would notice very distinct long locks of hair, carved with exquisite care, flowing down her back. The hair was so attended to by the sculptor that it feels like the predominance of his time was spent away from her face. The flow and placement of each shock of hair fills one with awe for the workmanship that does not appear elsewhere on the effigy. The love that is exhibited here is wrapped in great sadness, as all extraordinary loves are, if they exist at all.

∿

The shadow of maternity had hung over the shack for more than seven months before the fateful night arrived. Elwin could hardly wait for the birth of his first born. He had spent the last few years of his life anticipating this exact event and hoping this moment would come sooner rather than later. The only woman who had been willing to shackle herself to a dirt-poor farmer was laying in the next room screaming with pain. It had been Hell on earth living with her. After their initial sexual encounter prior to their wedding night, the opportunities to procreate had been few and far between. There had been no lovemaking or joy. Any sexual satisfaction he encountered had been in the bed of a neighbor. He had rejoiced that one of the quick awkward thrusts his wife had allowed him had completed its mission.

As she felt the pain from the poison course through her body, she realized it was time and revenge was tasting sweet. Her agony rose and fell like waves crashing and each time, catching her breath was harder and harder. She savored it, knowing that the last minutes of her life would be in her own hands. It was her call. It could be minutes or maybe hours, but it would be over soon enough.

"Elwin, go," she gasped. "Fetch the undertaker and be as quick as you can."

"Undertaker?"

She almost sat straight up in bed with the pain and her declaration.

"Yes, the undertaker."

"What? What are you talking about?"

"I'm talkin' about the fact that I'm gonna die and I'm taking your precious baby with me. You wanted me to carry your baby like some kind of breeding stock. Well, I did that. You took an oath to be true to me and you couldn't keep your damn pecker in your pants! I'm killin' that child by killin' myself."

Elwin began to cry.

"What did you do?"

"You cheatin' slob. There's only one thing you love more than yourself. You love this unborn baby, there's just not enough left over to love me for carrying it, is there? I believe your baby is already dead and I'm just pushing it out. I will be following it in death shortly after and with that I'll take your heart for all eternity. I take what you wouldn't give me!"

She winced in pain and then looked him straight in the eyes through her sweat and the heat.

"It makes me happy. It makes me really happy. I'm finally taking your heart, Elwin."

She shouted and grabbed her stomach.

"Oh God!"

Elwin stuttered a moment looking at his wife and then headed for the door.

"I'm going to get Miss Orpha," he said.

"Miss Orpha is a Yarb Doctor," his wife shouted after him. "She can't help you none. It's too late. I don't need no witchin' around my family. If it was illegal for her to be peddling her mumbo-jumbo, I would have had her thrown in jail. You're too late. Too damn late! Why don't you just run to your whore instead?"

She doubled up with pain and clutched her stomach as if it might explode. Her breathing was ragged and forced. Her face strained, turning darker in color. Sweat ran from her face in deep rivulets. Her voice now came out soft between the exhalations of her breath.

"You gave me pain first. Now I'm giving it back. I am ending my suffering and that of the child. I swear on the ghost of my Father, as I did on our wedding night, that you will find no pleasure in me or your offspring."

She practically rose up out of the bed in anger and spit at him as she spoke.

"I curse you! You will have nothing! You are a poor excuse for a man."

Then the pain grabbed her and knocked her back into the damp mattress.

"Death, be quick about it!"

Elwin ran to the barn where the wagon sat ready and left to fetch the midwife. His wife grabbed the sideboards of the bed and held on as tight as she could manage. She prayed the child would try to emerge before they returned. Then, if it were living, she could kill it with her own hands without anyone interfering.

While Elwin stood to the side helping with clean water and towels, Orpha worked on the child.

She leaned up between his wife's legs and her hands and trained fingers manipulated the baby inside. She cocked her head as if listening to something, but the only noise was the wife's laboring.

"It's coming," she said.

"The child?" he asked.

"Four, three, two. . ."

She paused and then the thunder rattled the cabin. She smiled at him.

"Wipe me," Orpha said. "The storm. Have you never waited for the storm by counting from the flash?"

He moved forward with a damp cloth and blotted the sweat from her forehead and out of her eyes.

"I hadn't noticed," he said, confused.

"You are negro scum," his wife shouted and spit at Orpha as she worked.

Orpha shook her head, more from what she was feeling rather than her running perspiration. She was unhappy with her discoveries.

"Kill me!"

His wife screamed throughout the ordeal, but Orpha paid her no heed. They had tied her ankles to the frame at the foot of the bed, legs spread wide. She would offer them no help and Orpha didn't want to be kicked.

"The child is in kneeling breech," she said to Elwin.

"Is that good?"

"No. It is a sign, like the storm. There's evil in this birth. She'd be better off dead."

Orpha watched his face. Clearly, he did not understand what she was saying.

"If the child lives it will be evil."

He walked in circles trying to get his thoughts in order.

"She must live! You must save her. She is all I've got."

"I have never willingly brought evil into this world."

"I'm the father. I can train her and teach her in the way of goodness."

"You are a poor excuse for a man," his wife shouted for the second time that night.

"The bond is here," Orpha said and with two fingers she pulled out a taunt section of the umbilical to the opening of his wife, showing it to Elwin. He turned his head away.

"Look," Orpha insisted. "The child is not tight inside. There is room for the cord to slip along the sides of the walls and come out first. I am trying to push it back up, past the child. The feet and the hind are coming out together. If they pinch the cord the child will suffocate before birthing. I will have no say in that. That would be God trying stop the child. If I try to pull the babe down and out before the cord can slip out sideways, the force will either pull loose the baby's limbs from the sockets or split apart your wife. I can't save them both."

"Save neither, witch!" his wife cursed at Orpha and tried to wiggle about.

"I am here to do what I have been trained to do."

"You are betraying my wishes, you old crone!"

She pulled out her hands and carelessly wiped her forehead leaving a splattering of blood and fluid behind.

"I am already betraying my own soul. Your crazy wishes do not concern me at this point," she said to his wife.

Orpha wiped her hands on the gingham rag she kept in her apron pocket.

"It won't happen. It can't happen," Elwin rocked his body and called to the heavens. "You must save my baby."

Orpha looked at him with disdain.

"That child should be buried while there is still life in her, standing up, so that God can take the child's soul before he loses it to Satan. You are making a big mistake here."

The thunder took another shot at gaining their attention.

"You are so simple. Even for being a man you are simple."

She shook her head.

"You understand nothing of the ways of the Devil."

"I understand that all I've ever wanted is a child. I will not have another chance. I'm poor, growing older every day and no woman looks to me. I have to save that child."

Orpha shook her head, then reached into the pocket of her apron and pulled out a handful of objects. She pushed aside the personal items from the top of the scarred wooden dresser and laid her items out instead. To Elwin, it looked like some dirt and a few bones and jewelry scattered on the wooden top. His wife screamed and he finally found his voice.

"What are you doing?"

"What I've been prepared to do," Orpha said as she placed certain items in their own small pile. "The Devil has given us a choice and you are stupid enough to take him up on it."

She took a pinch of the dirt. With two fingers, she spread the soil in a cross pattern on his wife's stomach.

"What is that for?"

"Blessed dirt to help counter the jimsonweed your wife ingested. If we are unlucky enough, one soul will remain with the body tonight. The bone yard shall make the choice."

"But my wife. . .you must save her too."

"I must do nothing of the sort," she said and with her finger and thumb spread the belly dirt out into a wider line. "Salvation is elusive."

Elwin was scared. He stepped up and pushed her dirt-covered hands back.

"I don't want any of your hoodoo magic in my house."

He was puffed up, asserting himself. Orpha spun on him, freezing him with just a look and causing him to shrink back against the wall into the shadows.

"You stay there," she hissed at him. "You stay there, little man and let me do my work! You fetched me. Now I am here. I am doing your bidding, not mine! So, leave me alone before I change my mind."

With a huff, Orpha turned back to her work.

"Yes, I am a midwife," she continued, frustrated. "I am also a Granny woman. I'll use every tool at my disposal. On a night like tonight, however, it may not be enough."

The thunder answered in response. She spoke low and slow.

"You stay out of my way whilst I try to save at least one Missouri life this evening."

She took a necklace from her pile and put it on herself. Her movements were deliberate, unhurried, and ceremonial, as if there were all the time in the world. Her fingers moved over the charm that hung from the beads, fingering the amulet's familiar surface, focusing on her ritual.

"Can you help her?"

Elwin's attention continued to be split between Orpha and his wife. He was growing more frantic by the moment, feeling helpless in this nightmare.

"I can," Orpha said. "But we don't know yet whether or not it is a girl. Do we?"

Orpha's toothy smile shrank him back yet again.

"All we know is that the babe is bedeviled and your wife has caused herself and the child great suffering. It must be removed. Then we can find how the poison has affected it."

She kissed the periapt and turned the necklace around so that the pendant hung down her back. She faced the bed, her countenance taking on such a dark tone and emotion that Elwin would not have thought it was the same woman who had walked through the door with him earlier that evening. The umbra that bisected her face seemed to be part of her skin and gave a great lurid depth to the lines that etched her appearance. From the other pocket of her apron, she pulled out a sizable knife with serrated blade. She paused and then looked at Elwin.

"You must be strong," she said, looking him up and down. "Although, I am aware that is counter to your soul."

He looked at the glinting metal and then to his wife.

"For the cord?" he asked Orpha.

"No," she replied. "For the womb."

In the years that followed the birth Elwin was visited often by Orpha to "watch the child's progress." While he was grateful for the assistance, he felt wary of their secret talks and long woodsy walks. But he couldn't deny that there were things, certain female-related things, that he just couldn't understand. Darkness draped the house and neighbors seemed to shun his land.

He had lost his position at the local feed-seller and needed to make do with odd jobs and farm pickup work. To help their income, he carved wood and chiseled stone, making things for people. Their house was in poorest of the poorest of areas.

Despite Orpha's continued warnings to destroy the young girl, she grew, thrived, and seemed generally happy. She would bring her father rabbits and squirrels along with any other small animals she had caught to help with their meals. She wouldn't trap them, but instead killed them with sticks and rocks in the most violent manner. It put him off, but he never turned down the food, for their needs were greater than his convictions. Whenever he would speak to Orpha about this, she would ask him if he was ungrateful for the food. He wasn't, of course. Beggars could not be choosers. He didn't want to lose his daughter's love and Orpha would shake her head, warning him the day of reckoning was well past due.

"The Devil is a strong demon," she would say. "And you are a weak man."

If Elwin attempted to offer excuses, he was put off by Orpha and charmed by his daughter. Mara was a charmer. Her jet-black hair carried the ghost of her mother and the shine in her eyes was as mischievous as it was lost. She had but to touch her father's arm to calm him or stroke his cheek to charm him to a happier unquestioning place. Elwin was always too tired to fight her while she was happy. The whiffs of a spirit that lingered in the cabin since the death of his wife rested like a blanket of foreboding. He could not get out from under the weight of it and it kept him silent.

He worried about Mara every day. In his heart he knew time was near. Were he a religious man, he might have prayed for guidance. Instead, once or twice a month he would hitch the wagon and go to the Joplin library. There, he found books on folklore, superstition, witchcraft, and children born under a bad sign. He would stutter his way through them, moving his lips as he silently read to himself, following the line of words his finger traced. He found that there were two options; the fight to win his daughter's soul, which he knew he couldn't win, and another he couldn't force himself to take. Either he would drive out all the bad blood from her mother and the poison that the jimsonweed had instilled in it, or he would have to bury her alive with her head pointed towards heaven. When the showdown for the soul of his daughter came, he told himself he would not lose from lack of preparation.

As she pinned the clothes to the line, Elwin watched the wind move Mara's shiny dark hair across her back in small waves. The glistening was diamond-like in its sheen and the volume was unworldly. When she turned and looked at him, Elwin smiled back in a learned reaction. Keep her happy. Let her know you were her rock, her only parent. He needed her to answer only to him.

But as she had gotten older, she understood her power more and more. She really could do anything she wanted, even if she was a little unsure of what steps to take to make that happen.

She removed the final clothes pin from her mouth and slid it over the dangling piece of material, holding it securely on the line. Then she stepped back to admire her work.

"Another job is finished, Mara," Elwin said. "Well done."

"Yes," she said. "That's the last time I'm going to do that."

Elwin watched her face cloud over as she sat in the wooden chair next to him. The clothes danced on the line.

"That's the last time I'll do anything I'm really not partial to."

"If only life were that easy, child," he said.

She turned to him, intense and meaningful.

"But it is, Papa."

She played with her hands for a moment, choosing her words carefully.

"I can make people do things if I want."

A statement made more chilling with the innocence in which it was spoken.

"What do you mean, Mara?" he asked.

But he knew what she meant.

"It's a feeling inside. It builds and builds until I want to pop. I have to let it go to make myself feel better."

She turned her head slightly and smiled at him with her eyes. She would be able to charm them all. He could feel that smile travel up his spine and sit between his shoulder blades, pecking the base of his neck.

"The other morning when you left to go to Alexander's store, I sat out on the front step and watched the woods. A squirrel, a fat red brown one, stood on the lower limb of the oak there."

Mara pointed at a branch some 40 feet from where they sat. Her head cocked slightly when she spoke as though she was reliving the entire incident over again.

"He chattered at me. I believe he was mad that I was sitting and watching him or maybe he was upset that I had killed and eaten his brother. I yelled out at him, 'Be quiet!' But he continued on with his talk."

She stood up from the chair as she told her tale and took a step toward the tree in reenactment.

"I said, 'Be quiet,'" and Mara continued her slow step to the tree. "I was so furious that I held out my hands, open wide, and screamed at the top of my lungs to frighten him off. He froze still for a moment and then dropped to the ground, still. I did it without stick or stone, Papa."

Mara turned back to her father, once again looking like the little girl she was.

"I just wanted to quiet him, but I killed him."

Elwin stood up and hugged her tightly.

"No, no, Mara. You didn't kill him. It was just a strange thing and he happened to die at the same moment you shouted. That's all."

Elwin put his arm around her shoulder and they turned to walk back into the house.

"Do you really think so, Father?"

"I do."

"That is odd. I thought it was me."

"No, no. Just strange timing. Life is like that sometimes," Elwin explained and stepped up on to the stoop.

Mara stopped and looked up at him.

"Yes, I suppose that's true," she said nodding her head. "So now that makes four strange things altogether this week."

She walked up the stairs past him and into the cabin. The chill returned to Elwin like an old companion.

When the first child's body was discovered, the news spread quickly through the hollow. He'd been found fresh as life, like he was sleeping there in the grass. The was no sign of violence, no injuries, not even any out-of-the-ordinary bug bites. It was just an odd thing that the doctor couldn't explain.

"Sometimes, these strange things just happen," was all he could say. "God calls us home to Him when we least expect it."

Elwin heard the talk at Alexander's Store and knew the boy's family. A layer of dread covered his heart as he walked the ridge to his cabin. When he arrived, he cupboarded the meager supplies and stepped out to look for Mara. She sat on a stump out back gazing into the trees.

"What are you doing?' he asked as he sat down beside her.

"Watching."

"For what?"

"Dinner."

"You don't have to today, Mara. I made enough chore money to buy us a few groceries."

Elwin pulled a long strand of grass from beside the steps and stuck it in his mouth. He looked at her face as he spoke.

"I heard about Paul today at the store."

She squeezed one eye tight for a split second as if he was giving her a headache but continued searching the trees.

"You know about your school friend Paul?"

She turned and looked at him.

"He was not my friend."

"He was ten and now he is dead," Elwin chastised. "He is much too young to be dead."

She watched his eyes for a moment and then looked back into the trees.

"He was older than our dinner," she said.

"That's true. But he was a person not a rabbit."

"The rabbits never laughed at me," she said and abruptly stood.

She walked into the cabin, leaving Elwin alone on the steps. He sat trying to figure what he knew for certain and what he did not want to know. It is hard for even the most rational of people to digest things that hang just outside of daily experience and Elwin decided he had more reading to do. That was it. That was all. He just needed more book learning.

Some weeks later, Elwin heard about the dead horse. He was sitting on a stone next to the road drinking some water he'd brought to the field with him when the county agent went by and stopped to talk.

"Just seemed like the heart up and stopped. Strangest thing. Doc can't figure it out. There had been mention of a young child being seen in the pen shortly before it happened, but nobody knew for sure."

Elwin knew for sure, but he didn't say so, not even to himself.

"Took you too many years to admit it," Orpha said. "But now judgment time is here ain't it? You conceived her during your spell of sinning and your wife tried to destroy her because she knew of your sin. It all says "devil" in great big letters."

"Can you help me? Another child cannot die because I was too weak to stop what needed to be stopped."

Orpha went back to whatever she was cooking. She poked at it with a fork to let the grease drip down the sides. It hissed when it hit the hot stove.

"You never want to let things heat up enough to pop. You can ruin a lot by letting it get that far. You allowed a cursed child to live."

She stood up and laid the big fork on the cutting board.

"I did warn you," she said. "It's true that all prophets are liars, but I knew what I was talking about. I've been through this before."

Elwin leaned his head against the door jamb of her cabin and began to cry.

"Orpha, you've got to help me. I can't do this alone."

She grabbed his face with both hands. Inches from him, he could smell the rot in her breath.

"I tried to help you! You rebuked me. Now things are dying and you come crawling back to me to fix it. Well, damn you! Help yourself!"

He jerked and pulled away when some of her spittle sprayed his face. He wiped his lips with the back of his sleeve.

"You've got to help me. I've got nowhere else to turn."

Her eyes seared through him like burning coals for a moment before she turned away and climbed back into her cabin. She walked to the corner of the room and grabbed a spade.

"You know what you have to do."

She tossed the shovel at him, and he grabbed it. He looked at it in terror realizing it truly was the only solution to his problem.

"God has already damned your soul, Elwin. Salvation is a fickle thing."

She slammed the cabin door shut. He stood looking down at his daughter's murder weapon.

Secretly digging the hole in the back corner of the cemetery was easy. There was no keeper, nobody to notice his activity. He had contemplated burying her somewhere out in the woods, but knew he needed consecrated land so God would take her soul or, at the very least, hold her down. Getting the Reverend to bless new ground would come with its own problems and suspicions, so he had chosen ground that was already blessed.

The night of the deed was cloudless and still. It was darker than the bottom of their well and Mara lay peacefully on her blankets. Elwin approached her with the clothesline he had torn from the trees out back. His work rag from the barn stuck out of one pocket. He tried to move without creaking the boards by stepping as close to the walls as he could where he knew the boards had less give. He crept to her side of the room and looked down at the only thing he had ever loved. She was beautiful. Her black hair even seemed to shine in the darkness catching light from some unknown place. He stood for a long time looking at her, remembering this moment.

With a final deep breath, he jumped on her before she could awaken in the confusion. Being sure to stay clear of her hands, he tied them behind her and began binding her legs together. She screamed and thrashed but he was too strong for her. There was no one to hear her cries. He ran the rope from the top of her leg bindings to her hands and over her shoulders, bringing it back down on the other side. She was now prevented from bending and had to remain in that position. He would lower her into the hole feet first, like a fence post, and she would remain erect, head toward heaven, as he shoveled the dirt in on top of her. He would save her, and she would wait for him in heaven.

Elwin retrieved the work rag from his pocket and stuffed it into her mouth. He secured it by wrapping a length of rope about her face. Then he picked her up, slung her over his shoulder, and took her out to the wagon in the barn. He laid her gently in the back and climbed up top.

BLACK IS THE COLOR OF MY TRUE LOVE'S HAIR

Giving the reins a shake, the horse began its journey to the stone garden and the final resting place of Mara.

At the gravesite, he lifted her out of the wagon and carried her over to the hole. She had managed to slip a couple of her fingers free and touched his arm. He turned, gazed into her face, and almost abandoned the entire plan. Her eyes pleaded with him and tears ran down Mara's cheeks. The child was begging for life. The rope he had wrapped around her head to keep the rag in place had chafed her fine white skin and she was bleeding. He stopped on the grass and set her down as his body heaved in agony over what he was doing. When his sobbing had subsided, he looked down at her and realized how much he loved her. He must save her. Her soul was all that mattered now.

Picking her back up, he carried her to the hole and laid her next to it. Elwin grabbed her under her arms, twisted her about until her feet were dangling over the edge of the cavity, and tipped her slowly in. He slid her down until she came to a stop with her head about a foot below the surface of the ground.

Standing up, he looked around for Orpha's shovel. Using the side of it, he scooped the dirt into the hole and over the head of his child. It fell into the pit, filling up, rising higher against her body. She wiggled and tossed as she began to breathe in the dirt through her nose. Then she was completely consumed by the soil.

He patted the mound flat and smooth, then set the spade aside. He knelt beside the dirt tomb and prayed to God. He was now a religious man.

"Thank you for giving me the strength."

There he left her in the Almighty's hands.

———✧———

Three months later, Elwin was carving on the slab of sandstone that he had set on top of her resting place, hiding the churned ground from any prying eyes. Some townspeople felt it was a memorial placed in the back of the old cemetery to a missing child who would never be found.

He was a sad soul and the local folks mostly left him to his own devices. It was later that afternoon when he heard the news. They had found another dead child.

After the learning experience of his first two anthologies, Editor Eric Miller really locked onto a clever idea which was to feature anthologies aimed at the thousands of truck drivers who crisscross our country every day. The books would be sold in truck stops and stores as well as online and contain genre tales with a trucker bent. Every story had to feature a truck prominently in it.

The idea for this story came from my mother. She'd run across an article in the newspaper about (I believe) an Indiana-based trucker who had this sort of misfortune befall him. I read the newspaper reports and thought the idea would make a good platform to dive off for an agonizing tale. Eric Miller thought so also and bought the story. Thanks Mom.

LUCKY

"Everyone has experienced that truth: that love, like a running brook, is disregarded, taken for granted; but when the brook freezes over, then people begin to remember how it was when it ran, and they want it to run again."

—Khalil Gibran

IT **WAS TO** be a short but annoying trip in shitty weather. It was always short and mostly annoying when you're running empty in one direction. That would be the first half of the trip. The shitty weather was a bonus. This was a drop and hook run with the dead head she was hauling for free in exchange for a supposedly preloaded double-tiered livestock trailer moving hogs south out of Indiana to a Tennessee packing plant.

She'd read something once that said if you lined up semi-trucks with the amount of grain it takes to feed the pigs in Indiana for a year, they would stretch from Indianapolis to Disney World. She believed it. There were a lot of hogs in Indiana.

Ray didn't much care for moving livestock. She'd done it a few times before, but never swayed her opinion to be positive. The shifting of the animals, the noise, the smell, plus it made her feel a little strange, emotionally. She was a meat eater, but loved animals. Hauling the pigs in weather like this made it even worse than putting up with the summer smells. The freezing cold would rush through the metal grids of the trailer with a nasty wind chill. Every time she'd arrived at the processing plant in the winter, there would be a few animals frozen alive, stuck to the metal walls. The workers would come out with tools and pry the pigs loose while they squealed and squirmed to get away. On several occasions, they would rip themselves out of their skins in the process.

She never would have taken this load except for the fact that she hadn't had a run in a couple of weeks, rent was coming due, and her cupboards were feeling a little bare. She was lucky to have gotten the job, no matter how shitty it was.

She had been lucky her whole life. Not life-changing luck but lucky enough; always getting by when things seemed their darkest. If Cullen would get off his fat ass and find a job, things wouldn't be so tight.

When money was low, the fighting at home grew worse. Maybe the break of being on the road would help calm things down. Cullen had called her every fifteen minutes since she'd left, probably to bitch. She never picked up. The idea was to get away for a couple of days and let things calm down. She'd let her voicemail listen to his rants for now. With the battery running down from the constant ringing, Rachel plugged her phone in and set the ringer to vibrate. She took the last swig of cabin temperature coffee and set the empty cup back in the holder.

The wind spun the snow around so hard that it appeared to be falling horizontally. The trailer bounced and swerved behind her, yanking the rig from side to side. Without any weight in the trailer, she had to keep her speed down to stay on the interstate. She was only about 50 miles out from her pickup dock. At this rate, she would never make it before they closed the gates. She grabbed the mic and double keyed it before speaking.

"Hey boys, any of you still in dispatch?"

She was met by the same kind of snow on the radio as she was looking at outside. She keyed it again.

"Hey, Pacer Trucking. Anybody there? This is Ray coming at you from the blizzard in Indiana. I'm northbound on the 69 just south of the Marion exit. Todd? Hello?"

Nothing. The storm seemed to be screwing everything up. She'd try again later, but in front of her were the flashing bubblegum lights of a police car. She hung the mic back on the radio and downshifted. Even picking up that small amount of drag made the trailer swerve and flutter as she slowed down to a crawl. Rachel could see the running lights of a couple of other rigs in front of her along with another couple of cop cars. There was an officer walking through the snow towards her with both hands up, palms flat, telling her to slow it down and stop.

She pulled up to him and brought the truck to a standstill. Ray rolled down the window and the officer stepped up on her running board. He wiped snow from his eyes and started to say something, then turned, and stepped back down on the snow. He waved on an ambulance, lights and sirens cutting through the snow. It drove past him and on down the road in the direction Ray was headed. The cop stepped back up to her window.

"Yes sir?"

"You can see what these conditions are like. You've got a layer of ice under a layer of snow. We've closed the highway at the next interchange. Too dangerous. You're going to have to wait there until morning, then we'll see where we stand. How are you on fuel?"

Rachel glanced down at the dashboard.

"I'm good for the night," she concluded.

"It's zero out right now and expected to drop another ten degrees not counting wind chill during the night. That should make it about thirty below. You'll need your furnace blasting all night."

He glanced inside the cab.

"Hope you've got something to eat. The truck stop at the interchange won't be open until about 5 in the morning and that's if their crew can even make it in to work."

He started to step down when he thought of something and turned back to the window.

"Do us all a favor and stay away from the pumps when you pull into Squire's. There will be plenty of drivers needing to fuel up first thing in the morning. There's plenty of flat lot space down the sides and around the back of the restaurant. Pick anywhere you want over there to camp out."

"No problem, officer."

Rachel smiled at him.

"I'll just snuggle down in the cab with the heater on and catch some sleep."

He looked her over one last time.

"You do that," he said as he jumped down from the truck, adjusted his plastic wrapped trooper hat, and waved her on.

As she rolled up the window, she could see him slowing down the next truck. I wouldn't want that job; she thought with a shudder. Even with the heater blasting, having the window open during that short conversation gave her the chills. She started driving toward the interchange. The wheels kept slipping on the ice-covered highway, but she gradually picked up momentum. She wanted to make the off-ramp incline without any problems. Hopefully there wouldn't be any stopping needed at the top of the ramp as she didn't have chains on. The road was becoming slipperier by the moment. Loose snow that was drifting across the roadway wasn't helping.

Her cell phone buzzed in the seat next to her. She didn't even bother looking at the screen; she knew who was calling. Ray reached over and shut her phone off.

"Tomorrow," she said to herself. "Tomorrow."

Through the snow and steamed windshield, she could see the red and yellow running lights of the trucks that had already managed to find their way to Squire's Truck Stop off on the rise to her left. Ray would have to climb the off-ramp and then make a turn at the top, cresting the bridge without stopping. If she had to stop for any reason, she may not be able to get the rig rolling again, unless she backed all the way back down the ramp and got a running start.

Considering the weather, that was not a good idea. She glanced at her side mirror to see how far behind her the next truck was. The headlights didn't seem to be moving. They were probably still stopped, talking to the cop.

Ray pressed down on the accelerator allowing her some more speed. Too much of a punch and her trailer would swing around and pull her off the road. Then she'd be fucked. The back end bounced and bucked but held firm on the road. The wipers merely piled the snow in long thickening strips on each side of her blurry windshield. Despite the defrosters working full blast, the steaming and icing of the glass threatened to take away all her vision. She kept wiping the inside of it with her gloved hand.

She gambled and pushed the gas a little more, swearing and fighting to control the truck. A white arrow on a sign with a green background, almost obscured by the snow, suddenly loomed to her right. She had almost overshot the ramp. Ray swerved, trying not to jerk the wheel.

"Easy, goddamnit!"

The ramp rose to her right and she had to get over further than she currently was or she wasn't going to make it. The vibrations from her tires changed up and she knew she had slipped off the asphalt and was thumping over the gravel and frozen grass. The trailer was dragging her left toward the snow-choked embankment. She would certainly be stuck. She might even roll over. It was now or never. She yanked the wheel to the right and as soon as she hit what she thought was the ramp, swung it back to the left. The trailer bounced and tried to pull her nearer the slope. At the last moment, the side of the rig's rubber hit the reflector rail. The force bounced the empty trailer straight behind her as she headed up the ramp. It all happened in a blurred frenzy of slow motion.

"Fuuuuuck!"

Ray made the top of the ramp and swung the cab to the left. The trailer stayed with her and together they crested the bridge. On the other side of the highway, she pulled into the truck stop and swung around past all the sitting trucks to the back corner of the lot, pulled the brake, and stopped dead. She dropped her head on the steering wheel and took a deep breath. She had always been lucky.

"Well, that was a Kansas City shuffle."

Rachel grabbed a cigarette out of their pack and lit it up. A couple of deep drags slowed down her pounding heart and she stared out the windshield at the driving snow, wondering why she was here instead of the bottom of the embankment in a bunch of twisted steel. Luck.

The snow came down in a white sheet in front of her headlights covering a mattress of ice.

She barely cracked the side window and blew out a long cloud of smoke. The trailer tire would have to be checked to make sure she hadn't busted the bead. Even though she wasn't a fan of sub-zero temperatures, it was better to check it now than in the morning. The same temperature always felt colder in the morning when she was just getting up. Awakening to a flat tire after white out conditions would suck.

Trying to find a reason to stall opening the cab door, Ray picked her cell up off the floor where it had bounced and turned it back on. It was still working. As it lit up it bleeped, announcing three missed calls. Cullen was tenacious if nothing else. Ray plugged the charger back in. She had a feeling that if she decided to call Cullen it was going to be a long conversation. She'd better be fully charged up and ready for it.

Gloves on, head tucked in under her hood, and coat buttoned tight, she was as ready as she was going to be. She took the flashlight from the toolbox on the floor, checked the beam, and put her shoulder to the door. The wind tore the door open into the breath-snatching blizzard.

The snow pushed past her into the cab as the vacuum that opening the door created sucked out all the heat. Ray's feet hit the ground, promptly shot out from under her, and she landed hard on the icy turf. Getting back up was difficult with the bumpy, glacial ground and the icy wind threatened to take her back down at any instant. She stood back up grabbing at the truck for balance. Then, hand-over-hand, she leaned against the trailer and made her way down to the rear wheels.

When she arrived, Ray bent down at the trailer tire. She was shaking with pain. She'd whacked her tailbone a good one. She pulled off one glove with the help of holding the finger tips with her teeth. Her flashlight shone on the wheel and she ran her fingers along the edge where the rubber and metal met to make sure she hadn't popped it. It seemed fine. The rubber must have slammed against the guard rail and bounced the truck back onto the exit ramp. She could feel the indentation in the rim, but it hadn't popped. Damn lucky break. She lowered the light and examined how the tire sat on the snow. It appeared fully inflated.

Slipping her fingers back into the glove, she pulled it down tight over her hand. Then, mimicking her previous trip down the trailer, Ray made her way back up to the cab. It took several tries against the wind, but the cab door finally pulled open and she flung herself inside.

Reaching back, she slammed the door.

Ray grimaced as she tried to find a comfortable way to sit in the driver's seat. She thought her butt was bruised, but didn't think anything was broken. There would be one hell of a mark come morning.

Great, she thought. *Bruised, stiff, and cold at the loading dock in the morning. I can hardly wait.*

As the trooper had mentioned, Squire's Truck Stop was closed so there was no getting something warm from inside. She had her cooler, some energy bars, and a pillow. Ray decided to hunker down and make the best of it. She only wished that she could pee out of her cab while sitting sideways in the seat with the door open like the male truckers. She could make it until early morning when the truck stop opened. There was no way she was going to crouch in that weather. The wind would probably blow it back over her as icicles.

Stripping off her gloves, she held her fingers in front of the blowing heater vent to warm them and noticed she had missed another call while she'd been out checking the tires. Ray took two aspirins in hopes of waylaying the pain in her hind end by morning. She knew it was probably a futile gesture. The truck was rocking her to sleep as the wind blasts continued their relentless buffeting. Like a baby, she drifted off to dreams of Cullen asking for forgiveness for arguing with her.

The lot was still shrouded in darkness when she jerked awake. The muffled outcry of the wind gusting against her empty trailer rose and lowered in volume as it pummeled the truck. The rig seemed to shudder and settle back to brace itself against the next onslaught. Ray touched her phone. The digital display told her she had a half hour before the truck stop was due to open, so she smoked another cigarette in the meantime. From where she sat, she couldn't see the front of the building. Ray had to pee. She needed to pull around towards the front so she could tell when the morning crew arrived. She unplugged the cell phone and slipped it in the breast pocket of her coat, then sat up straight and prepared to drive up around the side of the building.

Ray dropped the transmission into gear and stepped on the gas. The motor wound up, but she wasn't moving. Bumping it out of gear she dropped it back in and tried again. A lot of motor action, but no movement.

"Shit."

She knew what it was. Snow and ice around the brakes had frozen overnight, effectively seizing them up. She would have to crawl underneath the truck with a hammer and smack the ice off. The wind rocked the truck again.

"It's going to be colder than a polar bear's nuts."

The toolbox under the front seat had the hammer, so she pulled it out. She rechecked her empty coffee cup from last night with desperate hope that the coffee elves had visited while she was sleeping and refilled it with delicious bean juice, but it was still empty. Ray slipped it back in the holder and grabbed her flashlight. Taking a deep breath, she shoved open the driver's door and slid her feet out onto the snow.

"Fuck me," she muttered as her sore, screaming back reminded her of last night's fall.

Ray slammed the door behind her. At least she would have a warm cab to crawl into when she was finished. Stooping down at the side of her cab, she aimed the light across the width of the truck and across the backside of front wheel on the passenger side. The snow was drifting up on one side of the tire and the inside of the wheel looked packed with ice. She pulled her stocking cap down against the gale wind and then tightened and tied her hood over it as well as she could.

Dropping flat on the ground, Ray scooted under the cab and up on her side facing the inside of the driver's front tire. Even though her gloves were too light for this weather, they would have to do. She could feel the cold seeping into her fingers already, but they were what she had and she didn't have any extra money to buy a heavier pair. This was unusually cold weather for the area, so she would never wear a better pair often enough for her to justify spending money on them. She dug out the packed snow with her fingers. She could feel the wet and cold through to her skin. Ray grabbed the hammer and began to tap at the brake pads, chipping away at the layer of ice. When she was satisfied that she had knocked it all away, she rolled up onto her other side facing the passenger side. In that direction, the snow blasted her square in the face.

She used one hand to shield her eyes and belly-crawled under the truck to the opposite wheel.

Once she was at the tire, it hid her face from a direct onslaught of the wind.

It was now that she realized she'd left her flashlight on the other side of the truck. But the day was brightening up and she could see well enough without it. She didn't want to stay outside any longer than needed. Her fingers were stiffening up. Ray just wanted to get this ordeal over with. She lay on her left arm, so she dug out the snow one-handed. She picked up the hammer and was tapping the brake pads when a strong gust slammed into the truck. It creaked and began to shift on the icy ground. Before Ray could comprehend what was happening, the whole truck slid about an inch and then sank down into the snow, pinning her between the axel and ground.

Despite how she struggled to free herself, Ray was stuck on her left side with one arm pinned beneath her. Her free hand, cold and wet from the snow, was quickly becoming useless. She'd lost all feeling in her left arm as it fell asleep with her body weight crushing down on it in such an awkward position.

"Help! Help me!" she yelled.

Most of the trucks still had their engines running to keep their heaters on and probably radios or phones too. The wind sang and howled around the vehicles as if screaming a taunt to Ray to try and escape its icy clutches. There was no way anybody was going to hear her.

Then, her phone vibrated in her pocket. Cullen! He was up and had started his barrage of calling her again. The phone hummed in her pocket, but she could only move her top arm from the elbow out from under the axel. It wasn't enough to get to her pocket. She tried to twist and squirm but to no avail. The vibrations stopped.

"Help me! Somebody, help!"

The wind snatched the words from her lips and spun them to the artic ground. Her squirming made her become stuck tighter. It was as if the ground had reached up and grabbed her coat. The wind chill had caused the sweat she had worked up to freeze her damp coat to the ground.

Ray was packed against the truck axel on one side and frozen to the earth on the other side. The one hand she could slightly move had become leaded and heavy. It felt like a dead hunk of ice.

Then, the phone buzzed again. Cullen was trying to reach her. He knew. She knew he knew. It was like second sense or something. He must have felt she was in trouble and Ray shouted out to him.

"Cullen! Help me!"

If she could just figure it out, she might be able to get the voice activation function to work.

If she could bump it just right while it hummed in her pocket maybe. . . Then the vibrations stopped again. It had gone to voice mail. He'd call back. She knew he would. If nothing else she knew he was a persistent son-of-a-bitch. He had to call. He would. As Ray attempted to wriggle around, she realized she was freezing to the ground over a greater area of her body. Her movement was nearly stifled.

The wind whipped through the tires in the undercarriage; changing directions, blasting snow in a hodgepodge of directions. It took her breath completely away at times. By this time, she had shouted herself hoarse. Although she had lost track of time, she knew she had been lying there for at least an hour. Cullen's calls had come and gone. The phone had buzzed and rattled in her pocket, but she had been helpless to reach it.

Ray was in complete agony as her body began to shut down. Her clothes were frozen to her body encasing her in a numbing cocoon. She blinked at the snow and only one eye opened back up. The wind had frozen her other eye shut with her tears. Blinded in one eye, her line of sight had become extremely limited. The phone vibrated again and slowly moved in her pocket. It moved a little bit each time Cullen called. It would have moved further if she hadn't had her voice mail picking up the call, shutting down the vibrations.

Then she heard a snatch of conversation, human voices, and close. Cocking her head ever so slightly and looking out the corner of her good eye she could see the legs of two people standing beside her cab. Snow swirled and danced about them. They were facing each other, engaged in conversation.

"Help."

Ray shouted out, but her voice was weak and couldn't travel past the sound of her own truck's engine. She wasn't even sure she had said anything out loud, as she could no longer hear it herself. The wind laughed at her. It chattered her teeth and numbed her mind. She wanted to kick against the truck to get their attention, but she couldn't move her legs. She couldn't reach down and pick up the fallen hammer to slam it against the metal above her. All her struggles were internal now. Her mind was slowing, stumbling.

Her body was still. A cigarette butt bounced on the ground, got snatched up by the air, and carried past her. The two men walked past the back of her trailer toward the warm interior of the truck stop. Rachel cried and it froze to her face, never making zigzag track down her cheeks. She was getting tired. So tired.

The potbellied stove in the shed behind her trailer gave off a warmth that was both cozy and relaxing. All her tools had been laid out and a warm fire glowed through the grate on the stove's door. She was home and warm. She groaned and woke to the realization of the frost bite burning in her extremities. The phone hummed again. Cullen hadn't been in her dream. It hummed again and shifted in her pocket.

How long Ray had been passed out was a mystery to her. Was it night again? Everything was dark. Her brain took a moment to realize her other eye had frozen shut. It was okay. There was no feeling to it. Time drifted, meaningless now. She'd only just awakened yet was so sleepy. Surprisingly, she was warming up also. It felt exactly the way she had felt in front of that stove. It was lucky to feel warm. It must be the tire blocking some of the wind that blew across the parking lot. Maybe it was her frozen clothes blocking the air. She chuckled to herself that her frozen clothes were keeping her warm. Lucky for her.

Rachel had always been lucky. Her father said she had inherited that from her mother along with a strong sense of independence. Cullen called it something else. She smiled as her mind shut down and Ray lazily slipped back into her cozy warm dream. It was exactly where she wanted to be.

The cell phone in her coat hummed again. It vibrated itself loose from her coat pocket and fell out on the ice. Her voice mail picked up the call and the phone fell silent.

CRATE 156594

"Do we eradicate life because the history we desire to tell sounds so much better?"

—D. H. Altair

IT MAY HAVE been because of their military training. It might have been because they had been walking side by side for the last quarter of a mile. It could have been for a variety of reasons.

But whatever it was, their steps were in perfect cadence with each other, step for step, an echoing measure for measure as they made their way along the wide aisle of a warehouse at Silver Hill. This was where the aerospace items were restored, repaired, and returned to the Smithsonian Institute. There was a large area near the front of the building where tours and visiting dignitaries were shown staged mending efforts along with a lecture on the patching up of America's past. When items left this building, they were either good as new or their flaws were cleaned up and highlighted.

Here you can see the marks left from the burns where the capsule came back into earth's atmosphere.

The two men were well past that section of the building and were passing crates and containers all marked with numbers and letters identifying the contents. Even with the overhead fluorescents, this portion of the building appeared ghostly and removed. The man on the left seemed to be the guide. He spoke sparingly and had no doubt about direction. He wore a military dress uniform adorned with a gold leaf pin signifying the rank of an Army major amongst other ribbons and badges. To his right stepped a civilian in some official capacity. His suit was expensive and hand-tailored perfectly. His expression was slightly bemused as they made their way further and further into the bowels of the building.

"Don't deal with items back here with any sort of regularity?" one man asked the other as they approached the end of their walk.

"Not a high priority," the major replied. "Many of the people who work here don't even know this area exists or if they do, they don't know what it contains. What did it take for you to get permission?"

Suit considered his reply before answering.

"I needed to see what condition she was in after all this time. We may be moving her."

A heavy vault-like door with a pulley attached to the bottom corner sat on a metal rail. At the top it was a mechanically mirrored image. The major produced a key ring from his pocket and selected an odd cut key from the bunch. On the wall near the door was a metal box in which he inserted the key and turned it. There was a hum, a clack, a shudder, and the massive door slowly began to roll down the track to the side, revealing another metal door. A different key was inserted and the door swung open. Musty air, but not unpleasant smelling, was sucked out through the opening by the warehouse air conditioning system. There was the stale tinge of the room having been closed for some time. Like a living thing, it felt like it was waking up from a long sleep.

"After you, sir."

The major spoke with a sweep of his hand and the man in the suit stepped into the darkness.

There were times when the wind, funneling down through the mountain passes toward the ocean, blew so hot out of the desert that it evaporated any hint of moisture. The sand and grit that had been picked up in the flatlands found its way into her eyes, nose, and throat. She coughed, trying to rid herself of the invading dust. She needed a drink desperately. She smelled the air trying to fetch out water through her drying membranes. There was something to the south and she vaguely remembered having had a drink there before. The direction was good for her. It was away from them. They had been pursuing her. She had seen their smoke and smelled their meals, but they seemed to be able to keep pace with her. She'd had little time to eat on the run and at this point would welcome anything from meat to roots if her pursuers would only give her a moment to hunt or forage.

She searched for signs of others from her clan as she moved along but found none. There were no relatives, no family. She didn't know that now the clan consisted of one. . .her. The posse was on horseback, moving her in the direction they wanted her to go, and she seemed powerless to stop them. If she tired enough of this game, she would turn on them; catch them by surprise and kill them. But right now, she didn't want confrontation. She just wanted to be left alone.

Her instincts had been right; it was a lonely country. The air was free of their smells and odors. There were minimal inhabitants in the West during the turn of the century, mostly gathered in towns and cities. She had smelled the water and as she crested the hill the stream ribboned out through the tall grasses beside her. Sometimes when there was water, there were fish. She licked her lips in anticipation and nosed the air trying to pick up the scent of water.

For a brief time, all her worries were behind her.

The suit took a couple of steps inside the room and looked up at the lights flickering on. The major pressed a button next to the door and it silently rolled shut behind them. Crates and boxes with numbers stenciled on them filled the storage space, but these ones were stacked differently than the front hall. There seemed to be more space between them as if each container was equally important. The floor was tile, not cement.

"Climate controlled."

"She's been here all this time?" the suit asked.

"At least eighty years," the major said. "This way please." He looked at his handheld screen. "156594 is about halfway down."

The suit was happy for the guide as the boxes were not organized in any sort of numerical order.

Fucking government, he thought to himself. *Anything they can do to make shit harder.*

After about a hundred feet the major stopped them. He began walking around a bunch of the crates that were closely huddled together, reading each of the numbers aloud in his search for 156594.

Can't even face all the numbers out to make finding things easier.

"Can I help?" Suit asked.

"Sure, you can check some of the larger ones to my right. You may have to squeeze in between them to see a number. It's supposed to be right in here."

He looked back down at the phone screen and then moved to his left. He started mumbling as he waded into the crates.

"Yep, yep, mhmmm."

He stood up straight.

"Sir."

Suit stopped his search and walked over to where the major was standing. The number was stenciled in heavy black paint—#156594. He slapped his hand on the top.

"This is it," he said. "She's in here. How do we get it open?"

The major stepped up and turned the flashlight on his phone on. He pointed it at the mechanism on the container and tapped his phone screen again. The light turned from white to green and the container responded with a hushed click.

"Like that," the major said, smiled, and stepped back.

The suit was sweating. He could feel it run down his spine. He dug his finger under his collar and stretched it away from his neck.

"Climate controlled you say?"

The major allowed himself another smile.

"Yes, sir. I take it this is important, sir?"

The suit stepped up to the box.

"You don't know who she is?"

The major shook his head.

"No, sir. I'm not aware of anything except the crate number."

"So, you don't know what she represents. Have you ever heard the name Monarch?"

"Not that I recall. Was it an operation?"

There were no fish, but there was water and she was able to find some berries in the foliage along the bank. She drank away some of her weariness, but she did not rest. They were still behind her. Where could she turn to? The Mexican border was a long walk, but she knew nothing of it. Her main priority was food. Without food she would collapse where she stood; instinct told her that much. She moved toward the copse, seeking the shade to help her hide as her own shadows blended in with the ones surrounding her. A farm sat on the other side of the grove. She moved cautiously toward the house.

Standing there in the back edge of the thicket, she could smell honey. Its sweetness was ethereal like smoke. One moment it was there, the next gone replaced by the tang of fruit, watermelon freshly split. Her mind pictured the juices running pink down the green sides of the rind and salivation drooled from the corner of her mouth in response. It was there, sitting on a post that stood in front of the home. Bread smeared with honey and the beehive it came from next to it. The green beacon of the split watermelon lay at the base of the pole. The humming of the hive came to her as a beckoning song. It was a trap, but to her it was sustenance. Her fear was supplanted by her hunger, and she took the bait.

In one bite the bread disappeared. A swat of her paw broke the hive, smashing it open, finding the delicious center of the candy. The angry insects swarmed about her face and tried stinging her. At best, they were a nuisance. Her hunger was great. It had been days since she last ate anything. They had pursued her into a famished state, chasing her relentlessly, and she would take her due while she was able. Fear and adrenaline were fading with the rise of her hunger.

She could no longer wait to eat. She sat while she finished the nectar, making sure she missed nothing, like a child licking a bowl of pudding, and they closed in.

When she paused, her senses began returning to her. Her fear of her stalkers slowly entered her consciousness and she grabbed as much watermelon as she could carry and made her escape.

In the window of the house, the front curtain dropped back into place. The hook had been planted and it was time to reel her in.

"You've heard of William Randolph Hearst?"

"Rosebud."

The Suit smiled. It seemed the major had some life experiences outside of military service.

"Well, that's a different time. In the late 1880s, as a publicity stunt, he hired a journalist, a man by the name of Allen Kelley, to hunt down and capture the last California grizzly bear. It took a while, but he captured what turned out to be the largest bear ever held captive. He weighed more than 1200 pounds. Hearst named him Monarch and put the creature in a cage for people to come and see. He lived in that cell for twenty-two years and then in 1911 he died."

The major thought it over before speaking.

"Where did they bury him?"

"They skinned him. Took out his skeleton and shipped it off to the Berkeley Museum of Vertebrate Zoology. Then they stuffed the rest of him and housed him at the California Academy of Sciences. He's very special."

"Because he was the last?" the major asked.

"Because he wasn't," the man in the suit grinned. "No, he's special because he's the bear on the state flag of California. I was able to see him. The sun has faded his beautiful black hair into a dull brown. The hair on his nose has been rubbed away by years of people touching it. Inglorious, to say the least. His captor, Allen Kelley, later spoke of his regret in capturing Monarch, forcing him into over two decades of confinement."

"But he wasn't the last California grizzly?"

The suit shook his head.

"Only the most famous. Make no mistake, man extirpated the grizzly in California. It's what man does, but not until 1908. Sure, Monarch was still alive then but had been captive for almost twenty years. For all practical purposes, he wasn't the last California grizzly. That honor goes to Moccasin John here."

He turned and patted the airtight metal crate.

"You'll have to forgive the name. John was actually a female."

Earlier she thought she could smell dogs, but now she could hear them, baying while catching her scent. She had been on the move for miles hoping they would go away and leave her alone.

She had to avoid her hunters. She was tired and weak. Although the food had given her some energy, it had also moved her into Holy Jim Canyon, a box canyon, from which her only escape would be to turn and face her trackers.

There was no place left to run. Five miles into the canyon there was no place to hide. She turned at their approach, ready for the fight. She never saw the men who fired the rifles.

From the other side of the bushes three shots rang out, all from separate weapons. One struck her in the shoulder, turning her and causing the second to hit her leg. The third caught her throat and she went down, killed for the crime of existing. That's what men do. Her eyes stared blankly ahead. The dogs were on her in seconds.

"How much did she weigh?"

The major was looking with some concern at the metal cabinet. It was large but by no means large enough to fit even a small grizzly bear.

"600 pounds and six feet long," the suit said. "But she isn't here. They moved her to Washington to be near the leaders of the fools who dispatched her. Her skin and skull are well preserved in this airtight cabinet. No petting from visitors. No rubbing her nose hairless.

Despite rumors to the contrary, there has never been another proven sighting of a grizzly in California. She was the last."

The men remained silent looking at the box.

"Are you going to look at her?"

"I can't," the suit said. "Then it wouldn't be airtight, would it?"

"I guess not, sir."

"I just needed to pay my respects and then officially report that she is secure and should stay right where she is. We have done enough. We need to leave her alone."

After a moment, the Suit cleared his throat and gave one last look at the cabinet before turning away.

"You may close it back up, Major."

The major reversed the process he had gone through earlier including punching in the pin pad. There was the hushed sound of mechanisms clicking back into place. He stepped up beside the suit.

"All set, sir. We can leave now."

As they walked in synchronized step back toward the civilized world, the Suit turned to the major.

"We are a great nation, aren't we?" he said, mostly to himself.

"Indeed we are, sir."

It was a long silent walk back to the car.

When Editor Kasey Lansdale invited me into her e-only horror anthology Fresh Blood, Old Bones *in 2012 I knew which side of that title I fell under. I was delighted to be part of it. I believe this was her first anthology as an editor and she managed to put together quite a line-up of fine writers for the project. She can call me anytime.*

I had wanted to write another dark western story since 2004's "The Lost Herd," so I thought I would give it a try. I happen to be intrigued by the concept of betwixt and between and Liminality gave me a chance to run in that idea playground. I think that this feeling of not belonging anywhere is something we all have at some time or another. I just took that transitional approach to the extreme.

LIMINALITY

"It is a fearful thing to fall into the hands of the living God"

—Hebrews 10:31

THEY WERE LOOKING at me in a panic as they stood pressed against the side of the split rail fence.

The eyes are always the tell. Their emotion was palpable, an acrid smell of fear in the air, the sweat, the sexuality, the sensual desire that comes with the terror. She kept her daughter pressed against her side, ready to step in front of her for protection. She darted a look over to the man on the ground, who I presumed was her husband, and then back to me. His guts, some of which dripped from the long sides of my muzzle, were torn from his body. He had groaned only once after the initial shouting and was now unmoving on the ground. His body was covered in dirt and dust from where

LIMINALITY

I'd been slinging him about with my mouth as I ripped open the fleshy seal of his skin to get to his soft delicacies inside. The dirt yard where I'd been dragging him looked as if a giant broom had smoothed the surface and one could truly imagine that were the case if it weren't for the bits and pieces of body parts that had fallen off during the struggle and now lay scattered. It was hard for me to hold the food in my mouth with the shape I had been given.

The mother's eyes were large as poker chips and although she clutched her daughter to her with one arm, she tried to cover the young one's eyes with the other hand to protect her from the sight of the carnage, from her father torn asunder and from me.

I am something to see, I'm sure. Spotty gray fur covers most of my body and parts of my mouth, which is misshapen and grotesque with dripping intestinal matter leaking onto my arm.

That is correct, my *arm*. The appendage on my left is still human while a fully formed wolf leg protrudes from my right shoulder. My face must present the most alarming visage; eyes heavily veined and yellowed, nose shoved up top on to the base of what has apparently elongated into a snout-like protrusion that was of no use except to hold my upper jaw and additional teeth in place.

She continued to move backwards slowly, away from me and now was forced flat against the split-rail fence. She had quickly spun her daughter from her left side around in front of her and then to her right side, putting her closer to the gap in the barrier and a possible escape attempt for the house that stood about 25 yards behind her. She could dash for the wagon to her other side, but that is almost the same distance and offers no real protection. I can tell that she understands she will only have one chance. She appears to be a smart woman.

Even as I sit on my twisted haunches and make that horrible guttural noise in my throat that I have no control over, I want to reason with her. I want to tell her that there are things that I have no control over. My looks, my instincts, are now deep inside of me and they control me more than a twelve-year-old boy is controlled when he discovers his sexual drive in the palm of his hand. My mind can reason with, but not control my actions just as my vocal cords can produce sound without my being able to speak words.

I have no plans to attack her or her daughter. Her husband should satiate my lust for food and then I will leave and she will be safe to carry on with the lives I have spared. He was a sinewy farmer, but held enough fat for flavor. She looks sad but I carry no emotions for her or her offspring.

I am only sad for me, for my condition, for the spot I have found myself in. You would not recognize me had you known me prior; young and full of all the elixirs of life. I had traveled from the East out to this godforsaken dirt pile to take on the position of schoolmaster for a small town of silver miners and their families. The church and the schoolhouse were a single structure, interchangeable depending upon the day of the week. There were few single females, outside of saloon fodder, but I, with my personal proclivities, did not find the lack of the opposite gender a problem. I also assumed that as more of the ore was brought up from the earth, the town would grow in a symbiotic relationship with the silver. In turn, more miners would come in and the town would continue to grow and provide a larger and more varied population.

When I stepped off the stage onto the dirt street for the first time, I thought, *what have I done?* But I was here and there was work to be accomplished, so I found my rented lodgings and proceeded to make a home and profession for myself. Life was uneventful save an occasional drunken brawl in the street below my room or the moronic parents who felt their child was above learning and needed to be on the farm instead of sitting at a school desk. I never taught the children to swear, but used that sort of terminology in my own mind many times regarding the parents.

As I had predicted, the town grew parallel with the silver vein and the growth, though in spurts, was inevitable. I did not socialize much, save the parental talks about their offspring, church, and the occasional foray to the local eatery which was neat, clean, and served adequate breakfast. I preferred my time alone.

Eventually, the town gave birth to a crudely written but interesting weekly newspaper that reported all the gossip along with town hall information and the sheriff's arrest tally for the past week. This last section was more for the titillation of the locals, who all knew each other, than for any journalistic purpose. The people were simple and stupid, but gaining knowledge daily due to my direct and superior methods of teaching. I believed that my methods were totally novel and I intended to write a book about them during the next summer break. However, prior to my being able to gather that time for myself. One day I was approached by the local constable and summoned to attend a meeting with the heads of the town. Although wondering why they needed to speak with me (probably some problem beyond their limited comprehension), I gracefully accepted and that evening I headed over to the meeting hall.

The woman acts as if she is looking about for a weapon. I have seen that look in a crazed person's eyes before and, quite frankly, humans can be dangerous when their minds tell them that they are on the brink of extinction. Any animal can be. You should be careful of the little ones, like rats and prairie dogs, as they can get quite snippy. With her hip, she pushes her daughter slowly along the fence line while scuffing her feet in the direction of the opening. If she thinks she can make it to the house faster than I can run her down and catch her, she is sorely mistaken. Another growl sounds out, originating from somewhere deep in my chest, and her eyes shoot up to meet mine. She stops where the two of them stand and I can see her breathing from here and only imagine the sound of her own heartbeat in her ears. The stare down between us begins. She should not play games with me, but instead should remain still and let me finish my task at hand.

I attended this town meeting and was surprised to hear that some of the outlying ranches and homesteads had been devastated by the indigent people of our fair territory. Families had been slaughtered, with some members being killed only after the most deplorable sexual acts one could possibly imagine perpetrated upon them while other family members were forced to watch. Their houses were then ransacked and burnt to the ground. The crops were trampled and any livestock that existed was either taken back to where these savages lived or were set free.

To hear it told made it all sound revolting and extremely unpleasant. It was no wonder the white man needed to eradicate these crazed peoples. The soldiers at Fort Squander were many days ride away and could not be spared to just hang about the town hoping to catch these vicious criminals in the act. There was no help coming for us, even though it had been requested. It made me wonder if it was possible for anybody to help.

The mayor and his council had an idea. They claimed they had requested my presence at this meeting because I was the most learned person in town (which was true). They requested of me to write up a treaty or something akin to a local plea to get these heathens to stop hurting us. In return, the town fathers promised them some trinkets and a cow or two as compensation. There was even a backward kind of simple girl who lived in some abandoned mine shafts out the west end of town and ate off the charity of the locals whom the council said they would toss into the bargain as a mate for one of the uglier irreligious fellows. They wanted me to write this all up for them as a sort of contract and then go out to where they knew the encampment to currently be located to present the proposal. In exchange for this extreme act of bravery on my part, I was to be given a house of my own and a promise from the town's fathers to work quicker to construct my own school building.

Not being a stupid man (as you have probably noted), I thought it over for a moment and then asked whom they would send accompanying me out there, as I am not a gun-toting type of individual. I would need a show of strength to let these Indians understand I meant business.

They said that one of the deputies and one of the mine guards would escort me. I agreed and we all shook hands on it as a pledge of our word. I was to write up the treaty this week, let the fathers look it over, and approve the paper before heading out.

I heard a crack and noted that the woman had managed to push her opulent posterior hard enough against the fence to crack loose one of the crossbars from its post mooring. I, being lost in my thoughts the way I do after a satisfying meal, had not noticed the subtle but constant movement backwards applying pressure against the weathered wood. The loud snap of the timber brought me around and we stared into each other's eyes again trying to predict each other's next move. There was a slight shifting on her part, so I took a step closer and snapped at her, best I could with only half of a wolf's muzzle, and she stopped perfectly still as if portraying Lot's wife in the local church play. I ran my tongue out from under my top teeth and it lay out the side flapping along with my panting and dripping saliva and fluids that had come from the man onto the ground.

I don't believe she ever blinked.

Approvals had been made, the day had arrived, and I (in the lead of course) and my two companions were off to sooth the angry beasts. This would be my opportunity to show them how diplomacy is more effective than might. I was sure they had never been exposed to an opportunity like this; that is to attend a bargaining meeting with someone of knowledge. I was convinced it would be an eye-opening experience for them. The breeze was pleasant, the air was warm, and the day could not be any more serene.

As we got closer to where those people had made their obnoxious camp from animal skins and sticks, the deputy pointed out half naked men hiding in trees and atop of some of the cliff faces. I supposed they were watching us in fear of what we might do to them and they must have been frightened enough not to interfere with our passage. As we rounded a final clump of trees, the camp spread out awkwardly before us with no real geometric design or placement to it. The denizens stood on either side of the entry trail as we passed by and I felt somewhat like Christ must have felt as they placed palm leaves in the path for his donkey to walk upon.

I had expected to be met by a grey-haired chieftain who would be dressed in some sort of ceremonial garb and offering me a pipe of peace. But when he stepped from his bark and hide covered abode, he was small and brown. I would say he was almost shriveled and I was a bit disappointed that I would have to waste my time with this shrunken rucksack of a man. We pulled up a few feet in front of him and I stared down at the gnome. His eyes were intense. I remember that he never took them off me to glance at the other two riders. Not once.

I put my right hand up to show that not only was I not carrying a weapon, but that I was also pledging that what I was about to say was the truth. He spit once near the front hooves of my mount, causing it to snort and take a step back. He seemed unimpressed, obviously not aware of my keen insight and education. I turned to my right, figuring that maybe by introducing the deputy, it might make the reason for our visit a bit more official. As I pointed, palm up open handed toward the badge on his chest, a spear caught the lawman just below his head in the hollow of his neck and took him completely off the saddle. I heard the wooden shaft of the lance snap as he hit the ground. I could not see him as he'd fallen on the far side of his horse out of my line of sight, but I did see the tribe swarm him with rocks and clubs and never heard a single sound from him.

I was stunned, frozen in place, but the other rider jerked his horse's head about and scrambled back in the direction from which we'd come. The sheer number of arrows sticking out of his back within what seemed merely an instant resembled nothing less than a porcupine and he tumbled to the ground in a raggedy heap. I sat as stone still as if I had just been hexed by Medusa, for my entire body had gone numb and the mechanism that connected my brain to my muscles had ceased to exist. I could not move. I could not run. I could barely reason. I watched the tribe converge on me and pull me from the saddle.

Another snap and the wooden rail had broken free and was on the ground at her feet. Maybe, I thought, she is going to reach for that as a distraction while she gives her daughter a shove towards the front door. It might work for an instant, but not long enough. If she would have just stopped and let me finish with the man, I truly intended to go away. Some people are just too foolhardy for their own good. I took another step towards her and evidently her pressing thought to bend down and grab the wood dissipated. Again, she held her ground as we tried to stare inside of each other.

Bound with my hands trussed behind my back and laying on the ground inside one of their teepees, the only light that came in was from around the flap, the fire, the hole at the top where all the poles came together while the smoke streamed out. I could hear chanting and singing from outside. The drums beat a consistent rhythm. The flap opened and a garishly dressed savage approached me, beads were clacking around his neck while he shook some beaded rattle thing at me. He was followed by a couple of younger men who stood to the side while he danced about; waving, and shouting and making me dizzy.

He stopped suddenly and bent down to where I lay on the ground. He spoke some gibberish which one of his sidekicks translated.

He said, "You think you are a big man."

"No," I countered with a weak smile. "No, just a humble schoolteacher."

I tried to keep my speech from sounding shaky.

He said, "You think you are a great hunter who can lie to us with cheap trinkets and items to change our ways."

The medicine man had read the paper I'd authored and was not happy.

"Oh that," I started to explain, "was nothing. A trifle. The mayor and sheriff of the town forced me to write that."

He said he would make me a great hunter since that was what I desired; a devious hunter who slinks in shame during the moonlit nights. He would turn me into a wolf. But I would not be *just* a wolf. I would be an enchanted wolf; an especially sinister beast, hated by all who met me. I would exhibit the mark of a cursed species. This guy was crazy as a hoot owl.

I knew I had to get out of there. Someone untied me and the two strong fellows held me down while mad Geronimo chanted and sang. They stripped my shirt from me and began to rub me with some sort of balm. It stank, but he hadn't finished when I began to feel a tingle move past the top layer of my skin and deep into the frame of my body. My limbs twitched and throbbed while the nerves in my face jumped about like they were being stuck with hot needles.

The pain was incredible and I needed to do anything within my power to escape. He pulled a knife out, for God knows what, but accidentally dropped it and as one of the strong boys turned to pick it up for him, I seized my chance.

I reached over with my suddenly free arm and grabbed a burning wood faggot from the fire.

Knife-boy turned back just as I swung the flaming weapon. It caught him on the side of the head and sent a shower of embers across the tent. My other side was suddenly free and people were screaming. The sage's hair was on fire and he was rolling about on the ground. I pulled up the bottom of the teepee behind me and crawled out. I ran faster than I'd ever run before. I felt different, awkward, and mean at the same time. I didn't stop for quite a while. I must have collapsed at some point.

I next awoke when it was dark and I was burning up. I desperately needed to drink and I thought I could smell water nearby. I sat up and started off in that direction when I fell in on myself. My legs weren't working correctly and when I reached down to them, I found that they were misshapen and covered with a thick layer of hair. I fearfully brought my hand up and in the moonlight it looked fine. My other arm moved, discomfited from the shoulder and bent precariously wrong. My control of my muscles was spastic at best and I felt as if I had to learn to use my muscles and tendons differently just to get my arm to move. As I brought it into sight, I saw that it was lupine in shape and also covered in fur. I let out a scream, but the sound was muddled and guttural. More groaning than human speech, I could hear the canine in me. I put my good hand up to my mouth and realized it had also transformed. My bottom jaw was the same and shaped as it always had been, but my upper lip hurt and was stretched out across what can only be described as the top half of a mutated wolf's muzzle.

I forced myself up on my haunches and tried to walk or drag myself toward the water I smelled. I was parched and would die without some water. As I became acquainted with my newly malformed body, my muscle movement became more fluid and although not perfect by any means, I had to practically remain on all fours. It soon required less effort from me both mentally and physically to move about in the direction my mind was telling my body to go.

With some effort and a keen sense of smell, I managed my way to a stream that moved slowly and calmly out along a pathway it had carved through the forest and onto a wide flood plain.

There in the moonlight, reflection mirrored in the water, I saw myself for the first time. It was hideous. I was an appalling amalgamation of two beings: part wolf and part man, ultimately neither. As a beast I was neither here nor there. While the realization set in, I discovered that my tear ducts still worked. I drank and cried, my voice reaching new heights of volume and echoed in the clearing as I raised my head and screamed. I was a beast in agony, an abomination of God. The moon mocked me by lighting my reflection and I knew I had been hexed. Why hadn't I been transformed completely into this creature or remained a man? How did I get stuck betwixt and between two worlds? Neither animal nor man, I would be forced to roam as a legend; a creature to be spoken of when telling campfire fables.

It was many months before I finally worked out what had happened. The witch doctor must have died that night. I saw him on fire, rolling and screaming as the others tried to help. He had only partially completed the transitional ceremony when I had made my move. I had literally cursed myself and become stuck on this threshold, never to be allowed all the way inside the soul of the beast or back the way I'd come.

Now I was old and the grey threads that weaved themselves

throughout my fur felt physically heavy. I desired to carry this burden of life no longer, but I was looking into the face of a very scared woman. She was complete. She would never know the agony that coursed daily through my veins. She neither knew nor cared about the decades of pain that drove me along with the animal instinct to survive. She flinched and I knew she was going to make her move very soon to run to the cabin. There was that telling twitch near her eye. I'd seen it before in poker games.

There is always a tell.

I had intended to leave and let her be, but the man had grown cold and dirty and my inner beast was stronger than ever. I was not yet satiated and she was not yet inside the house.

So many times, I've gotten myself in a world of shit by trying to do what I thought at the time was the right thing. Most of the time I can laugh about it afterwards. But what if the results were deadly? I played with that and decided to take the most helpful people I know and have them screw up. This story has never been published and some of my beta readers have become upset at me for writing it. But it is legit, human, and possible. As with many good tales, the creation of my story is "what if?"

Heated discussions have occurred from people reading this story and exchanging their feelings concerning it. This is not my happiest piece.

FOR MOTHER

"The most merciful thing that a large family does to one of its infant members is to kill it."
—Margaret Sanger

THE MACHINES SPOKE. They clicked and hissed. They beeped and hummed. Lights flickered and flashed while digital numbers danced on their displays. A tube extended from one bedside contraption across to the bandaged head of the person in the bed. It covered the mouth in its entirety. The bellows in the equipment rose and fell, forcing air into the mouth and lungs. Her chest rose and fell in time with the machine. It was breathing for her. It was breathing for his mother.

She had always been strong for him growing up.

"Quit trying so hard," his mother would tell him. "You are who you are. You're a good boy. You're my good boy. You can't control the way other people feel."

She would wrap her arm around his shoulder and pull him

close. Then she'd hold a tissue at his nose. "Blow. Always do the right thing in your heart and everything will turn out okay. When you see somebody in distress, help them. If they are sad, try to cheer them up."

As he grew older, he knew he was different. People looked at him funny, like he was some sort of exhibition. Everybody else had friends. Everybody else was smart. Everybody else was, well, everybody else. Wayne looked in the mirror and didn't think he looked different. He said hello to everybody he passed, but a lot of times they didn't say hi back. He'd made it through high school, but he wasn't smart enough to go to college. His mother didn't have the money for it, anyway. It wasn't her fault. She worked hard.

A car horn jolted him out of his thoughts. He had walked backwards into the lane with all the shopping carts he had collected. He waved at the driver. "Hi!"

"Get the fuck out of the way, dipshit."

He looked around and then realized that he was who the man was yelling at. He pushed the carts with all his might back into the corral and out of traffic. The front cart turned and hit the metal railing, scattering them in different directions.

"Sorry, Sorry."

The driver gunned the car and passed him by.

"Asshole."

Wayne watched him drive away. He touched his chest.

"I have a good heart," he said to the rear of the departing car. "I try to be helpful."

His manager stepped out of the store and shouted, "Wayne, come here!"

Wayne always got rattled when an authority figure spoke to him. He tried to pull the carts together and just kept banging them awkwardly. He looked up at his manager who was standing with his hands on his hips.

"Wayne."

"I'm trying Mr. Reynolds. I'll be right there."

"Leave the carts there. Come up here. You need to leave."

"Wha..? What?"

Mr. Reynolds waved him in. "Take that apron off and grab your jacket." One of the boys is going to drive you to the hospital. Your mother has been in an accident. You need to go see her in the hospital right away."

Wayne ran up to Mr. Reynolds.

"But who will take care of the carts, Mr. Reynolds?"

"Don't worry about that. I will. Just go grab your stuff and meet Michael at the loading dock."

Wayne pulled his apron off and looked around. The carts were still haphazard about the asphalt.

"But it's my job," Wayne pointed to the runaways.

"Oh, for Pete's sake," Mr. Reynolds said and held out his hand. "Here, give me your apron."

Wayne handed it to him.

"Thank you, Mr. Reynolds."

"Yeah, yeah. Now go and meet Michael."

He brushed Wayne away with the backs of his hands. "Just go!"

Wayne looked back and forth for a moment and finally turned and ran into the store, nearly bumping into a full cart being pushed out the door. The lady shrieked. He stopped and reached out his hand.

"Sorry lady. I didn't mean to. . ."

"Wayne!"

He turned and looked.

"Yes, Mr. Reynolds." Then he ran through the store.

Reynolds shook his head and tossed the apron across his shoulder. He walked over to the cart corral and started pulling them out and fitting them together.

The hospital was a frantic scene with gurneys rolling past, groups of white coated doctors clustering in discussions, and families hugging in the emergency room lobby. Michael had dropped Wayne off at the front door and driven away. Wayne was on his own. His mother had taught him that whenever confusion set in, he needed to stop and gather his thoughts before moving on. So now he stood, staring at the automatic doors. They reminded him of a space lock in a science fiction movie. A man rushed past, knocking him to the side.

"Out of the way, please. Don't just stand there."

The man turned and waved to people behind him.

"This way, folks!"

Wayne had to step back as a large group of people pushed past him. He moved against a wall. It was all so active. Colors and sounds. Things blurred in his mind then gradually came back into focus. He started humming to himself. Mother. He was here for Mother.

"Can I help you?"

A pretty girl in a red striped uniform stood next to him. She was older than he was, but smiled nice. Wayne smiled back.

"I'm Susan. I help around here. You look lost."

"No! I belong here. My mother is here. She is hurt."

Susan reached and took Wayne's hand in hers.

"It's okay. Let's see if we can find her for you. They'll help us out at the desk over here."

Mother lay on her back, eyes shut, hands at her sides. Her head was wrapped like in an old Mummy movie they had watched together. A tube was taped to her mouth. Something was clamped on her finger, which peeked out from the bandages that encased her hands, while other wires ran from the tall bank of machines behind her to under the covers. There was electronic beeping and something that sounded like a pump that Wayne had heard coming from the well in their basement. He stood at the side of the bed, occasionally bending down, and whispering in her ear.

"She can't hear you."

The voice startled him. He forgot that Susan had walked with him up to the room. She came further into the room next to the bed and fluffed the pillow. She pulled the blankets up snug around his mother. She did a quick look around as Wayne followed behind her. She motioned to a chair on the other side of the bed.

"Why don't you have a seat?"

"I can help," Wayne said.

"I'm sure you can."

She pointed at the chair.

"Please have a seat. I have a routine. It will be much faster without you trying to help me. But thank you for offering."

Wayne moved around and sat down.

"I want to talk to her. I'm scared."

"She can't hear you because she is in a coma."

"What's that?"

"They've put her to sleep."

"Can we wake her up?"

"No, if she is asleep, she doesn't feel the pain. That's when the healing happens."

"What is that?"

He pointed at the tube in her mouth.

"That's a ventilator. It's helping her breathe. Without it she would die."

The machine continued breathing with the bellows exhaling through the whisper valve.

"I don't like these machines," Wayne said.

The aide picked some things up off the floor and threw them in the waste basket.

"Neither would your mother if she were conscious."

Wayne watched her intently. His mother moaned from the bed.

"I think she is waking up."

"She's not, but maybe she's dreaming."

"What are you doing?" Wayne asked.

"Cleaning up a little. Just trying to keep her as comfortable as possible. She can't say anything, but we know what signs to look for."

Wayne stood up. He wiped his hands on his thighs and then held one out to her.

"Wayne. I'm her son. That's my mother."

"Nice to meet you again, Wayne."

She shook his hand and then went back to straightening up. "I'm sorry it had to be under these circumstances."

He made a sound in his throat and looked about the room uncomfortably. Finally, he sat back down. Susan made a couple of notations on the chart on the back of the door and noted the time.

"I'm sure I'll see you again if you are here during my shift."

"Is my mother going to be better?"

"I don't know, Wayne. I'm not a doctor. I hope so."

She turned to leave.

"How do I know it is my mother?"

Susan turned back.

"I'm sorry, what?"

"How do I know it is my mother?"

Wayne did a head nod in the direction of the patient.

"They call me a dummy. Mother said I am a good boy. Mother said I should help people. They say I'm slow. Maybe I am. But I'm not stupid."

Susan looked at him square for a moment. "Of course, you're not." She took a step towards Wayne. "I must tell you, if they removed the bandages, you still wouldn't know for sure it was her."

Wayne looked back and forth between his mother and Susan.

FOR MOTHER

He stood up and walked over to the bed. Face bandaged, hands and arms bandaged, there was nothing to go by for identification.

"Why?"

"The fire."

The machine took what seemed like a big breath and pumped. The lit-up numbers flickered and the graph bounced on the screen before settling down. A tone beeped four times and went silent. Mother's chest rose and fell. Her fingers twitched. Wayne looked over at Susan who shook her head.

"It's just. . .things. She looks like a mummy. Mummies are dead. It's not her."

"It's her, Wayne."

"Will she be alright?"

Susan smiled sadly at Wayne.

"I'll check back in with her later. Doctors and nurses will be looking in on her all day. They do their best. Don't touch her."

"I won't. I try to help."

Susan smiled and left the room. Wayne settled into a cold, plastic, cushioned chair and tried to get warm. It was chilly in the room.

Days passed and then a couple of weeks. Then one day, Wayne came to the hospital and his mother's room was empty. He stood in the doorway, confused. Backing up, he double-checked the room number. Convinced it was the correct room, he walked back through the door and looked around, but there was no sign of her.

"She's been moved."

Wayne turned around. Susan was standing there.

"Why? I almost lost her."

Susan put her arm around Wayne. They walked over to two chairs in the hallway and sat down. She reached over, taking his hand.

"Wayne," she paused realizing he still didn't understand. "You did lose her. She has passed away."

He stood back up and began walking in circles.

"No, no, no. You mean she's dead? Like a mummy? Mother cannot leave me! I've been good."

"She didn't have any choice, Wayne. Her injuries were too big for her to fight through. Then when infection set in. . .Well, that was it."

He stopped circling, trying to process what he was hearing. Wayne was shaking his head. He looked down at her in anger.

"I don't know!" he shouted. "I don't know what you're saying about half of the time."

"Yes, you do," Susan said. "You just don't want to. I understand that. I really do."

He dropped back down in the chair and Susan pulled him against her chest. She stroked his hair while he sobbed.

"Was she in pain? Don't lie to me, I'm not stupid. I'm a good person. I try to help people."

"I would never lie to you, Wayne."

"I want to see her."

"You can't see her," Susan said. "We already have her identified, so you don't have to see her like that. You don't want your last memory of your mother to be this."

"Was she in pain?"

"She was in a coma most of the time and they gave her drugs to try and mitigate, stop, any of the really strong pain."

"I heard her moaning in bed."

"That was a reaction. We don't know that she felt any pain."

Wayne looked at the form on the clipboard that Susan had handed him.

"Then why give her the drugs? Why keep her in a coma?"

Susan looked down for a moment and then sighed.

"I agree that maybe they could have let her go sooner after she got here, but they didn't know for sure that she would pass back then. They were trying to save her. The doctors always try to save people. Maybe she could have gotten better. Maybe she could have had a regula. . ."

"You said you would never lie to me! You're lying!"

Wayne walked away to the other side of the room and started pacing. She watched him.

"I'm sorry. I didn't lie. I was trying to spare your feelings."

"Everybody is always trying to spare my feelings. I'm not STUPID. I just want to do what's right and have people be honest with me."

"I know," Susan said. "I'm sorry." She walked over to a counter by the sink and picked up a pair of scissors. "Come here."

Wayne went over and she cut off a small lock of his hair. "A gift for your mother. I will have them put this with her so that you will always be with her."

FOR MOTHER

<hr>

Wayne and Susan stayed in touch over the years; holidays, birthdays, and lonely grey rainy days. He was living in a state-run facility since all the money they had went to pay for his mother. Wayne still worked at the market. Even though he had a good heart, he never had a girlfriend, was never married. He made other people happy, always joking around and smiling.

Even though he always tried to help people, in the back of his mind he felt like a failure. He felt he could have, if not saved his mother, at least shortened her painful times. While he could forgive the world, he would never forgive himself.

Mr. Reynolds came to him in the grocery store break room. Wayne was standing, staring through the glass at the vending machine with all the potato chips and cracker sandwiches.

"Wayne," he called out.

He spun around and put his hands behind his back.

"I'm sorry, Mr. Reynolds. I wasn't doing anything. I was just looking. I'm a good person."

Mr. Reynolds took a step towards him.

"It's okay, Wayne. You're fine. But unfortunately, your friend Susan is not."

"What? What's wrong?"

"She's had an accident and is in the hospital."

"No, no, no," he said and held his hands to his head. He started looking all around the room.

"What am I gonna do?"

Mr. Reynolds walked a little closer and pointed at Wayne's locker.

"Take your apron off and put it in the locker and then grab your jacket. When you're ready, come out front and see me at the manager's desk. We'll make sure you get to the hospital."

Wayne stopped for a moment and stood, head bowed, looking at the floor.

"Did she burn up?"

"Did she what?" Mr. Reynolds looked confused.

"My mother burned up. Then they put her a machine that killed her. I tried to help but couldn't."

"I don't think that's true, Wayne, but no, Susan did not burn up. She was in a car accident. She was hurt very badly."

Every detail of the hospital was seared into Wayne's memory. He went to the big desk, and they put a sticky badge on him that had the room number of where Susan lay. They also made him wear a mask.

"Are you okay?" the man at the desk asked.

"I'm good," Wayne said, and he made his way off to the elevators.

There were no lights on in Susan's room. A girl in a red and white striped uniform was bent over the bed.

"Susan, are you okay?"

The lady turned around quickly at the sound of Wayne's approaching voice and smiled. It wasn't Susan, but she was pretty, too. She stepped aside and Wayne could see Susan lying on her side facing him.

"I'm Lily. I'm an aide here. I'm just straightening up and trying. . ."

"To make her more comfortable. I know," Wayne said. "That's what Susan did too."

"Oh, she was an aide also? I didn't know that. I'll keep her comfortable, so she'll get better.

Wayne looked at the machines. "That's a lie. Susan lied to me one time too."

"No, it's the truth,"

Wayne approached Susan's bedside. Her skin was red and black and scraped all over. There were bandages. Lots of bandages.

"Why is she so dirty?" Wayne asked.

Lily smiled.

"That's not dirt. That's bruising. It's like when you bump yourself and get black and blue marks. Maybe I'll talk to you later if you're still here when I come back." Lily went out the door and down the hall to the next room to continue her rounds.

Wayne turned back to Susan. It was all there; the wires, the beeping machinery, the flashing lights, the numbers on the display. There was the breathing machine. Her chest rose and fell as the air moved through the whisper valve, gently whiffing.

He walked over to the ventilator and watched it force the air into her. In his head, the noise of the machines grew louder as if somebody was huffing and puffing right into his ears. He put his hands over his ears, but that didn't muffle the noise. WHIRL. BEEP. WHOOSH. WHIRL. BEEP. WHOOSH. On and on and on. Stop! Make it stop. This was what killed his mother. He wouldn't let it kill Susan.

He looked all over the machine. Where was the button? How could he make it stop? And then he spotted the plug. He knew that if he pulled the plug out of the wall the machine would stop. The noise would stop. Susan would get better.

"I'm a good boy. I help people."

He got down on his knees and reached through the legs of the cart until he reached the plug. It was stuck. He had to wiggle it back and forth, loosening its hold in the wall. One final yank and it came free. He couldn't help his mother, but he could help Susan. She was already gasping.

He wondered if the hospital people would get mad if they knew it was him that had saved her. He could come back later, but he needed to leave now so he didn't get caught. He ran out the door to the hallway.

Susan kept gasping and gurgling. Her breathing became shallow, her chest twitching and trembling. A moment of sanity. A moment of consciousness. Her eyes fluttered open and through the open doorway she saw Wayne out in the hallway. He was jumping up and down with his arms raised, like Rocky Balboa. He was shouting.

"I'm a good boy. I help people. I'm a good boy!"

He turned and ran out of her sight as Susan's eyes closed for the last time.

THE WITCH POOL

"Human nature is potentially aggressive and destructive and potentially orderly and constructive."
—Margaret Mead

IT WAS DARK and smelly inside the trashcan. A sheet of paper that was wet with soda or water or some other he-dare-not-imagine-what liquid stuck to the side of Jimmy's face. He could hear the laughter from Artie and his cronies as they walked away leaving him upside down in the waste receptacle. He thumped around, but with all the weight in the bottom he couldn't get enough leverage to topple over.

So now what? The bell would ring and he would be late for class. *Sorry, Mr. Laimer, but I was stuck in the hallway trash can and couldn't get out. No sir, it won't happen again.* But he knew it would, indeed, happen again.

Somebody grabbed his legs and leaned him to the side. The can fell over and Jimmy crawled out backwards. He looked up to see his best friend Frank looking down at him. He was stealing glances furtively up and down the hallway.

"Thanks," Jimmy said.

"We'd better get out of here before they decide to come back," Frank said.

Jimmy peeled the paper off his face and tossed it back in the trash. He tried to smooth his hair down, which was sticking up by way of some kind of gel-like substance that had been down in the bottom with him. Just then, Amy walked by on her way to class.

"Hello, Jimmy," she said, wiggling her fingers at him in a little wave.

He turned red and gave her a sheepish smile. Frank kicked the can to the side of the hall.

"Why can't those guys leave us alone? They've been hammering on us all semester."

"I don't know," Jimmy said, and he brushed himself off. "This has got to stop. I've got to think of something."

Frank slapped Jimmy on the shoulder and pointed.

"Well, you'd better think fast. It looks like they're coming back for more."

The two boys turned and ran down the hall while the sound of laughter echoed off the tiled walls behind them.

They parted the bushes slowly, making as little noise as possible. The moon, which stood out large and round like the glass on the face of a grandfather clock, reflected in their eyes. Although the air had cooled with the onset of darkness, they shivered more from fear than from the temperature and pulled their jackets tight around them. Jimmy, the youngest at fifteen, stepped in front to lead the way, for this was territory he was familiar with. As they made their way toward the water the wet earth squished beneath their sneakers.

"This is it," Jimmy said and stuck out his hand to stop Frank. "Can you hear it? Can you hear the bell?"

Frank stopped and cocked his head struggling to hear what Jimmy heard. The water was as still as a cat about to pounce. He thought he could hear a low, muffled, metallic clang that floated in the mist which shrouded the pond. The sound was smothered and finally faded out. Frank wasn't sure it was a bell, but there definitely was a sound. Their breath rose to mingle with the moisture in the darkness. Frank pushed himself up on his toes to see over the dry cattails that stood sentry duty around the shoreline.

"So?"

"So, nothin'," Jimmy said. "Just shut up."

After five minutes of waiting, Frank was growing restless.

"What's supposed to happen?"

"Nothin'."

"Nothing? Then why are we down here?"

Jimmy made his way to a fallen tree and sat down. He waved Frank over and gestured for him to sit down beside him.

"To show you."

He held out his hand toward the water.

"See! Nothing, absolutely nothing. No noise at all. Not a living creature."

He indicated the tree and cattails.

"Even the plant life near the water is dead."

Frank hadn't noticed it before, but Jimmy was right. All bushes of any size stopped within twenty feet of the pond's edge. The shore grasped the water with fingers of mud that stretched out from the dead vegetation. Where lush tall grass touched the mud, it was brown and stiff like a bristle scrub brush. There were no tracks or signs of animal life that Frank could see. The entire scene felt like nature's vacuum. There was an overwhelming absence of movement and sound. One lone leafless tree stood on the opposite shore silhouetted against the night sky. A huge, gnarled branch stretched out over the water like an arm with the palm flat up, fingers pointing at the sky.

"That's it," Jimmy said, indicating the tree. "That's where the challenge will take place."

Frank mumbled, "I don't know. I don't like the looks of it."

Jimmy rose and moved along the shore cradling the lump inside the pocket of his sweatshirt.

He headed toward the tree and waved at Frank.

"Come on, follow me!"

Frank took another look at the water as flat as the glass top on his mom's coffee table. He stood up and ran after Jimmy, not wanting to get caught alone in the reeds even on this bright moonlit night.

Jimmy turned on Frank as he caught up with him.

"Spooky, huh?"

Frank stared at the tree, his eyes growing as he thought about what Jimmy was planning.

Jimmy found some footholds and began climbing the gnarled trunk. He turned and looked back at Frank who was still firmly rooted to the ground.

"Yeah, you bet it's spooky, Jimmy. You couldn't get me to do this in a million years or a double dare."

"Me neither," Jimmy said, smiling at his friend. "Just come up a step or two so I can show you something really weird."

Frank looked at the still water and then back at the tree.

"I don't know. I really should be getting back."

"Let me show you and then we'll go back. Or are you gonna walk back alone?"

Jimmy fished in the bloated pouch of his sweatshirt and pulled out a small high beam flashlight he'd been carrying. He motioned to Frank to step up.

"You won't be able to see if you don't get a little bit off the ground. This is a great light. My dad uses it sometimes to find addresses on houses when he needs to make a night run."

Frank scooted up behind Jimmy as high as he could with the other boy in his path. He hugged the tree like a long lost relative and turned his face toward the water. His cheek pressed against the rough bark so hard he knew he was making marks on his face.

"Look," Jimmy said, and he turned on the beam and shone it down into the water. "You can't see anything during the day because the light reflects off the surface. But at night the entire town is there still, just waiting to pull somebody down to live with the ghosts."

Jimmy moved the light slowly over the surface and the beam bore through the water. Small fish and floating bits of silt crossed the light. Jimmy scanned across, searching for something.

"See that?"

The light passed over something white, deep in the water.

"That's the church," Jimmy said. "At night the bell rings, calling for people to come to the church of the dead."

Frank's eyes grew big as plums and he grasped the tree harder.

"I don't believe it's haunted. That's just a local legend. My dad told me so."

Frank sounded more like he was trying to convince himself.

"All I have to do is get Artie to think this place is haunted," Jimmy said, "He'll back down in a second and lose face. He's been pushing me around all year. After this he'll never bully me again."

"But suppose he doesn't back down?"

Jimmy looked out over the black, still water and then back at Frank.

"What if he calls your bluff?" Frank asked. He shook his head and gave a little shiver.

"It scared you, didn't it?"

"Yeah," Frank agreed. "But I'm not Artie."

Jimmy took a long deep breath of the humid air. He smiled down at Frank.

"Come on, we'd better get back."

They picked their way down the tree and through the weeds back the way they'd come.

Frank looked at the lake one last time and then, suddenly feeling very alone, turned and scurried along behind Jimmy back towards the road. As they walked away the water moved lazily, as if it were stretching. It lapped gently at the muddy bank and somewhere out in the darkness something splashed.

The classroom doors flew open as if they had a direct connection with the period bell. Kids spilled out into the hallway in anticipation of the weekend. Jimmy walked down the crowded corridor talking to Frank and another friend of theirs, Harvey. As he turned the corner heading toward his locker, he bumped into Artie head-on. Artie knocked Jimmy's book-carrying arm causing his textbooks to fly outward in an arc onto the floor only to be kicked and scattered about the hallway by hundreds of moving feet. Papers slipped out from between the covers and became instant floor mats beneath dirty shoes. Jimmy just stood looking down in disdain.

"Hello, Fartface," Artie said with that smug smile he always wore.

Frank, almost as tall as Artie, stepped towards him with a sudden lack of restraint.

"Hey Artie, that wasn't very. . ."

Artie took a step toward Frank.

"Wasn't very what, Shit-for-Brains?"

Frank realized he was alone in this. There would be no help from either of his friends. To cover his own butt, he turned to face Jimmy while talking to Artie. He pointed his sweaty hand at Jimmy so Artie would look at him instead of keeping his focus on Frank.

"Jimmy's got a deal for ya," he said shakily.

"No kidding?" Artie inquired, pushing Frank to the side and stepping up to Jimmy. "I love deals. What have you got in mind, Needle-Dick?"

Jimmy's neck tensed up and he swallowed hard before speaking. It was now or never. He moved in closer to Artie and tried to puff himself up to a threatening height, falling far short of his objective.

"The Witch Pool."

He took a deep breath and looked relieved that he had gotten that out. Artie stood with his mouth agape, staring at Jimmy. He formed his hand into a fist and advanced directly toward Jimmy's face.

"Who're you calling a Bitch, Fool?"

"Witch Pool," Jimmy clarified and backed up rapidly, "I challenge you to the Witch Pool, the lake out near Salva's farm. It's haunted. Nothing that goes into the pond can live."

"Really?" Artie sneered, causing flecks of his spit to land on Jimmy's face.

"Anything in that water gets pulled down into the town below. There were residents who never escaped when the limestone gave way from the weight of the town on top and the natural springs carved it out below. The people were warned but not all of them moved before it collapsed. They're still down there. Waiting."

Artie leaned down. Jimmy could smell the stale cigarettes he'd been smoking in the bathroom on his breath.

"You stupid fart! I'm gonna slug you so hard your ass will fall off!"

"Don't believe me?"

Artie grabbed him by the shoulder and Jimmy could swear he heard him growl.

"There's a big tree that hangs out over the water. I dare you to climb out onto the branch and dive in."

He twisted away and threw his words at Artie while pointing at him very dramatically.

"Are you chicken, Artie? Scared of ghosts?"

There was a crowd beginning to gather around the pair and Artie was feeling the pressure to save face. Jimmy shouted like a boxing promoter, heroic with all the attention.

"Here's the bet. If you don't jump, you'll never screw with me again. If I don't jump, I'll be your slave for a year. You know, carrying your books, cleaning shit for you, whatever you want."

"I could make you do all that right now," Artie said and tried to grab Jimmy again.

Frank turned to Harvey and spoke loud enough for the entire gathering of high schoolers to hear.

"I think he's afraid! He knows there are dead people in that underwater town. He's heard the church bell, haven't you Arthur?"

Artie turned quickly and grabbed Frank. He pulled him up so close that their noses almost touched.

"You don't know who you're messing with, Asshole."

The crowd could feel the power in their numbers and wouldn't let Artie intimidate them.

They started jeering and yelling, laughing at Artie and making chicken clucking noises. Artie, still holding Frank, turned and looked at the crowd. They laughed and pointed, flapping their elbows like they were trying to fly. A large evil smile crossed Artie's face and he turned back to Jimmy.

"Haunted city bullshit. There's just a bunch of old rotted boards left for the frogs to fart in. That's all."

Artie let go of Frank's shirt.

"When?"

"Friday night at nine o'clock. We'll meet at the corner of Salva's property near old Breck Road. Those who remember to should bring some flashlights. It gets awful dark back there if there isn't a full moon. Makes it hard to see anything coming to carry you down into the water. There's a path where we can walk in from there."

Jimmy looked out at the crowd of people standing in the hallway.

"We'll need witnesses," he said. "Everybody who can show up, be there! Mister Macho's going to show us that he ain't afraid of no ghosts."

The excited voices growing among the students suggest that this challenge would be the talk of school for a while. The bell broke the spell and students all scattered to go home leaving Artie and Jimmy to stare at each other in the emptying hallway. Artie pointed his finger up under Jimmy's nose. He was bold again now that they were alone.

"You just make sure you show up, Booger."

Jimmy snapped his teeth at Artie's finger, making him pull it back.

"It was my idea, Asshole, of course I'm going to be there."

Artie stepped towards Jimmy like he was going to punch him, but Jimmy turned and ran off down the hall with Artie laughing behind him.

"You'll get yours, Jerk Face," Artie yelled after him. "You just make damn sure that you and your ghosts are there!"

He stood, pointing his finger at the retreating figure when he realized he was alone in an empty hallway shouting false bravado that only he could hear. He shook his head and turned towards the exit.

"Ghosts," he said.

The crickets stopped chirping at the sound of the approaching footsteps. Their silence would add to the invisibility the darkness already provided them. Jimmy, Frank, and Harvey walked to the fencepost at the corner of the Salva property and stood huddled together. Harvey looked at his watch.

"Ten minutes to nine, Jimmy."

"I told you guys; he isn't going to show. Ten more minutes and I have my freedom from Mister Bully Butt. This was the greatest idea I've ever had."

In the distance, a low murmur wafted through the night. It was the sound of voices, quite a few of them. The three guys looked at each other and then down the road toward the sound.

Golden pools of light flickered back and forth as a group of students walked into view. A pretty blonde in a windbreaker walked up to Jimmy.

In a seductive, teasing voice she said, "Where's Artie?"

"He's not here yet. I don't think he's gonna show up at all."

"He'll be here, Jimmy," she said as she pulled a towel out from under her jacket and handed it to Jimmy. "You're going to need this. It's chilly tonight."

Jimmy took the towel from her.

"Thanks Amy, but I don't think it will happen."

"This is for luck," she said and gave him a kiss on the cheek.

"Hey Jerk-off, are you ready to get on your hands and knees to lick my ever-lovin' boots?"

Artie and two of his sidekicks walked into view. Jimmy turned and looked at Frank with a *what do I do now* expression on his face. Frank stared at Artie with disbelief for a moment and then shrugged his shoulders.

"It's your party, man."

Artie held out his hand to one of his friends and snapped his fingers. The buddy unslung an athletic bag from around his shoulder and handed it to Artie.

"I've brought along a little something to make the evening even more interesting."

Artie set the bag down on the ground and unzipped it. He reached in and pulled out a long rope of thick coils.

"I figured that as long as we were going diving, maybe we could have a contest to see who can get further out into the pond."

Jimmy turned a little pale and looked at his friends while a noticeable tone of excitement danced around the crowd. Artie slapped Jimmy on the back.

"Lead the way, Slave."

Jimmy took a deep breath and prayed for a miracle. He knew everyone's eyes were on him, so he reluctantly started off through the tall grass toward the pond. The group made their way around the fringe of the pond to the dead tree that hung out over the water. When Jimmy stopped, everybody stopped. All sound stopped; maybe even a heart or two stopped.

The water lay mirror-still, reflecting the moonlight from above; even though a breeze brushed the tall grasses they had just walked through. An owl hooted from some perch nearby.

Everybody froze. There was the momentary sound of wings brushing the night air and all was quiet again. Artie walked around the base of the tree looking up at the large branch.

"This it?"

Jimmy nodded and Artie stepped back, holding the rope in one hand behind himself like a cowboy. With a grunt, he tossed the rope up and over the branch. The end dangled out of the reach of the people on the ground.

"You might as well get used to following my orders so why don't you climb up that tree and lower the rope on down to me?"

Artie placed his hands on his hips like Errol Flynn in a Robin Hood movie. He turned and laughed, directing his comments loud enough for the entire crowd to hear.

"Unless you're afraid the tree is going to eat you up like in Poltergeist."

Artie's friends laughed among themselves. Jimmy looked at Amy standing in the crowd. She looked scared and turned away from his gaze. He walked to the base of the tree and began to climb.

Artie, loving every moment of attention he was getting, made a big show of taking his shirt off and stepping out of his pants to reveal the bathing suit he had on underneath. He nailed a Muscle Beach pose, flexing his biceps to the crowd.

"Eat your hearts out, ladies," he crooned.

The comment was greeted by moans and groans.

Jimmy had gotten to the large branch and called down to the group.

"Wait everybody. Quiet down. Listen."

Artie and his friends stopped laughing and looked up at Jimmy.

"What is it?"

"The church bell. Can't you hear it?"

Quietly, but nonetheless distinguishable, the low metal clang of a town square bell could be heard. It was muffled, like somebody playing a recording under a pillow. Artie blew out a huff and raised his arms above his head.

"Church bell, my ass. I don't hear anything. It won't do you any good to try and screw with me. It will just make it harder on you later, Slave. Now get moving."

Jimmy shimmied out on the branch until he got to the rope. Scooting it over the limb, he lowered it down into Artie's waiting hands. Artie tied the end of the rope in a slipknot and pulled on it until the hemp was tight against the tree branch. The branch groaned and creaked in response. He held the long length of rope and walked backwards until the end of it almost slipped out of his fingers. He looked up at Jimmy, who had been watching from his perch.

"Since we're both going to get wet, I say the person who lands the furthest out into the water wins the bet. Is that okay with you or is the Loch Ness Monster going to eat us up?"

Laughter rippled through the crowd as Jimmy started to scoot backwards off the branch toward the trunk. Artie jumped up into the air and started running at the pond as fast as he could.

"Geronimo!"

As Artie reached the shoreline, he jumped up grabbing up the rope as high as he was able. It felt like slow motion as he swung out over the water, rising higher and higher into the air. Just as the rope reached its maximum height, he let go. His hair trailed out behind him as he stretched out his legs like a long jumper, trying to reach as far out in the pond as he could. He splashed through the water's surface almost flat; such was the distance he'd attained. His friends broke into a cheer.

"Try and beat that, Jimmy," they shouted at him.

Jimmy's bag carrying buddy pointed at something in the water. "We'll mark it by that reed growing out there."

He indicated the cattail growing out from the water not far from the wave rings created by the splash. The cattail swayed and bobbed with the ripples.

The area where Artie made his entrance into the water began to boil and foam. It churned violently from the center and worked its way out, growing at a steady pace. Jimmy stood up on the branch, pointing at the thrashing.

"The Witch's Pool," he screamed. "The Witch's Pool!"

The students began to back away from the pond, never taking their eyes away from the swirling water. The concentric circles grew as the water seethed and foamed. Suddenly, Artie belched up from the center. He rose with both arms straight above him, screaming at the top of his lungs.

"They've got me. Don't let them pull me down! Don't let them!"

His skin was white, almost blue in the moonlight. Several water moccasins clung from his face and neck, thrashing violently. Small cascades of blood ran down the side of his face. They looked like animated streamers. As he rose higher out of the water, more and more of the snakes could be seen on his body. Their fangs were deep in his flesh. Blood mixed with water and washed over his torso. Several serpents dangled from the meat under his arms and he flailed about trying to dislodge them. He finally, mercifully, went back under, as if he were being pulled from underneath.

The crowd was frozen in place, staring at the smothering water. Nobody moved. There was nothing they could do, anyway. He had swung out too far from shore for them to help. The vipers' nest was too large. Local legend claimed that everybody stopped breathing at the same moment that night at the Witch Pool.

Another plume of water and Artie surfaced once again, shooting upwards as if being vomited from the very belly of evil. Although snakes clung to his face and parts of his lips were missing, his mouth was open in an effort to be heard. He reached his hands toward the people on shore, but they could not hear him over the foaming of the water. For the last time, he sank beneath the surface of the Witch Pool.

As the waters stilled at the center, the rings reached shore and lapped at the muddy banks. Somewhere, off in the distance a church bell rang.

Here was my third outing for editor Eric Miller. He was doing an anthology entitled 18 Wheels of Science Fiction. *It was part of that trucker series he was selling mainly to truck stops. Now I'm the first to tell you that I am not a lover of the science fiction genre. I tend to find it cold and impersonal. It's just not my cup of tea. Eric knew that and was a little trepidatious about having me write a tale for this grouping. There was also the added challenge that the science fiction tale had to prominently feature a truck for the series.*

But the challenge intrigued me, and I felt I should add a science fiction piece to my collection.

To counter my aversion to what I perceived as the coldness of the genre, I decided to take the Ray Bradbury approach and make sure it was character-strong and not the Isaac Asimov approach and make it machine-oriented. Then, I set it in an apocalyptic landscape. But I couldn't leave my horror roots too far behind. It seemed to work and Eric bought it.

A FLICKER OF BRIGHT LIGHT

"The insanity of darkness can be calmed with just a flicker of bright light."

—D. H. Altair

"I CAN'T GO on eating dust and being. . .nothing."

Estrella kicked a stone along in front of them as they walked the dirt road. She squinted against the wind that was carrying particles of sand, the fine grit blowing into every open orifice.

"Not much choice," Susan said, kicking the rock back in front of Estrella. They stopped and Estrella picked up the stone and threw it into the desert. It burst up a little sand cloud into the wind when it landed. The dust swirled then dissipated quickly assimilating itself into the air and vanishing with the wind.

"That is us," Estrella said, and she used her hands to simulate an explosion. "Poof, we're gone. We are nothing."

A body truck rolled past them churning up a dirt cloud from the road, forcing them to turn their heads away and shield their eyes. Estrella pumped her arm and the driver responded by blowing the horns. The driver leaned out the window and waved at them. It was a game between them three times a week when the truck made its run carrying the load of carrion. He shouted out to the girls. Susan did a mock curtsey.

"He's lucky," Estrella said. "He'll be sleeping in the City with a full belly."

As he passed, the rotted smell of death choked them and Susan gagged, spitting into the dirt.

There was a damp trail of spotting that drizzled from the vehicle as it passed along. The sun created a momentary rainbow in the puddled liquid before it soaked into the loose ground leaving a black spot. Estrella watched the spectrum swirl in the moment before it was absorbed.

She thought about how long it had been since she'd seen rain, let alone a rainbow.

"One more stop and then he goes home. No wonder he is always so happy when he goes by. I wish he'd take me with him."

"Beeman," Susan said and nodded. "They have a body pick up there."

"Oh yeah," Estrella said to herself. "That's the last point in Zone B."

Estrella continued watching the truck.

"We're going to do it," she said.

"What?"

Estrella turned and smiled at Susan.

"Our way out."

Susan looked at the distant cloud of dust. Estrella placed her hand on Susan's shoulder.

"When tomorrow's truck comes will you come?"

"Where?"

"With me to Beeman, to freedom."

Susan's eyes grew wide as she thought of the possibility of escaping Zone B by body truck.

She shook her head.

"We'll die," she said.

"We'll die if we stay."

Susan stared at her. Estrella was serious. She was always serious. She looked down at her feet.

"I can't."

Estrella cocked her head and took a step towards her only friend.

"Why?"

"I'm only twelve."

"So am I. We got nobody but us."

Susan kept looking at her feet.

"I can't."

Estrella reached out and turned Susan's face up. She studied her eyes and could tell that what Susan was saying for herself was true. Estrella kissed her full on the lips, not impulsively, but endearingly. She wiped away some of the grime on Susan's cheek with her index finger. It was damp. Mixed with Susan's sweat and tears, they had made a small muddy trail on her face.

Estrella started down the road in the direction of the disappearing truck.

"Will you help me escape?"

Susan nodded her head.

"I don't want to leave you."

Susan began to cry. She turned away and wiped her dirty arm across her lips.

～

Susan walked along the side of the road alone. She could see the truck churning up a cumulus of dust behind it as it raced towards her. When the driver saw her, he began to slow until he was up alongside her, where he came to a stop. The dust the truck had churned continued moving past them and Susan shielded her eyes until it swirled past.

"All alone?" the driver shouted from the cab.

"She's sick," Susan shouted back up to him.

"I hope she is okay," he said. "I don't want to be hauling her in this truck someday."

Susan managed a weak smile.

"She'll be okay. She's just a little weak. We haven't eaten for a while."

The driver studied her for a moment and then turned back into the cab.

"Hang on."

This was good. Susan wanted him to spend as much time as possible talking with her. The driver leaned back out the window with something wrapped in his hand. He reached down to Susan.

"Here."

She scrunched her face up.

"Go on take it. It's food. It will make your friend stronger; help her to get better sooner."

"I can't reach," Susan said.

The driver threw the brake and popped open his door. He climbed down and handed the package to Susan. The was a clunk from the other side of the truck and the driver turned his head. There was no other noise, so he turned back to Susan.

"Probably just the bodies shifting."

"Where do you take them?"

He looked down the road where he was headed.

"I've got one more pick up in Beeman. Then I go to the City."

"I'd like to go someday," she said.

"Wish I could, but it's against the rules. The only way to get into the City now is to be born there. Not enough food. Not enough resources. Very few outsiders ever get let in. You must have merit. You have to bring something that's a plus for the City. They would never let in a little girl with no skills. We have enough little girls."

Susan accepted this proclamation. She had heard it all her life.

"What happens to them?" she asked pointing to the body truck.

The driver glanced at the truck before he responded.

"Those are resources. After I pick them up in Beeman I take my load to the City, and they're rendered. Even cadavers can provide something to help the people in the City live. They are put in a machine called a Scythian Vaporizer."

"Scythian Vaporizer?"

"Yeah. It breaks the bodies down into their six essential elements to be reused. Nothing is wasted."

She looked at him like she didn't quite understand what he was saying.

"You, little girl, are more useful to the people in the City dead than alive. You will never get in. Not alive, anyway."

He turned and climbed back up into the cab.

"You be sure and give that food to your friend so that she can get better."

"I will," Susan said. "Oh, my name is. . .."

"No!" He stopped her. "No names. It makes you real."

He reached down and let the brake go. She gave him the pump signal and he blew his horn for her. They both laughed and the truck began to pull away. Susan smiled at the food she held in her hand. She would have to eat it. Estrella was leaving.

❧❧

Were it not for the bodies piled so haphazardly on top of each other, like an elder's game of Stackman, the air would never have reached Estrella under the canvas. It was hot from the sun and tasted of rotting death, but it was air. The area above the top of the mound of bodies and the liner shield was minimal at best. Estrella wondered if others like her were inside. How many other souls had climbed inside the body truck, hiding under a stretched canvas, and trying to breathe the fetid air of survival? Maybe there were none. She could have been the only person crazy enough to chance it.

She slid her knee up a bit to help relieve the pain in her thigh from an awkward position. A throbbing ache from being unable to move or straighten out since the bodies from Beeman had been dumped in and burned into an angry pain that threatened to numb her entire limb. It wouldn't be good if she needed to make a run for it at any point. She couldn't hop to freedom.

Estrella had survived her entire life in Zone B, but was now starving as an outcast with the rest of the sector's population. For months she'd watched the trucks roll past, headed for their terminal at the gathering place. She knew that workers brought bodies to the various yards like Beeman and filled the trucks by dumping the bodies on conveyer belts. They were carried up the incline and then dropped like pus-filled rag dolls into the beds of the trucks.

In the past, she'd heard stories of people who climbed into the trucks, unseen by the loaders, or lay on the belts like a corpse to be dropped into the trucks. When the trucks had been loaded, she'd even heard of other scramblers making a late run becoming trapped between the conveyor belts and the truck trailers. Parts of them landing outside the trailers, severed from slipping into the gears, while inside the rest of their bodies slid into the pile to quietly bleed to death once their screaming stopped. They couldn't be heard over the sounds of the loading. Maybe they could be, but it didn't matter. Nobody cared. It was one less stowaway for the Guardian Protectors to mess with. Somebody else would pitchfork up the overkill and throw it in the trailer of the next truck. There were workers for that.

This truck was only one of hundreds taking bodies to the city. Upon arrival at the facility, Estrella had heard that the trucks were dumped, filling enormous cargo containers with bodies.

Those were sent to the vaporizers. It was one big continuous operation.

She had often wished she'd been born before the Earth wanted for room. She had seen a cemetery stone once, beaten and destroyed, and heard tales of burying the dead in the ground with the stones as identity markers to those who lay beneath the soil.

But now there was no room left to bury people in the ground and no fresh air to be further polluted by burning the dead. So the containers, which were filled with bodies brought in from all over the country, were dumped into a container convoy to be converted into a reusable chemical mist. They were no longer the Earth's problem. They were a solution. The future was missing for the people outside the City. Death was a constant occurrence. Life was merely a waiting game, waiting for it to end.

Estrella had a plan. She would escape the container once the trailer began dumping the bodies out of it. Using the corpses, she would climb up and over the side into the waiting arms of freedom. She'd heard that just outside the container yard was a utopia. If she made it to the City, she would be free. It was her shot at life. If she did not take this chance, she would die in the dirt next to Susan.

One time, a body truck broke down on the road near where she lived. She looked at it really closely and it appeared to her that the trailers dumped from the front end lifting and the bodies sliding out the rear and into the containers. She needed to make her way forward and find something to hold onto at the front. Her thought, as uninformed as it was by tales of people who had never tried this escape, was to hold on when the trailer was tipped and not drop down into the container until the very end. Her fall onto the body piles would be the shortest and softest as she plopped onto the rotting mass. There, on top of the pile, Estrella would climb up and out of the container. Maybe she would even be able to find work at the processing facility. She could keep that job forever, she imagined, as there would always be a steady supply of bodies. Maybe she could become a truck driver and visit Susan on her weekly runs in the body trucks. She, too, would be able to live on death.

The smell inside the trailer had almost disappeared for her, the stench being so common as to not assail her senses anymore, unnoticeable in its ever-present grotesqueness. She pulled her leg loose from the cadavers and let her sleeping limb's nerves work themselves awake. The darkness was deep with only flickering slivers of light creeping in from where the canvas was tied down on the top of the trailer. The truck rumbled along the road, a long steady humming. In the darkness of the giant metal coffin, they could have been going in any direction.

Estrella reached out and began to feel her way through the soft moist mass in front of her.

There were various shapes and she only knew they were bodies by touching an occasional limb or skull. It mostly felt like she was crawling through heavy gelatin. She was frightened and tried to ignore her thoughts of disease, doing her best not to contemplate what everyone she was sliding past or through had died from, or what had been in their stomachs or bowels when they had died that was now dripping and oozing out into the pile. Sometimes she would slip through something warm and slick making it hard to maneuver and then she would have to force bodies and bones that were impeding her advance aside.

She pushed an unidentifiable body and a spear of light from outside shown directly on a clouded eyeball gazing through a milky lens that stared her down. Estrella pushed the head aside with her forearm and a brown liquid ran down from the socket over the lip and into the mouth that was withered and pulled away from its teeth. The face held a death grimace that seemed to be laughing at her, at her possible exercise in futility.

"Don't worry about me, mister. Between the two of us I'm the one who still has a chance," Estrella said aloud, just to hear her own voice.

A whimper answered her statement. Not from the skull in front of her, but somewhere to her right, somewhere in the pile. She stopped moving and listened, trying to make sure she had definitely heard it, that it wasn't truck metal or body shifts in the pile, but a living noise. She held her breath and waited. It was the rhythm of the truck as it bounced along the rough roadway, the shifting of the bodies as they slipped in place and nothing else, possibly nothing else except ghosts or souls departing.

She knew about the death breath, that final exhale of life that departed the empty cocoons of our bodies when we passed. Here, in this darkest of places, life's last breath floated about only to escape when the metal lid was lifted and the souls floated away. The officials did not need people to be fully dead before throwing them on the conveyer to transport, only the appearance of death.

There it was again, a whimper and the sound of shuffling that didn't match the normal settling of corpses. It was faster, more frantic, and more desperate than the sound of bodies bouncing to the road music. It was possible that it was another scrambler, stuck deeper in the pile, slowly suffocating in the rotted air of death. Against her best instincts, Estrella began to pull herself deeper into the trailer toward the sound. There was still time to find out what was making the noise and then to make her way back to the front of the rig before it arrived at the dumping station.

"Hello?"

She called out as she dragged herself toward where the noise was coming from. The whimpering and shuffling stopped at the sound of her voice. Estrella paused trying to pinpoint the sound.

"Hello? Can you hear me?"

The truck drove over a patch of washboard road. The trailer bounced and screeched, metal screaming against miles of abuse, and a scared yelp from the pile in front of her rang out in surprise. It was maybe ten or fifteen feet in front of her. Estrella reached out into the corpses to pull herself forward when the truck made a sharp right turn. The trailer, playing crack-the-whip, snapped around throwing her sliding across the bodies and smacking into the wall.

"Easy! Goddamit," she shouted out to the driver who couldn't possibly hear her.

She used the metal wall as leverage to push against and right herself. A random shaft of light pierced through the area where the wall met canvas and she struggled to place her face by the fresh air. She was rewarded with a mouth full of dirt and sand. Estrella spit back into the pile and wiped her arm across her face leaving more draggle smeared across her lips from the suppurated remains she been dragging herself through than what she was able to remove. She raised her head up and wailed once out of frustration. Pulling the material of her dirty shirt over her mouth she tried for one more breath of filtered air. At least the heavier grains of sand would stop before she swallowed them.

A bellow came from the stack in the direction she had been crawling and she tried to use the light coming in from behind her to scan the pile of carrion. She was shocked when the return of light came back at her from the pupil of an eye that was watching her. The sound it made was a half-hearted bay. Maybe it was dying and just too weak to respond anymore. But it never took its eye off her as it made another nondescript noise in its throat. There was something wrong with the way it looked at her.

It was a dog. It looked in the direction of her noisemaking as opposed to seeing her. Perhaps, she thought, it was blind. The back three-quarters appeared to be stuck down in the pile, tangled in the sludge of decaying humanity, drowning slowly in a quicksand of remains that slowly sucked it down with every movement of the bouncing trailer. With most of its body being trapped and slickened by the seepages that continued to ooze from the cargo, it had no chance of pulling itself free.

She thought the dog realized that there was another living animal in the trailer with it. Friend or foe, it couldn't know. It didn't matter, as the animal was in no position to help itself and was beginning to resign to its inevitable fate. It was too weak and too destitute of vision at this point. The dog laid its head down on the damp pile. It was giving up.

"No, no, no," Estrella cried out. "Don't. . ."

She struggled for a word. Being surrounded by death she couldn't use that term.

"Don't quit." She said softly, the words getting lost in the metal slamming of the bouncing truck and she continued her crawl towards the dog.

Estrella crawled through the slippage, the movement of the

truck in direct contrast to the movement of the personages shifting and settling. The question of whether the souls were trapped in the trailer with them crossed her mind as she struggled to reach the dog. Once, while crawling, her arm plunged down between the assembled bodies and she dropped chest flat on the rancid mass. But she was almost there. The dog was still turned away from her. With a sucking sound, she pulled her arm up out of the boodle and flicked it to throw off most of whatever gruel was sticking. The last couple of feet seemed to take the longest, as if the driver was purposely swerving and bouncing the truck to make her trek difficult.

As she came upon the dog, it laid its head completely back on the top of its skull so that it faced her upside down. In the darkness, she couldn't tell if the dog was injured. Being covered in ooze from the ulcerated bodies surrounding it camouflaged the possibility of any wounds it may be carrying. She had to pull the dog loose from the pile and drag it up on the top of the stack to check it over better. She knew that if the animal was hurt, there was the possibility it may bite her when she went to touch it. If it did and it happened to be carrying rabies, then this entire ordeal could be for naught, both for the dog and for her.

She began to speak to it in low soothing tones that she hoped were calming above the racket from the trailer. The dog continued to look toward her through the tops of its eyes.

"Hey, Slick," she said. "I'm not gonna hurt you. I want to help you."

The dog gazed, wide-eyed, as she slipped her hands around its chest and up under the armpits of its front legs. It didn't move, just stared straight into Estrella's eyes. She lifted, but the leverage was wrong and her knees slipped on the mass, toppling her to one side and pulling the dog over with her. It didn't try to wiggle away or get angry, but lay without movement save the head following her every motion. She would not be able to pull upwards with any heft while her knees sank down into the gumbo of cadavers. Like the dispersal of body weight on a bed of nails, she would have to lay on her belly and work the dog up and loose that way, back and forth, a little at a time, until most of it was out and then she could pull it free.

How long had this all taken, she wondered? The outside light that had shone through the cracks and holes in the trailer had gone away, leaving only blackness both inside and out. She used her memory in the darkness—what the dog had looked like and how it was tangled in the bodies. Lying on her belly, she held the creature firmly but gently and began to work it back and forth while pulling steadily upward at the same time. Estrella began to feel it slide loose and the pile lost its grip when, simultaneously, something quickly slithered across her arm. She screamed and released the dog. She was shaken, but realized that whatever it was had been leaving the scene of the extraction. She had disturbed it and now it was heading for another damp wet spot to hide. . .or feast. A rush of ice ran up her spine. She had gooseflesh and pulled herself in tight, shivering in repulsion. What else was living in the cluster beneath her? What reptiles and insects had been scooped up with the bodies and deposited in this small space with her? Whose feeding had been disturbed by the jaws of machinery and then tussled again by her efforts to free the dog?

In a way she was glad it was dark so she could not see the other denizens moving about the trailer. Estrella was running out of time. She could feel the dog moving, whining with the effort. If it did manage to claw its way out it might run in the other direction and then she would never be able to grab it and take it to safety with her. In the darkness, they were both blind. She crawled back to the dog.

"Easy, Slick. Shhh."

She tried calming the dog with slow movements and gentle talk. It was all extremely difficult with the truck banging and bouncing around. Estrella wrapped her left arm around the dog's chest. With a singular smooth pull, she slid the animal up and out of the bodies. It wasn't quite as difficult as she had imagined. All the liquids and goop made the movement straightforward.

She dragged him over the top of the bodies and pulled him in close. Estrella held him against her so he could feel the heat from her body and her breathing. She rolled on her side and rubbed his face with her free hand. She couldn't see him, but he wasn't struggling to get away.

"Shhh. It's okay. We're together. I've got you."

He lay perfectly still as she spoke. Her breath went directly to his face so that he would learn her scent over the extreme fetidness of their surroundings. He seemed settled with the human contact; she didn't want to make him any more nervous than he already was. She had lost Susan by leaving her behind. She had lost everyone she had ever known by leaving them behind. It was the two of them now.

She knew they were at least halfway down the length of the trailer and she had to get the two of them back up to the front end before they arrived at the processing center. They needed to crawl to the front through the darkness, over the bodies and whatever else lay in wait. She tried to roll back onto her stomach. Estrella wrapped her arm around the dog as tight as she dared.

There was nothing to hold him by except his slippery hair, but she needed him to come with her.

"Trust me," she whispered closely into his ear. "Believe in me."

She began to crawl to the front one-handed. She pushed bodies and fragments aside to make space to crawl through beneath the cover as she pulled Slick along with her. He seemed to understand that they were together. The trailer shuddered across rough road and her knee sank into something that made a wet squelch. She slid her leg away and kept moving forward using one arm to grab in front of her and both legs to push with. Sometimes Slick got stuck on some obstacle that she had to pull him around or sank down in the morass from which she'd yank him up and continue onward. She was battling an unknown deadline. Estrella was determined to move forward until she touched the metal wall at the end.

Her body was as flat and long as she could make it to keep gravity and the shaking motion of the trailer from pulling her down. Snagging a body part, Slick slipped out of Estrella's encircling arm and began to slide off to the side. She frantically grabbed at him and managed to clasp his foot and hold him until she could maneuver over and pull him close. She laid still, hugging him against her, breathing heavily in her panic.

"Sorry," she said. "Sorry."

She regained her bearings and started moving on towards the front end of the truck, clutching the dog to her side tighter than before. Estrella was starting to predict the swaying of the trailer motion which helped with her balance. It was like the sea legs she had heard that the pirates of old managed from being aboard the ships for long periods of time. Together, they reached the end of the trailer and she turned them around and sat in a soft spot, her back against the front metal wall, Slick in her lap.

"Nothing can stop us now," Estrella said to the dog.

As she sat, Estrella felt tiredness overtaking her. Slick was at her side. The motion of the truck rocked her to sleep. The clanking of the metal and constant rumble of the road became a lullaby droning her off to dream of beautiful green landscapes and blue waters. She hadn't slept this deeply in years. She hadn't felt this safe in a long time. As she slept, a many-legged insect crossed her lap. It dropped down by her ankles and tunneled into the rot beneath her.

The truck jerked to a stop, its brakes giving a high-pitched shriek as it fought the weight of the filled trailer. She awoke disoriented and then the realization of where she was sank in. It was light again outside and the rays of sun came through the cracks. There was a slamming of a door and someone was walking past the side of the trailer. She could hear voices clamoring above them. This was the transfer point. This was where they would need to make their move. Their. Them! Slick was not in her arms. She called out in a strong whisper to not alert the people outside.

"Slick!"

Off to her left and in the darkened light she could make out the dog crouched. It appeared to be relieving itself in the bodies. Somebody banged something above them that made Estrella jerk. She could hear metal sliding.

"Slick, come here."

She tried to sound calm so the dog would not move away from her. The canvas was unhooked at the far end of the trailer and slid back. Sunlight flooded inside. Estrella squinted against the sudden intrusion of sun. The light and noise combined to frighten her even more. Estrella needed the dog. She began to crawl toward it speaking gently. Estrella reached out her hand, hoping to draw the dog to her. The animal didn't move. She kept crawling, reaching out. The few feet between them felt like a mile. There was more noise of the hooks letting go of the canvas. The far third of the trailer was now uncovered. Estrella was hoping nobody looked in while she was pursuing the dog.

"That's it, my last run of the week. I can't wait to go to my quarters," the driver said.

A FLICKER OF BRIGHT LIGHT

There was an unintelligible reply and then the two men laughed and made small talk while they worked.

Then there was a hum and the mechanical sound of hydraulics. The trailer rocked and the end Estrella and Slick occupied began to lift. No ceremony, no preparation, just a slow rise.

Slick cowered about three feet from Estrella's grasp, evidently too frightened to move. Their end of the container continued to rise. There was some shifting of the mass down at the low end. Estrella could hear liquid running off and splashing on the ground. Some of the more precariously perched bodies tumbled from the top near her to flop down to the end and out the gate into the waiting container.

Estrella grabbed the dog's leg. Slick tried to pull his leg free and roll toward the exit, but Estrella would have none of it. She held on to it so tight she was certain it would break. She crawled closer to Slick and pulled the dog to her across the cadaver stack. Once again, Estrella was able to clutch the animal to her. Their eyes held each other. Now they were together.

"Don't you ever leave me again. Ever."

Slick just stared at Estrella and then everything beneath them began to shift again with the rising floor and they slipped slowly towards the opening. One tumbling body struck Estrella as it rolled on past, but she held onto Slick with every bit of her will. She looked up at the wall rising behind her. They had to be over there so that they could land on top of the falling bodies and not become trapped in the midst of them. With one hand, she began to claw her way towards the upper end of the trailer. Each grasp only seemed to pull whatever was loose in front of her down to where the two of them lay. Slick slipped and wriggled in her arms. Their progress was slow, but Estrella felt like they were making headway, inch by stench-filled inch.

Slick was suddenly yanked out from her arm. The dog began to spiral down the incline, out of Estrella's reach. She lunged for the animal. She grabbed him as her motion took the two of them down the embankment, scrabbling and spinning with various faces, arms, and bodies joining them on their descent out the back. She reached out to stop them but everything she grabbed was soft, wet, and moving in the same direction she was. Just as Estrella instinctively pulled Slick in tight, her head cracked against the tailgate at the bottom and it all went black.

It was dark again. It still smelled like a garbage pit. Estrella had the image of her face being washed by Slick while she sat crumpled in a corner of a different metal container. They were lucky they weren't dead. They could have been suffocated by an avalanche of corpses. She could have died by smacking her head on a metal wall. Lucky.

She had no idea how long she had been out. There were no bearings for her to get. The container they lay in was sealed fully, leaving no light for direction. No sense of up or down except for gravity, no forward or back. There was only here. She began to cry while she rubbed the side of Slick's muzzle. The dog laid the side of its head against Estrella's chest.

It was too late. They were waiting to be taken to the vaporizer. Would it hurt? Would they implode? She couldn't let the dog die like that.

"I wonder if there are rainbows in the vapor, in us," she said to Slick and scratched him under his chin. She was crying. She had failed her only friend. Now he was going to die. With a scream she quickly twisted Slick's neck. There was a cracking noise and his head dropped awkwardly to the side. His eyes still watched her.

"Hello?! Hello?!"

The voices were from above the container and she could hear footsteps on the metal lid.

"Open it. Open it now, damn it," somebody yelled.

The motor hummed and the lid began to slide open. Once again, the sun invaded the interior.

The shadow of the driver crossed Estrella's face. She looked up at the black silhouette above her like an angel.

"I told you I heard something," he said to a second silhouette that joined him at the edge.

"Oh, my God," the second man cried. "Oh, my God."

The two men looked down into the hold. Sitting on top of the bodies was a young girl clutching the body of a decayed road-killed dog.

Editor Tom Piccirilli (one of the nicest guys I ever shared a drink with) had an idea to do an anthology featuring actors writing horror, alone or with Horror writers, and he titled it Midnight Premieres. *He knew I'd been in a couple of "C" movies with actor William Smith (in fact, playing Renfield to Bill's Dracula in one of them) and asked if we would like to submit a story. It sounded like fun, so I approached Bill.*

He said okay. He wrote beautiful poetry, but wasn't a story writer. So, we made a deal. He'd come up with the story idea (which he did in the form of wanting it to feature a version of his "Angel" character from the motorcycle movies) and laid out the skeleton of the tale. I would work it into a full-blown tale. It was accepted into Eric's anthology. The result you'll find below.

THE HUMPS IN THE FIELD

Co-written by Actor William Smith

"I'm not in this world to live up to your expectations and you're not in this world to live up to mine."
—Bruce Lee

IT BEGAN THE way most absurd arrangements begin; too much alcohol and too little brains. It was night and the following day was a holiday, so the parties would run late and heavy. No one was concerned with time. There was always so little of it available for fun. Tonight was the night.

As the music grew in intensity, the voices in the tavern rose to match it. Red faces at crowded tables drained large mugs of amber, frothy liquid shouting at the waitresses to bring more.

Women sat on men's laps as, here and there, a quick grasp of flesh created squeals of phony protest and mutual delight. Some people danced. Some people staggered. Some people drank and watched other people.

The games of chance moved at a slower than normal pace as dart players argued about tosses, billiard players fought over poorly called shots, and people along the bar yelled at each other.

At the same time, two teams struggled on the television in some muddied sports field. The night was just reaching its full stride when the stool next to Mr. Deaver was vacated and a stranger sat down on the still-warm padded vinyl. Though, nobody stayed a stranger long on a Friday night inside Champion's Sports Bar.

Deaver eyed him through the relaxing blur of four pints consumed in the span of an hour. He had paced himself. It was going to be a long night. The stranger was well dressed and his long coat gave off a cold draft of air as he removed it, folded it, and laid it across his lap.

"The temperature is dropping like death out there. That's why I hunker down in here."

Deaver grinned through yellowed teeth. The stranger looked at him coldly as he ran his hand across his coat, brushing the material smooth. The bartender arrived and the stranger ordered a cup of coffee and a shot of Amaretto. He exhaled into his hands, rubbing them together. The bartender walked off to fetch his order.

"Yes, it is," he said, looking up at Deaver. "And I forgot my gloves. I've been getting awfully absentminded lately." He blew on his hands once more and placed them under the folds of his coat.

Deaver nodded, feeling silly with the beer warming his gut, while acting like somebody meeting his favorite celebrity for the first time. "Yeah, yeah," was all he could say. He knew the grin covering his face made him look like an idiot. It certainly made him feel like an idiot. He had never been any good at keeping secrets. He was too impulsive. He looked away, taking a gulp of his brew. The bartender returned with their drinks and the stranger snatched the coffee from the bar almost as soon as it hit the countertop. He drank it down without pause and asked the barkeep for another. The bartender stared at the stranger.

"Was it not hot sir?"

"Yes," the stranger replied. "And I was cold. Now, could I have another please? Don't fill it all the way as I need the space for my Amaretto."

"Certainly," replied the bartender as he left to refill the mug.

Deaver was looking at the stranger in the mirror behind the bar until the bartender left. Then, he turned and faced him with his mug held up in salute.

"My name is Deaver. Albert Deaver. But everybody calls me Deaver. Cheers."

The stranger gestured to the bar space in front of him.

"I have nothing to salute you with. The shot's for the coffee."

"Oh yes, right," said Deaver, feeling foolish as ever. "Well, here's to cheers when your drink comes." He pushed his mug a little higher in the air.

The stranger stuck out his hand. "The name's Edward. Edward Falcon."

Deaver froze with his mug stuck up in the air. His eyes traced over the face in front of him putting the name and the body together. Slowly, he lowered his arm and did a quick take over both shoulders. Finally, he set his mug down on the counter. The bartender arrived with the new cup of coffee and Deaver used the moment to try and pull himself together. Edward poured his Amaretto into the mug and mixed it together with his spoon. Holding it aloft he said, "Salute."

He brought the mug up to his mouth, inhaling the aroma deeply before taking a healthy sip.

"Mmmm," he said, sniffing in another whiff of the scented steam. "This will bring warmth back to a dead man. It's the elixir of life. Add to it the warm glow from the lamps and the conversations of the drunks and memories of one's hometown. Yes, Deaver, all is right with the world." He warmed his hands on the side of the mug.

Deaver looked at him straight on and spoke very deliberately. "It's been a long time since I've heard mention of that name around here. If that is who you really are, why would you risk coming back here?"

Falcon grinned as he stared at his mug. "So, I'm not forgotten?" The question was more of a statement. Deaver thought Edward must have become prideful in his freedom. Time makes things feel less important to those who are lucky enough to forget.

Deaver drained the last inch of his coffee and motioned to the bartender to bring a third.

"Forgotten? You are a sort of urban legend," he said to Falcon. "Those of us who heard the story as it was passed around were told it was true. But it had been passed through so many people that we never knew what parts were fact and what was fabrication. As I've heard tell, you are a murderer; you and your friend what's-his-name. We've never heard from him again either. They couldn't find enough proof to charge you. That was all we ever talked about in high school that year."

"So, that's what it's come to, is it? I'm a murderer?" Edward took a sip of his mug and finally set it down on the bar, taking his hands away for the first time. He looked up at Deaver and took a deep breath, like a man beginning a journey. "The story has passed through many mouths, hasn't it? Not long after it all happened, Billy disappeared. I haven't heard from him since. The truth is, the real *urban legend* was the genesis of all that transpired. The story isn't a story, but the truth. What would you have done in my place? Would you have denied the girls their fun?"

Deaver waved his hands in front of his face. "Whoa, whoa. Back up a moment. Which story? What fun?"

"It's true," Falcon said. "You were young at the time. You're bound to be confused. If you wish, I will tell you my story. It will keep us warm on this holiday's eve. Plus, confession is good for the soul, they say."

"I'd like to know."

"Then, Mr. Deaver, it will be your job to keep the drinks coming."

The bartender arrived with Deaver's drink and Deaver sent him back for another shot and another coffee for Edward. Once it had arrived and the men had settled in, Edward was ready to tell his tale. He leaned in towards Deaver as if imparting a very important secret.

"Do you remember the Sand Val Drive-In Theater just on the outskirts of town?"

"Sure," Deaver said. "Even though the giant screen and speaker poles are gone, the field's still there and some of the walls of the projection booth/snack bar are still there, too. The land was sold to a developer, but after the stock market bust, nothing was ever done with it."

Edward stared into his coffee. "No kidding? I thought all of that would be gone by now, like a bad dream. I guess it's hard to build on haunted land."

"What do you mean haunted?"

"Any land that has soaked in the blood of the innocent also consumes the souls of the victims into the soil. The killer that stalked that area, or still does for all I know, shed the blood of many folks. The land is poisoned. Maybe they'll never be able to build on it without consequences."

Deaver leaned back on his stool. "Don't give me any crap, Edward. I never heard of other deaths out there. Don't try and get out of what you two did by passing it off as some kind of woo-woo shit."

Edward laughed and shook his head.

"Of course you never heard of any other deaths out there. They can't trace them to there, or to him. They were just disappearances. People disappear all the time. No bodies are ever found. No murder cases are ever opened because they are just disappearances. I've checked out the newspapers on the computers and microfilm at the library. In a twenty-mile radius in the last sixty years there have been almost a hundred and fifty disappearances. That's over two a year!

"What did we do out there that night? I'm not quite sure." Edward tapped his temple with his finger. "But think for yourself and don't let others tell you what happened. Were the girls murdered? I don't know. I think so, though. Were there bodies? Hell no. They just walked to the concession stand and never came back. Why would we have killed them? We were at the drive-in for Christ-sake! I wanted to spend some time in the backseat. Instead, I spent some time in jail while those idiot authorities tried to sort things out. Which they never did, by the way!

"They had to let us go because they had nothing on us. We were the ones who called the cops in the first place. But they wouldn't listen. They didn't believe us when we told them that the actor with the eye patch was there. They said we'd been watching too many cheap films."

Deaver shook his head as he thought the story out. "That actor from the biker films hasn't been acting sixty years."

"True, but maybe *it* just takes a form you'd recognize. Maybe *it* looked like someone else before."

"You mean like the frightening specter of Fred Astaire?" Deaver chuckled.

Edward didn't even react. "Laugh if you want, you weren't there."

"But Edward, that theater hadn't been open for years. Why were you there?"

"It was open for us. He did it or *it* did it. That's how he lured people in. An illusion? That's how he found his victims. The ones you never heard about. The others that just disappeared. He starts with your mind. You know, like mass hypnosis or a dream or something. I can't explain it. It was probably even easier for him when the theater was open. Back then there were lots of people waiting in the dark. He could have his pick. Or maybe he just dragged them there from another location after hours, when the night was finished and everyone else had gone home. The land needed to be satisfied."

Edward was becoming more animated as he told his tale. Whether it was from the drink or because he truly believed in what he was saying, Deaver didn't know. What he did know was that Edward was getting into it. So, Deaver ordered another round and kept the pump primed.

Edward was using his hands to shape the giant marquee in front and above him.

"It was lit up, just like the old days. All four of us saw it. Two of the actor's classic biker flicks were playing; "Angels Die Hard" and "Run Angel Run." Billy said he'd seen the films, but I'd only seen one of them and Gloria and Joanne just thought it would be fun to go. Would you have denied the girls their fun? We figured it was cool because the girls would probably get bored and we'd have a better chance with them. Plus, if we couldn't get anywhere with them, we could still watch the films and have a decent time. Either way was fine with us."

Deaver took a slug of his fresh beer. "So, you went in?"

"You bet your ass we went in. It was weird and cool at the same time. The guy in the drive-up ticket booth was dressed just like the actor in the film. You know, all in black with a patch over one eye. He looked just like that actor who was head of the biker gang. The girls were kind of creeped because of the old tales of the killer actor who had stalked the place in the past."

"You mean the disappearances you were talking about?"

"Yeah, the urban legend. We just thought the management was using it as a publicity stunt for their opening. Hell, we figured that's why they were showing the films that they were, with the biker gang legend and all. You know, kind of tie everything together and kick it off with a bang. Maybe even get the newspapers talking."

Deaver gestured with his beer. "So, did you say anything to the guy, or did he say anything to you?"

"Say anything? Hell no," Edward shook his head. "Son-of-a-bitch didn't even smile. With that patch and being so tall he really fit the part. But that wasn't what creeped me out."

"Why, what did you see?"

Edward put both his hands against his chest. "I didn't see anything, but the girls did."

Deaver smiled. "Sure they did, they were already freaked out."

"Yeah, in a way. We were the only car there. We just figured we were the first and a little early. I thought it was a little closer to dark though. Maybe that's the reason the guy in the booth was ticked at us and acting so unfriendly.

"So, anyway, we parked in the back, about seven rows behind the food stand. I thought it might be easier to get it on if there weren't a lot of cars around us. I didn't know there would never be any cars around us. So, while Billy and I were getting the speakers in the car, we parked in the middle of two speaker stands so we could have one in each window, the girls went up to get some dogs and drinks."

"And they never came back," Deaver said. "Yeah, I know the story."

Edward pointed at him. "Wrong! Say, who's telling this story anyway? They came back, but they were freaked. They said the same guy who'd been at the ticket booth was the one who took their money for the goodies."

Deaver laughed. "They were crazy. What, was the guy going to run back and forth between the ticket booth and refreshment stand?"

"That's what Billy told them. He said that all the theater's employees were probably dressed-up like that for the promotion. They just all looked alike. It was getting dark by then and the film started. We really didn't pay attention to the flick, because we were trying to make out. It wasn't until later, when I talked to the cops, that I realized I couldn't remember if any other cars showed up.

Edward paused his narrative to take a long sip of coffee. "I can't remember that. I can't remember," he said. He launched back into his tale.

"I do remember that once or twice during the first film, I looked over and could see that actor look-alike watching our car from the door of the concession stand. Just staring."

Edward took another long sip of the liquor-laced coffee, as if to drive away a chill of some cool air from the past that Deaver couldn't feel.

"I was thinking of just watching the movie, Joanne was bitchin' at Billy for groping at her and this was turning off Gloria, so I was getting nowhere. The girls kind of got pissed and when the first movie was over, they went off to the bathroom together."

"Girls do that, you know," Deaver said.

"Oh, don't I know it."

Deaver laughed. He realized he better cool it on the drinking a little as he was also a sheet or two into the wind at this point. He'd started drinking first, at least in Champion's Pub anyway. He had no idea where Edward had been prior to walking in here.

Maybe Edward was loaded. Maybe Edward was crazy. Maybe Edward had a death wish. But Edward was just telling his tale. He wasn't asking Deaver to believe or not believe it. He only wanted to tell it, to purge. It was up to Deaver to accept it or not.

"Anyway," Edward continued. "The dancing hot dog cartoon on the screen ended and the second movie started. No girls. I finally got out of the car and told Billy to stay there in case they showed up. I walked up to the concession stand to look around, no girls, nobody. I mean it was all set up for stuff. There was popcorn in the machine, candy in the glass counters, and hot dogs spinning on the rollers. But the girls weren't there.

"I walked over to the Ladies restroom entrance and hollered out for them. Nothing. No answer. The guy, the same tall guy with the patch or another look-alike, was in there with a mop bucket and the floor was all wet and soapy. He kind of grunted at me, I asked about the girls, and he just shook his head like he'd never seen them.

"I went back to the car to check with Billy. He was there, but no girls. He hadn't seen them. Billy said maybe the girls had been really pissed off and decided to teach us a lesson and walk home to make us worry. Hell, we thought they could have walked out of the theater to a nearby burger joint or something and caught a ride from there. I said we should call and see if they'd gotten home, but Billy said it was late and we'd wake their folks and then everybody would be pissed off. So, we just ended up going home."

Deaver took another swig of beer. "Had they gone home?"

"That's just it," Edward said. "The next morning, I called Gloria's house and her little brother answered. He said she hadn't come home the night before. I called Billy and he called me back after trying to get hold of Joanne, same story there. That's when I called the cops."

"And hilarious complications ensued," Deaver said and took a long slow swallow of beer. He looked at Falcon. "Sorry, I've been drinking a lot," he said.

"Yeah, forget it," Edward waved him off. "Just a silly story told over some alcohol. What difference does it make anyhow?"

Deaver watched the foam swirl about in his beer as he spun the pint in his hands. He sat it back down on the napkin. "They never found them, huh?"

"Not even a trace to this day." Edward finished his coffee and set the cup back down. "But you have been thinking I'm a murderer."

"You have to admit," Deaver said. "That story of yours is a little hard to swallow. The ghostly grounds of a drive-in theater. Woooh!" He raised his hands up like a stalking ghost. "It sounds like a bad rip-off of a rotten seventies slasher film."

Edward reached down and unfolded his coat. "Yeah, well, thanks for the drinks. I'm back to the Big Easy in the morning. I was just visiting what little family I still have."

Deaver grabbed his arm as he turned to get off the stool.

"Wait, wait. I would really like to know. If nobody has ever been connected to all these murde. . . disappearances, then the guy, the perpetrator is still out there."

"So?" Edward looked at Deaver.

"So, if I'm the only person who even remotely believes you, maybe you should try and convince me a little more."

"What are you talking about?" Edward seemed ready to slip away.

"I'm thinking that maybe you and I should go out there tonight and see if we find anything."

"Tonight? Are you nuts? What are you going to find out there tonight? Besides that, it's colder than a lawyer's kiss out there."

"A better time would be, when?" Deaver leaned in towards Edward. "Are you coming back later just to show these town cops up? Maybe you'd rather let this little label of murderer hang over your head for the rest of your life."

He dropped back into his seat and threw up his hands.

"Fuck it! You're probably right. No skin off my ass. Go back to Mardi Gras and disappear into the crowd. That's why you moved there in the first place, isn't it?"

Deaver turned back towards the bar and looked up and down as if he were trying to find the bartender. Edward stared at the blank space of room between Deaver and himself. Then he sat.

"Shit," he exclaimed. "Shit, shit, shit!"

Dirt and debris blew across the road in front of the headlights making it seem colder than it was.

Deaver drove, hands at ten and two with a death grip on the steering wheel, head leaning forward, staring into the blackness. Edward Falcon sat next to him, head back against the rest, cheeks puffed up with a solid stream of air blowing through his puckered lips. Deaver was looking for the place to turn off. They were lucky that it hadn't rained, as it was taken to this time of year. The ground should still be solid, and they wouldn't have to worry about getting stuck in the mud.

Finally, the entrance appeared in the weeds and Deaver made a left into the tall grass. Edward pressed his fingers into the padding near the door handle and hoped that Deaver could see better than he could. Deaver's aim was true and the car bumped into the wide-open field illuminated only in the strip of brightness from the headlights. They could see the humps in the field and the shadows rose and moved before them as the car bounced its way further away from the road.

Pieces of walls with ragged edges stood about three-quarters of the way into the field, centered among the speaker humps. There was no roof left on the concession stand and the gutless cinderblock building stood like a sentinel against the wind. The tall grasses beat against its peeled paint walls. Deaver cut diagonally across the rolling ground making the car ride feel like they were cresting waves before sinking back down into the troughs. He stopped the car with the headlights pointed at the building some forty or fifty feet in front of them.

"Come on, let's get out," Deaver said and popped open his door, stepping into the cold wind.

Edward crawled out on his side and pushed the door softly shut while looking around.

"Nobody is gonna hear us out here! You could shoot off a gun and no one would hear it," he gestured at the open field. "Especially with this wind."

The old theater grounds were speaking to Edward and he seemed frozen in place. Deaver walked around to the back of the car.

"I've got a flashlight in the trunk," he hollered against the wind. "We can use it to scan the ground for anything and inside the concession stand. The headlights cast too many shadows."

He unlocked the trunk and took out a long black police-type flashlight. He turned it on and waved it back and forth across the ground a couple of times to get an idea of how large an area it lit up. Deaver held the flashlight up in front of him and pointed it at Edward's face. He shaded his eyes with his hands.

"Fairly new batteries," Deaver said. "We don't have to worry about this thing going out." He patted the flashlight. "Let's go check out the building."

They walked back past the front of the car towards the building. Edward trailed a few feet behind Deaver. The headlights cast long shadows, like arrows pointing from their bodies toward their destination. Plant parts, dirt, and debris blew against their legs and underneath the sound of the wind was a low mournful moan that rose and fell in intensity. Edward turned his head this way and that, trying to pinpoint the sound, but could not quite get a bead on it. Deaver scanned the ground in front of him with the flashlight as they made their way up towards the building. At the stand, Deaver handed the flashlight to Edward.

"Here, take this and go ahead inside. I'm gonna take a leak first, too many damn pints. Great for courage, but bad for the kidneys."

Deaver walked around the corner of the building unzipping his fly while Edward turned towards the lit doorframe. An empty box blew against his foot and he jumped, turning in fright and shaking his foot to knock its cardboard grasp loose. He was scared and pissed at himself at the same time for being so afraid.

As he stepped through the doorway, the moan rose to the volume of a freight train. He dropped the flashlight and its light blacked out as it hit the ground. Clasping his hands over his ears he spun in a circle trying to see shapes in the darkness. It was their cries! The girls were screaming at him! Then as the gusts of wind died down, so did the moans, and he realized it was only the air rushing through the many openings of the shattered and weathered walls. He laughed at himself and let out a breath in relief. Edward bent down and picked up the light from where he'd dropped it. He clicked the switch back and forth a couple of times until the light shot out the end. It was fine, still working like a champ. The yellow-white light brought him a modicum of comfort.

"Weird place, isn't it?" Deaver asked. "Does it bother you? I was so hoping that you'd still enjoy the fact that the theatrics never leave an icon of drama, like this old drive-in. Once an entertainer, always an entertainer."

Edward stood his ground. "What are you talking about?"

The dirt and debris spun and smashed against the inside walls of the structure almost like a small tornado. Edward kept turning his head and putting up his hands to protect his eyes from the dirt.

"Look what I found, Edward." Deaver held up his hand and from it, on an elastic band, dangled a black eye patch. "How does it look on me?"

He began to slip it over his head.

Edward reached out to him in warning. "No!"

"Don't worry," Deaver said as he finished adjusting the patch in place. "But I do hope you'll forgive the fact that I lied to you tonight. . .several times. I didn't find this patch at all. I've had it in my pocket all along. I was waiting for the appropriate dramatic moment to put my costume on. Tah-dah." He held out his arms and did a little spin in place.

Edward turned and ran back out the door. There stood the two girls; Joanne, and Gloria. They were between him and the car but cast no shadows. The bright headlights were visible right through them. The wind gusted through the field and the two girls opened their mouths in a collective wail.

Gloria drifted closer to him and he noticed that the wind didn't seem to affect her clothes.

Nothing moved, not her dress or hair or. . .nothing. It was as if she stood in the eye of the storm. Her voice came out clipped and low as if she had trouble speaking. Her expression never changed, and she stared directly at Edward like a sniper lining up her target.

"You didn't spend an excessive amount of time looking for us, did you, Eddie?"

His mouth opened to answer, but his thoughts didn't seem to connect to his vocal cords.

"Did you!"

The wind and her moan coincided once again. The sound cut like a knife through Edward and he shined the flashlight at her hoping to snuff out the noise. The light reflected off the grill of the car behind her. She seemed to have her own internal illumination. He could only blink at the sight in front of him and the sand blasting around his face.

"In fact," Gloria's voice rose in volume. "You didn't bother looking for us at all! Did you?"

She reached out her arm as if she had a desire to touch him. Edward stepped backwards until he was against the outside wall of the building. He tried to flatten himself against it.

"I called the police! I called your house!" He was crying now, and the wind smeared the tears across his face.

"You didn't even want to come and look for clues tonight, Eddie. It's been so many years." She moaned low and savagely.

"I thought you were mad at me!" Edward buried his face in his hands and broke into sobs.

"Well, I'm glad you're here Eddie. We've all been waiting a very long time for you to join us." Joanne spread open her arms as if to encompass the entire field. Edward looked up from his hands.

"What are you talking about?"

He saw Deaver standing next to the car.

"All of us, Eddie," he said. "All of them are here. Many of whom you've known about all along but couldn't convince anybody they existed. We're all here and we're so lonely. And the ground is so thirsty."

Joanne threw back her head and moaned a death-rattling moan along with the wind. It grew in intensity until Edward was positive the ground was shaking. The dirt on the rows of humps began shifting and crumbling down into the roadway aisles. Cracks appeared along their tops and sides while fingers and hands began to claw their way out of the ground. Deaver began to laugh hysterically and Edward glanced in his direction only for a moment before being drawn back, afraid to take his eyes off the corpses pulling themselves from the earth.

Deaver was yelling now. "I do think that the graves look so much neater when they are lined up like that, don't you?"

There was a sound of motorcycles being kicked to life and Edward turned to see what he thought were the headlights of a car separate as two dead bikers began to pull around on both sides of him. Deaver's voice carried above the engine noise. He spread his arms out in the cabaret display of a ringmaster starting a show.

"The intermission is over!"

Chains of Love was inspired by a Dave Berg cartoon strip in Mad Magazine. *It is the only piece of flash fiction I've sold or even tried to sell at the time. It wasn't a piece of flash fiction originally, but it was a short, short story, making it easy to cut down.*

Editor Stan Swanson asked for flash fiction from many authors, and they submitted for free as the book Stan was putting together was a charity anthology entitled Slices of Flesh.

At this point I cannot remember the charity, nor did I ever learn how much money was raised.

I do know that the book was a lot of fun to read with some top-notch writers donating their talents. Hunt down a copy. It is hard to find.

CHAINS OF LOVE

"Silence is better than unmeaning words."
—Pythagoras

"IF YOU DON'T HURRY, Harold, we will never get there on time." She had honed her ability to insult and complain into single statements over the years of their marriage. She tossed off offending remarks like dandruff, spewing her verbal hatred wherever she went.

From the front door of the house, Harold watched her leaning out of the passenger side window of the car to ensure that he could hear her yelling at him. Oh yeah, he could hear her.

After all this time, her taunts still poked about in the acid area of his chest. He bent over slightly to make it easier to take a breath.

"I'm sorry, Maggie," he said. "I just wanted to throw in an extra pack of cigarettes for the trip."

He slammed the door behind him and scurried into the car. Maggie had rolled up her window, but reached back down demonstratively and pushed the button, cracking it back open.

"I don't know why you bother to shower and brush your teeth. As soon as you light up one of those stinking rolls of rope you start to smell like pig crap, anyway."

By then, he was turning from his street and onto the highway. He twisted sideways to help shift the burning in his chest. He slammed his right hand against the steering wheel and shouted at another driver.

"Come on, idiot!"

He took a deep breath.

"Settle down, Harold!"

"Maggie, it is Sunday. Relax, for Christ's sake."

Even after all these years of marriage, he had never quite created a strong verbal defense to her fine art of inflicting pain with words.

"I bust my butt and scrub my hands raw so you can have clean clothes and a fresh appearance. Do you even care? You'd much prefer to stink like an ashtray."

She looked over at him.

"Buckle your seatbelt or you'll get a ticket, or you'll end up in an accident and go flying through the windshield leaving me with no way to get home and nobody to depend on. Honestly, Harold, sometimes you are such a selfish jerk."

Harold groaned and pushed at the center of his chest where the flames were running like a volcanic river up from the bottom of his throat. He reached into the console and pulled out a package of antacids. Taking out two, he chewed them into mush.

"How can you eat that chalk? Just don't expect to kiss me after filling your mouth with that disgusting crap."

She turned back to look out the window and, in a deeply pitiful voice, took another swing at him.

"Not that I'd agree to be kissed by a stink weed like you, anyway."

As they passed a sign announcing their entrance to the Angeles National Forest, snow began to appear on the ground alongside the road. Harold cracked his window for some cool mountain air. He took a deep breath, momentarily feeling better from the combination of medicine and oxygen. Maggie shuddered to show she might be catching pneumonia and turned on the heat control.

"You know they're going to require chains to get over the mountain. You and your stupid shortcuts. If we'd only left earlier, like I suggested, we could have taken the desert road and still been there in time. We certainly wouldn't have had to stop and put on chains. Do you even have chains with you? I hope you had enough sense to bring them with you."

"Of course, I've got them with me, Maggie. They're in the trunk. Maybe we won't need them. We'll deal with it when it comes to that."

Maggie laughed.

"Who are you trying to fool? You know damn well that we're going to need the chains. Look at all the snow and we're not even that high up. You know as well as I do that you are going to have to put the chains on."

As they rounded a curve, a sign stood in abject mockery to Harold. "Chains required beyond checkpoint for all vehicles. One mile ahead." Harold moaned somewhere deep inside while Maggie let go of a small self-satisfied sound in her throat.

"I told you they'd make us put the chains on. You never listen to me."

"How could I help but listen to you?"

She dropped her voice an octave in a poor imitation of Harold's tone.

"I'm a man. I know more than a woman."

She snorted. "Well then, I guess you know what you have to do now."

They approached a dirt side road. Harold turned off and continued driving away from the main highway.

"I think you're far enough off the main road to stop and put the chains on now, Harold. You can stop anywhere along here. Harold, Stop! Where in the world are you going?"

They came to an area that could have passed for a scenic turnout. It was covered with an untouched frosting of snow. It had been a while since any traffic had passed this way.

"This is just great, Harold. Three inches of wet snow to kneel in when you could have just pulled to the side of the highway at the checkpoint where the pavement was scraped clean."

Harold turned off the engine and stepped out of the car. Everything was cloaked in a white blanket. He stopped and took a deep, cool breath. He walked to the back of the car and popped the trunk. Maggie rolled down her window.

"I suppose you have to remove everything in the trunk to find the chains! Hurry up, I have to go the bathroom."

Harold slammed the trunk and walked back up the side of the car. Opening the car door, he leaned in holding a dirty wad of balled up chains in one hand and began unrolling them. Maggie was visibly disgusted as the greasy chains made black marks on the upholstery.

"Harold! What are you doing with those filthy things in this clean car?"

He smiled at her.

"I'm going to put the chains on just like you want, Honey."

Maggie's eyes widened as he reached across the seat. She began to scream as soon as the first cold steel link touched her skin.

THE NECROSIS FACTOR

"No amount of experimentation can ever prove me right; a single experiment can prove me wrong."
       —Albert Einstein

"WHAT WE ARE dealing with here is programmed cell death," Dr. Slade scanned the room full of students trying to ascertain who was awake and who was napping.

"Programmed cell death", she repeated. "Mr. Niles."

A young man in the fifth row snapped his head up, trying like hell to look as if he was in the same classroom as everybody else.

"Yes, Dr. Slade."

Slade stepped out from behind the podium and stood in front of the overhead projector so that the bright light illuminated her like a mad scientist in her laboratory.

"Now that you've concluded your study into sleep deprivation, would you be kind enough to inform the class as to what I mean when I speak of programmed cell death?"

Niles looked back and forth at his fellow students trying to glean a hint. He looked up at the screen, but Dr. Slade's shadow obliterated most of the words. He was lost and his expression acknowledged it.

"Okay," Dr. Slade said deliberately. "Let's break it down to make it easy for you, Mr. Niles. What is cell death?"

"The death of cells?"

The class chuckled among themselves, but Dr. Slade continued.

"Very good, Mr. Niles. And why do cells die?"

"Well," began Niles, gaining a little traction as his sleep-filled fog began to clear. "There are a variety of reasons. . .injury, age, illness; any of these could cause cells to die."

Dr. Slade stepped back behind the podium.

"All true, Mr. Niles. But what about a child? What about a newborn? What about a healthy embryo with no injury to it or its mother? Does cell death occur under these conditions or," she looked about the room, "do we not lose any cells until there is an unfortunate event?"

"I'm. . .I'm not sure," Niles said, feeling very on the spot. "I guess so."

"You guess so!" Dr. Slade smiled. "Fair enough. Rules begin as theories, which begin as postulations, which begin as guesses. So, figuring we are back at the beginning, and you guess so, what would you guess would cause cells to die at those stages?"

"I don't know, Ma'am."

Dr. Slade pointed at Niles. "No, you don't know. At least you're being honest. And you won't find out by sleeping in class. Now pay attention or you will discover more than cell death. You will discover grade death."

The class laughed again.

"Yes, Ma'am. Sorry, Ma'am."

"Apoptosis is a cause of cell death in an embryo. Apoptosis is also known as programmed cell death. Maybe you've heard it said that you get a new body every seven years because your cells are constantly refreshing themselves?"

The class stared back blankly.

"No? Well, stay with me, as this leads us into a fascinating exercise in unraveling the complex interactions of the genes. Apoptosis is the deliberate elimination of cells; deliberate, on purpose, programmed. Genes, different kinds of genes, cause apoptosis and my personal favorite of these is the Reaper gene. This purposeful killing of cells occurs in a morphologically distinct manner that leads scientists to believe that this is an active, gene-directed process."

She flashed a drawing of the Grim Reaper in all his glory with hood and sickle up on the screen. Taking her marker, Dr. Slade wrote "Reaper Gene" next to the picture. She began tapping on the projector as her voice rose dramatically.

"This little fella's job is to kill your cells. He's a protein gene and he doesn't do it alone. The rest of his team is called Grim and Wicked."

The class chuckled at the names as they might at a horror film.

"That's right," Dr. Slade continued. "Science is not filled only with nerds. Scientists know who Freddy is and who Jason and The Creeper are. They are killers, just like the Reaper. Only less effective."

Dr. Slade stepped down from the podium and moved among her students like a creepy ghoul.

"Not only are they killers, but they kill inside the embryo. . . scattered subepidermal death. They kill in the embryo so that the embryo can grow and live." She took in their confused faces. "Sounds like a contradiction, doesn't it?"

Standing behind one of her seated students, she reached around and grabbed him by the nose.

"If the genes did not do their job on your face, your nose would not have any nasal passages."

She let him go with a pat on his shoulder.

"Thank you, Carter," she said walking away while he rubbed his nose.

"Your hands would end up being oven mitts instead of having individual fingers and your feet would be clubs. These genes are the sculptors, the artists with the hammer and chisel for the block of flesh we call your body. Inside every block of flesh is a human. All that needs to happen is for the other parts to be chipped away like a sculpture. But instead of chipping them away, they are not allowed to develop in the first place. We need apoptosis. We need those cells to die.

"We will be studying more of this in the future, but at least this gives you some food for thought. If something hadn't carved out your eye sockets by killing some of the cells that form your face, your eyes would be useless. There would be no hole for them. The eyes might even be in there, but they would be covered up with flesh.

"But what triggers this process? What turns on these killing machines and what turns them off? What targets them toward a specific part and away from an undesirable one? In private studies I am working on those questions. What if we discover how to turn these proteins on and off so well that there is no need to use a scalpel or laser for plastic surgery? We'd merely turn on the genes and let them reshape you into your idea of beauty or to heal protruding bones and nodules or burn scars. The possibilities are endless."

She paused and looked the class over.

"The most gifted of you may be asked to work with me in these studies. And that, Mr. Niles, is why I suggest you stay awake in class. With a little more sleep at night and a little less during the day, you just might be a part of history in the making."

She walked back up onto the stage and clicked off the projector.

"Class dismissed. I'll see you all on Tuesday."

"Michele, how's it going?"

Professor Williams joined Dr. Slade where their paths crossed in the quad. He had a briefcase full of papers to grade, which seemed to weigh so much he leaned to one side. He compensated by craning his head back in the other direction, as if the weight distribution would keep him upright. On the other hand, Dr. Slade rarely took any work home with her. Her experiments and caretaking of her invalid husband kept her busy enough.

"Fine, Will, and how about you."

"Lovely," he said in that persnickety way he spoke, "absolutely lovely."

Michele never understood how he got all those dates with the undergrads. The power of the grade point she guessed. William Williams. Two first names. She'd heard some of the female students refer to him as Wee Willie Williams. He did a little dance around some exploded asphalt, not only keeping himself from tumbling over on his side but also managing to match Dr. Slade step-for-step.

"I think that my lecture on the importance of foodstuffs in 15th Century literature went over quite well," he said. "I may try to expand that idea next semester." He was the type that stared at you when he spoke to catch every reaction, no matter how inadvertent.

"You could have each student prepare one of the dishes you're talking about. That would give it more of a hands-on feel. I know how much you enjoy hands-on."

Williams giggled. "That's brilliant, Michele, absolutely brilliant. I'll invite you over to taste test when that happens."

"I can't wait," she smiled. "Oh, here's my car."

"Michele?"

Dr. Slade straightened from unlocking her car and turned to face Will. He had dropped the load he was carrying a little bit lower and had put on a sympathetic this-is-in-confidence-best-of-friends face.

"How is Lee doing?"

Michele opened the car door and put one leg inside. "Fine, Will, he's just fine. I'll mention you asked about him."

She sat down in the driver's seat and slipped the keys into the ignition. Williams reached in and put his hand on her shoulder.

"Really, Michele? Please don't soft-soap me. I know it's been tough for you since the incident. What's it been now, two years?"

"Three," she said starting the engine and pulling the driver's door shut. She looked through the glass at Williams wearing his puppy dog face and mouthed, "I'll let him know you asked."

Then she backed the car out of the space and drove out of the parking lot. Professor Williams watched her turn off school grounds and out of sight. He sighed and stood for a moment looking at the empty space, the smell of exhaust still hanging in the air. Shaking himself out of his dream-like state he looked around the lot, trying to remember where he'd parked his car when he'd come to work that morning.

Michele thought about Lee while she drove, the radio tuned on to some white noise that slowly slid to the back of her head as her thoughts spun.

They'd had a few drinks in them and Lee was a lot less reserved than he usually was. In fact, he was giddy with the booze. As is natural, between a man and a woman, the talk turned to sex.

"I have only seen one woman naked in my life prior to you."

"Really?" Michele seemed unconvinced although she was a bit let down having thought all along that he was a virgin. However, she couldn't help picking at the scab.

"Was she good-looking?"

He almost did a spit-take in attempting to get the glass away from his mouth. He laughed and coughed into his napkin. He wiped the tears from his eyes.

"Please don't do that to me again."

"I'm sorry," Michele said. "I didn't know how you felt about her."

"You want to know, huh? Okay, here's the scoop."

He leaned in towards her as if sharing a big secret.

"She was the most gorgeous woman in the world. Tight buns and a slight but toned build."

Michele wiped her mouth and put her napkin down on the table.

"Maybe that was more than I really wanted to know."

"Now, now, Michele," he said, reaching out and holding her hand on the tabletop. "Don't get all mopey on me. She wasn't going to be a big-time doctor like you."

Michele had been smitten and now she felt dashed.

"Yeah," she said and pulled her hand away.

"Michele! It was some girl in an old science travel magazine. Honest to God. It's the only time I'd ever seen a naked woman. She had breasts that looked like a couple of socks with a golf ball in the bottom of each one. But what an ass!"

She smiled to herself as she turned the car onto the two-lane blacktop. She was glad to be off the highway. This was the part of the drive where she could relax. She chuckled again at the memory. He had gotten her good that time. The laughs had been nonexistent lately. She guessed that was why she was dredging up humor from the past, trying to make the present disappear. Trying to make everything disappear. It was so hard sometimes just to face life, harder to face death.

The house always felt cold without any lights on. In the deepening twilight, the darkness reached shadowy fingers out from the corners and from around the edges of the curtains and furniture.

Michele clicked on the floor lamp that stood next to the overstuffed chair just inside the front door and bathed her favorite reading area with an isolated pool of warm yellow light. She leaned her briefcase against the footstool and looked through the hallway towards the staircase. He was up there, waiting for her, and some days it was easier than others. It was just that today she felt tired and worn from her classes, wrung out like an old washcloth.

They had loved the house when they'd bought it. It was big and classic with lots of old dark wood trim. The staircase leading up to the bedrooms reminded Michele of some old black-and-white movie set in a southern mansion.

"A little paint to brighten up a few of the rooms," Lee said spinning around in the vestibule like some television show decorator. "Strip some of the wood and stain it fresh. I can't wait to get started."

Michele smiled at his enthusiasm. "Better you than me, baby. It is all yours. Just keep a hard hat by the front door so nothing falls on me when I come in at night."

It was a dream they were going to create together. Unfortunately, some dreams have a way of becoming nightmares.

He would know she'd arrived. The sounds of the car in the driveway, the opening of the front door, and her footsteps on the hardwood floors, all of which would cause his anxiety to rise with anticipation. He'd been thinking about her all day. His blood pressure would climb. His breathing would grow shallow with excitement. His muscles would begin to twitch and spasm involuntarily. She was the highlight of his day. She was his day. He was her last duty each evening before she could claim some time to herself and her experiments.

She thought about going straight up, knowing he was waiting for her, but decided to head into the kitchen first to get something to drink and wet her mouth, which had felt dry all day. She needed to put a cushion between her reality as a professor and the surrealism of her home life. Maybe tonight she could spend some time in the laboratory. She knew she was close; painfully close.

The house had gotten that smell; like a sickroom. It was a combination of medicine and stale air. In Lee's case it was also dead skin, decay, and the stench of open wounds. Burns took a long time to heal. Chemical burns were worse. There weren't many left, only the ones that had started out deep. They had to heal from the inside out to keep them from becoming infected. The scrubbing off the surface of dead skin every day with Lee screaming in pain was hard enough.

They had used maggot compact bandages to remove the dead skin that was down inside the wounds. The maggots were harmless and painless, eating away only the dead tissue, but the process was psychologically devastating. She would remove the bandage and clean him up before they had sex. Afterwards, she would replace it with a fresh maggot pack.

Michele swallowed the last of the water with the tranquilizer and thought about how she'd been repulsed by him when she first saw him. The accident had turned her handsome groom from a light that shone deep inside her heart into a monster that stirred repulsion.

She had forced herself through the memory of it time and time again. It was her fault. She had come home that night and, seeing the light upstairs where he was working, rushed up the stairs to tell him the good news of her appointment. She could smell the fresh paint and varnish and knew he had been at it all day. She pushed the bedroom door open. The open tub of paint thinner with the soiled brushes sitting in it must have been right on the other side of the door. He had just sat down and was lighting a cigarette when the liquid splashed across his face and body.

The initial whoosh of the flame knocked him over and Michele saw him squirming and rolling on the ground, a blazing bonfire. She knew she needed to smother the fire and grabbed the first thing she could see in the barren room. Knocking the ladder to one side she scooped up the plastic drop cloth and wrapped him in it while he rolled and flailed back and forth. The hissing of the fire on his skin was so loud it was the only sound she could seem to remember. She didn't realize the plastic cloth would burn and dissolve on him, fusing as one. It melted and flowed like rivers of liquid forming pools of plastic that burnt deep into his body.

During the healing process, she had come to accept his appearance. Maybe she'd just gotten used to it the way a battered child begins to think the whole world is ugly. In fact, there were times when she closed her eyes and lay next to him and could imagine the accident had never happened. Inside the cocoon of horror that he was trapped in was a beautiful soul. Sometimes, though, he spoke too much, and his flights of fancy revealed the crazed mind that had grown during the three years of scars and decayed flesh and melted plastic.

She sat the glass down on the sink and headed for the stairs. He never rang the bell or thudded on the floor or called out when she came home. She knew he was awake and he knew she'd come up. There was no hurry. They had all night to make love. He liked it that way, lots of foreplay, a long slow build to her climax and a shuddering, clenching orgasmic release. Lee claimed that the sex, the orgasms, were the only things that pulled him through after the accident. Even with all the pain pills, it was only a heavy convulsive climax that made him forget the pain. After, he would talk about their future that her experiments would bring them and what it would be like; simple things like day trips and shopping excursions. Their future.

It had been impossible for her in the beginning. He was too tender and injured to be touched, but he had demanded that she lay next to him on the hospital bed and touch herself until she came. She would cover her fingers with her wetness and scent and run them over his lips and inside his mouth. He couldn't even move his own arms or bend at the waist because of restraining scar tissue, but he could cum like a freight train, just from watching, just from tasting her, just from savoring her.

At first, his screaming would bring the floor nurse who would turn and leave, repulsed by what she saw. After a while, the nurse quit responding. Once they could leave the hospital and bring Lee home, there was no need to be discreet. Michele knew what her husband needed.

He'd begged her for it enough. As he healed and the thick scar tissue formed, she began to be able to put her weight on him. But she had to be careful how her body rubbed against him lest she remove patches of newly grown skin.

Michele had used a method of skin replacement with cadaver skin as the base to grow new skin on his body. But sometimes the skin didn't adhere strongly and if it was too new or the sex was too rough, she would push herself away from him and find large patches of dead skin stuck to her and Lee with a raw open place where it had once been. Like new sod on an ill-prepared field, the epidermis would shift and turn and slide. He never complained. Many times, afterward, Michele would find herself in the bathroom splashing water on her face, forcing herself to keep her Happy Hour drinks in her stomach.

She always smiled at him. She always made him feel like everything was going to be fine.

Her lust burned, almost as insatiable as his. Riddled with guilt, she was still a sexaholic who happened to be another sex addict's dream. Their life was going to be perfect, until. . .

With time, the healed scar tissue made him strong against her, he could take more now than he ever had. After three years, he was almost healed; even the deep tissue injuries that had needed to be reopened constantly and scraped and cleaned daily were nearly closed.

But his beauty was gone, covered over by a monster awash with purple and pink scars that bubbled and rippled like a topographical map across his entire torso. His nipples were missing, replaced, or covered over by a thick vein looking scar that ran down from his jaw line and across his chest before twisting and turning behind him. Some of his fingers were fused together and when he touched Michele it was like having a warm bumpy skin mitten trying to penetrate her musky dampness. She'd grown used to most of his deformities. Once he was inside her, she could close her eyes and time would reverse itself.

She paused before going upstairs, turning the lock on the front door and removing her suitcoat.

She folded it and draped it over her arm as she reached over and snapped off the floor lamp.

She could see a light in the upstairs hallway that must have been coming from his room. He was ready and waiting for her. She placed her hand on the large wooden phallic fennel at the end of the banister and started up the stairs.

"Hey Professor, I'm coming up," she shouted cheerily and then took a deep breath as she continued to mount the stairs.

No matter what food they were serving, the lunchroom at the university always smelled the same. It was somewhere between old stew and fresh hash browns. Michele had been sitting staring off into space while Williams talked on incessantly about the semester's latest dark-haired beauty. There was one every year that Wee Willie picked out to be his "special assistant."

Michele was lucky enough to snap back by the end of a sentence.

"William, one of these days you're going to get your ass in a sling," Michele said. "You'll lose your tenure, your position, and you'll end up flipping burgers down at Top Hat's."

"Yes, but what a glorious run I'll have had in the meantime." Williams laughed and then leaned into Michele. "So how is the research coming? How close are you?"

Michele used her fork to poke at a gummy slab that was supposed to be a Salisbury steak, but was grease holding together bits of fatty hamburger. She had poured steak sauce on it to try and fool herself into thinking there was some real beef involved, but it had been to no avail. She took her knife and cut through the mass; it was too congealed to use the side of her plastic fork.

She'd already lost one tine in the futile attempt.

"I haven't been able to work a lot on it lately, but I believe I've found the fuse that will ignite the Reaper into action. My biggest problem is trying to control the gene's actions and speed once it kicks into gear. But I'm close, Willie, really close. I'm close enough that I can feel confident about starting experiments on real subjects."

Williams swallowed a lump of his potatoes and washed it down with milk from a carton that had been opened incorrectly. It dribbled down his chin and onto his shirt.

"Do you think Dolan will give you permission to use the lab animals for this? I mean, all of the research on this has been outside the auspices of the school."

Dolan was the science college foreman who doled out the rights to use the facilities like they were a gold standard. He was notoriously cheap, making him best friends with the school board and headmaster and equally made him dreaded enemy number one of the research professors.

His job would be secure at Broxton for a long time.

"I'm not going through Dolan," Michele said.

Williams stopped mid-chew. "What other option do you have?"

"I'm keeping the entire experiment at my home and in my personal lab, and I don't want you saying a word about it; not a whisper!"

"But where are the rats going to come from? What are you going to do, catch them yourself?"

Slade pushed her plate aside.

"Lee volunteered. I won't need many more rats."

Williams was getting excited, spitting potato like a mini snowblower as he spoke. "You can't experiment on your own husband! Are you out of your fucking mind?"

"Listen to me, William, and keep your voice down."

Some heads at nearby tables had turned at the sound of William's outburst. He gave them an apologetic smile and turned back to Slade.

"Lee cannot continue to exist like this," Michele said. "We can't continue like this. His looks may be gone, but his desire is well intact. Now that he is getting some restricted mobility, he won't even get up or look at himself in a mirror or try to live a normal life. He can't stand to touch himself. I'm the only one he lets near him. It's the only time he feels alive."

Willie tried to wrap his thoughts around what Michele was proposing.

"But you haven't conducted any trials yet," he said. "Or any controlled tests in a safe environment. Just what exactly do you think is supposed to happen when you. . ." He looked up at Slade. "When you what, inject him?"

"No, it's an oil-based liquid that I've mixed the gene hybrid into. I'll squirt it down his throat with an eyedropper."

"Much like giving a pet some medicine," Williams said by way of comparison. "You do a couple of Petrie dish experiments and you think you're ready to dose your husband. This is insane, Michele."

"Listen to me. I'm damn close. I think I'm close enough to do this. If I don't, he ceases to live anyway. He feels he has nothing to lose."

"But does he understand the risks?"

"Absolutely. Probably better than the rest of us do. I'm going to need you to help me. Tonight."

Williams shook his head. "What are you asking me? I can't sanction this by being a part of it. I may not only lose everything here I've built, but I'm pretty sure it's illegal too."

Michele stood up and picked up her tray. "But you'd rather take the same risk by fucking some Fiona Floozy from your third hour class? Do whatever you want then Willie. But stay out of this. I'll do it on my own. And stay out of my way!"

She turned and crossed the cafeteria, leaving her tray and going out the far door without looking back. Williams sat at the table with his cold food wondering why he was even there.

Michele rose up and could feel Lee sliding out of her; bringing his semen and whatever other lubrications might have been caught up in their lovemaking oozing out of her with him. Her hair was stuck to her forehead and her teddy was drenched with sweat. His labored breathing became a laugh as he shouted, "Yes, yes, my god. That was so good!" She lifted her leg over him dripping across his belly on the way. She grabbed the towel she had lying on the floor and wiped between her legs without looking.

"Lee, I think it's time to begin the treatment."

"Right now?"

He leaned up on his elbows and looked at her.

"I thought you needed help to prepare it?"

"I've figured out a way around that," she spoke as she walked into the bathroom. "Late Monday night I'll set everything up in advance so I can get the heating and mixing done together in the short time it needs to be prepared in."

"How many treatments will I need?'

"I don't know. A few. A lot. I don't know."

She stuck her head out of the bathroom. She was wiping her face down with a washcloth.

"Maybe it won't work, maybe it will. These genes need the full forty-week term to do their work on an embryo. If it's going to work on an adult, who knows how long it could take?"

She threw the cloth inside the bathroom behind her and walked over to Lee.

"Lee, are you sure you want to go through with this? What if I can't control it? What if it doesn't work? What if it kills. . .?"

He grabbed her face between his knitted hands and pulled her close to him, shushing her. He pulled her cheek down next to his.

"I'm ready. I love you and can't continue living like this. I want my life back, and yours. Please, Baby, help me out of this living tomb. Please."

She began to cry.

There were no problems with the preparation and administering of the solutions. For a long while afterwards, Michele felt they were getting no results. Even though Lee would tell her he felt different inside, there were no visible changes to confirm anything. All of his blood tests appeared normal. She adjusted the mixture to give her more catalyst, to push the gene into doing its work faster.

One morning, she rolled over and saw that the color of her husband's scars were changing.

They were growing lighter and, if she wasn't mistaken, the raised area from his chin down across his neck was less swollen. She ran her hand across the area and felt the topography becoming less radical and smoothing out. She could swear that the skin was moving beneath her hands like the movement she had felt holding his testicles. She was thrilled and scared at the same time. The anticipation of a miracle is one thing, experiencing the actual miracle is a whole different experience. She rose from the bed and walked over to yank open the bedroom curtains. The bright morning sun beamed into the room creating a yellow glow. She took the desk lamp on the nightstand and twisted it so that it shone brightly down onto his face.

"Hey, what the hell are you doing?" He held his hands up in front of his eyes.

She grabbed his face by the chin and twisted it to one side. "Sssh, give me a moment here, Professor."

It was working. The experiment was a success! She quickly unbuttoned his pajama shirt and ran her hands over his chest and torso. Smoother. It was all so much smoother. It wasn't just her imagination. She grabbed the elastic of his waistband and pulled. The raised scar that ran from his chest diagonally down to his thigh was now disappearing somewhere between his navel and his pubic hair.

"Pick your ass up," she commanded and promptly pulled his pajama bottoms off.

He was smooth. The hair on his legs shone in the lamplight and skin above the hairline at the top of his thighs was utterly, miraculously smooth. She ran her hands over his skin, delighting in the results. Many of the scars were gone and the rest were disappearing; collapsing like groundhog tunnels on a beautifully kept lawn. He moaned from her touch and pulled her down on top of him.

"I really think I'm going to like this treatment, Doc," he said.

She sat back up and quickly pulled her clothes off. She walked her fingers up his stomach and across his chest feeling the last remnants of a horribly disfigured human. Putting a hand on both sides of his head, she pulled his face up to meet hers in a passionate embrace.

"Me too," she laughed. "Oh my god! Me too!"

The curtains fluttered in the window. The train roared through the tunnel. The dates ripped themselves off the wall calendar. They made love for ages and for all eternity and when it was over, they lay side by side. Exhausted and as close to satiated as they had ever known.

Eventually, Lee rolled over on his side. He ran the back of a single finger along the soft downy hair by her ear. He played with her lobe until she playfully slapped his hand away.

"Well, what do we do now?" he said.

"I can think of two things." She wrapped her arms around him and gave his ass a good squeeze.

He looked at her quizzically.

"Write an article to help with my tenure and fuck; not necessarily in that order."

Professor Williams slid his tray down across the table from Dr. Slade. He fussed with his briefcase and sweater for a moment before he plopped down in the chair.

"I see we're back on speaking terms," Michele said. "Does this mean all is forgiven, Professor?"

"Michele, I may not agree with you, but it doesn't mean I have to ostracize you."

She took a large bite of her salad. "Getting lonely, huh?"

"Yes, fine. Even nerds like me need contact with our peers sometimes; whether we agree with them or not."

He took his dishes off the tray and sat them on the table in front of him, then slid the tray onto the empty table beside them.

"Anyway, your experiment seems not to have killed Lee despite my misgivings."

"It's true, Willie. Lee is looking marvelous and feeling even better. Physiologically, nothing could have turned out finer."

Williams stuck his fork deep into the creamed spinach and lifted it up in a giant swirl of steam. The smell drifted towards Michele and she immediately gagged. She grabbed her napkin and held it to her mouth, choking. Willie held the fork suspended in the air trying to grasp what was going on as Michele pushed back from the table.

"Excuse me," she mumbled through the napkin and took off running to the bathroom.

He dropped his fork and stood up at the table.

He called after her. "Michele, are you alright?"

With her free hand she waved at him as she pushed through the double doors leading to the lavatory. He sat back down and picked his forkful of spinach back up. Giving it a good sniff, it appeared okay to him, so he popped it in his mouth.

Lee was in the kitchen when Michele arrived home that evening. He heard the front door close and shouted out to her.

"Hey babe, how are you doing?"

She dropped her bags next to the reading chair and then plopped herself down, exhausted.

"Horrible. I'm pregnant."

It sounded like a load of pots were dropped in the sink. Lee came hustling around the corner.

"Horrible? That's great! I'm ready to take on the challenge of being Mr. Mom."

"Lee, listen to me. This child may be forming inside of me, but it is sharing your genes too.

This is beyond the scope of my experiment with you. I never counted on this. A million things could happen to this fetus if it is allowed to form inside me because of the treatments I've been administering to you. I'm not sure that cycling my blood and genes through it is enough to keep it safe."

"You're contaminated, Lee. We can't trust your sperm. We just don't know what will happen. I have to have an abortion."

Lee sat down on the floor in front of Michele's chair. He reached up and held her hands in his.

"Couldn't we just monitor the pregnancy? You know, be on top of it in case anything happens?"

"Oh, baby," Michele said and pulled his hands up to kiss his knuckles. "We don't know how fast or slow this gene thing might happen. We're probably talking four or five weeks already.

There's no way to tell what's going on with the fetus at this point. What if we don't discover anything until six or seven months in? Then what? I just don't think we can take that chance."

She smiled at him, hoping he'd understand.

"The therapy saved you, Lee. That's enough for me, really it is."

He stared at her awhile longer and then laid his head in her lap. She stroked his hair and tried to set everything straight in her mind.

That evening he beat her to bed and was already snoring while she stood at the bathroom sink removing her make-up. She knew there was no going back on her decision. Even as her blood filtered through this child, it may not be enough to cleanse the effects of her experiment. It had worked, to a point. But in reclaiming one life she was jeopardizing another.

She pulled her nightshirt over her head and a sudden pain shot through her left breast. She reached over and pressed her hand against the side of it with her fingers inhaling through her teeth. She could swear that she could feel the fatty flesh ripple, giving way beneath her touch and then pushing back, just a bit. There was something at work under the surface. A gift from Lee; a little something to change her life forever.

My wife and I always enjoy working together. I mean in the same house, not necessarily on the same project. However, she does come to me with story thoughts and ideas. This one was particularly intriguing.

When a writer/director acquaintance heard her idea, it intrigued him as he was working on a series of scripts for a horror television anthology under the Dark Delicacies moniker at the time. The series never came to fruition so I asked him if I could write a short story based on my wife's idea and his script. He gave me his blessing.

The story has never been published until now. So here is the tale after filtering through three people.

CALLED TO THE SEA

"The Siren waits thee, singing song for song."
—Walter Savage Landor

FOR OVER ONE HUNDRED years the Blue Fish Restaurant clung to the narrow finger of land and pier between the windswept coastal highway and the majestic Atlantic Ocean. The pilings that had held the wooden structure in place for all these years were weathered grey and barnacle covered; a living display of marine art. Visitors would stop in their tracks to marvel at the variety of ocean life. On beautiful days such as this, the sea lapped casually, toying about the base of the pier like a child beckoning somebody to come and play. The blue of the ocean matched the cerulean of the sky blending the horizon. The occasional cotton cloud that drifted by added to the lazy feel of the day.

The popping sounds of a sports car muffler cracked with ear-splitting sharpness. A rust-resistant grey convertible rounded the curve and sputtered into the parking lot where the driver ripped up the handbrake and killed the flow of gasoline to the engine. He was James Dean, eternally young. He looked to be in his mid-twenties, brooding, handsome, wearing aviator shades, which he took off to have a better look at the weathered sign that swung from its hooks in the breeze.

THE BLUE FISH
FINE SEAFOOD SINCE 1923

He smiled, jumped over the driver's door, and strode from the large gravel parking lot into the dimly lit interior. The room, festooned with all sorts of fishing nets and buoys, could have been no place else other than the oceanside. He paused, letting his eyes adjust to the shadowed interior. Taxidermized fish were attached to the walls on wooden plaques. Behind the bar was a large aquarium. Those fish were living.

The tables were sparsely populated at that time of day. Behind the bar a twenty-year-old boy wearing a white apron ran a few glasses left over from the lunch crowd over the soapy, spinning brush. Behind him, another worker restocked the glasses on the mirrored shelves. The dishwasher looked up, saw Austin Lott standing in the middle of the dining room smiling at him, and froze. Then a smile began to crawl its way across his own face and he hurried out to give his cousin a big bear hug.

"No way," he let out a laugh as he squeezed him. "You are kidding me, man! How'd you get here?"

Austin held his cousin out at arm's length to get a better look at him.

"Holden, geez man, all grown up." He turned and looked toward the parking lot. "I've got my Ghia out there."

"Hah! I can't believe it. You made it! Where's Annie?"

Austin dropped his arms and shook his head. Holden studied his cousin's face for a moment and then nodded in acknowledgement. He grabbed him by the arm and began to pull.

"Well, come on. There are people I want you to meet."

Austin laughed at his cousin's exuberance and let Holden lead him towards the kitchen.

"Hey Carrie," Holden called out to the waitress. "This is my cousin, Austin. Austin, this is Carrie and that's Joe over there."

He pointed to the man stocking glasses who nodded in greeting.

181

"Joe, this is Austin from Boston." He looked back at his cousin. "Man, I haven't called you that in forever."

Holden pulled on Austin again and pushed their way through the double-doors into the restaurant's kitchen. As they entered all the heads turned to see what the commotion was about.

"Hey Mom!"

Holden spun around and pushed Austin in front of him.

"You are not going to believe who just walked in the door."

Holden's parents, Mike and Meg, gave each other a quick furtive glance. This initial coolness did not go unnoticed by Austin whose smile faded for a moment. Somewhat deflated, he managed to press on with a smile.

"Hey, Uncle Mike, Auntie."

Mike looked at him for a moment and then wiped his hands on a towel. He crossed the kitchen to give Austin a hug. His smile gave off that "Aw shucks, you didn't notice what you think you just noticed" air.

"So, Austin," Mike said as he hugged his nephew. "Where the heck did you come from?"

Mike let go a little too quickly.

"I guess this was my idea of being spontaneous," Austin shrugged.

He walked around his uncle to his aunt and gave her a quick kiss on the cheek. She smiled like it physically pained her to do so.

"My mom sends her love."

Austin stepped back and looked at the three of them standing there.

"Good to see you guys."

Aunt Meg wiped her hands on her apron and then walked back to the preparation table where she was putting together tonight's special. She looked down and began to remove bones from the fish filets as she spoke.

"Good to see you, too, honey. How long can you stay?"

Austin shrugged again. It seemed to be his signature move. Mike walked around the table and began to work next to his wife while he waited for Austin to answer.

"Hadn't thought about it."

"Yeah, well don't." Holden walked over to his parents with a big smile on his face and gave both a hug as he answered Austin.

"It's boring as hell out here in the summer, even with all the tourists. You couldn't have picked a better time to drop in."

Austin stared and said nothing while his aunt and uncle gave that knowing glance between them again. His cousin grinned like a monkey who'd just discovered his own genitals for the first time.

"You can put your things in Holden's room." Aunt Meg looked at her son. "Holden has work to do. We'll see you later for dinner, dear."

<center>~~~</center>

The Atlantic Ocean coast of the United States had great sunrises, but lousy sunsets. California, Washington, and Oregon reaped the benefits of the orb's travel across the sky with beautiful scenes at the end of the day. The Atlantic water, late in the afternoon, had turned more of a steel grey than blue. There was a coolness that had settled on the ground down by the shore. The water's edge was a little further out as the moon pulled the liquid away from the sand. The full moon in daylight was always an interesting site to see and Austin stared at it as he walked past the pier toward the shore.

Austin spent the day in town, getting his bearings again in relationship to the restaurant. He was back at the house now, awaiting dinner, and wondered why the mussels and shellfish hanging on the piling weren't part of the menu. There was a noise behind him and he turned to see Holden scrambling down the path from the restaurant. He stopped next to his older cousin and looked out at the water.

"Welcome to Mariner's Cove."

Austin looked at him and shrugged. Then he picked up the flattest stone he could find and skipped it across the tops of the retreating ripples. He got four good skips in before the stone leaned to one side and took a header into the water. Holden looked up at him, sensing he was disturbed.

"Don't even try and figure that out back there, okay? When you showed up, the folks were just a little busy getting things ready for tonight's dinner. They're trying out some new specials and they're a little on edge wanting to make sure the food is right. They're perfectionists, you know?"

Holden smiled too big at Austin, so Austin pretended to look around for another flat stone.

"Be straight with me, Holden. Did I come at a bad time?"

Now it was Holden's turn to shrug. He looked about and indicated the sand with a sweep of his arm.

"This summer the beach is off limits. All of it. Just ask them." He chuckled to himself. "They get kookier the older they get."

Austin just glared at Holden. He knew there was more. He didn't speak, waiting instead for Holden to get comfortable and finish what he hoped would be the truth.

"Okay, it might be Sammy," Holden said sheepishly. "It is seven years this summer."

Austin closed his eyes, tipped his head back and let out a frustrated breath.

"Come on, man," Holden said, "did you hear me? It was seven years ago."

Austin opened his eyes and looked at Holden.

"I know. Yeah, I know. But I didn't know it was like an anniversary or something."

Holden nodded back at the restaurant, clearly anxious to be off the beach before his parents saw them.

"Life goes on, right?" He slapped Austin on the shoulder. "I think that wherever he is, he'd want us all to be living our lives, you know, like a traveler not a tourist."

Austin held his cousin's eyes with his own, trying to decide if he was being lied to or manipulated. Finally, Holden picked up a stone and tossed it into the ocean. It skipped twice and disappeared into the water. Austin watched the circles spread out from where the rock went under.

"Damn, you were always better at everything," Holden said indicating where the rock had sunk. Austin let the statement hang in the air a moment before answering.

"Annie and I called it quits."

Holden looked up at his cousin.

"When?"

"Last year." He paused, trying to put his thoughts together. "I screwed up, bad. I was stupid and. . .you know. . ."

Holden nodded and then put on that overly big smile.

"Well, there are lots of hot, sunbaked, golden brown women in town, especially right now. I mean, if you want to drown your sorrows in nubile flesh, you showed up at the right time."

He laughed conspiratorially. Austin looked out at the darkening water. Clearly this wasn't what he came for.

"Always the peacemaker, Holden."

Holden pursed his mouth and started back up the path to the restaurant. When he realized he wasn't being followed, he stopped and turned back to Austin. A foghorn began its long bellow somewhere off in the distance.

"Thanks for coming, man. I mean it."

Austin continued to look away, seemingly embarrassed by the sentiment.

"After Sammy disappeared? You were my brother, Austin. I used you as my rock. That's how I thought of you."

A puff of air left Austin's lips.

"Thanks, now I really feel like crap."

"Hey, you met Annie, you were in love."

Austin finally turned back to his cousin.

"I blew you off for years, man, you didn't hate my guts?"

A small smile pushed at the corner of Holden's mouth.

"Maybe a little."

"Never heard anything about him?"

"Sammy?"

Austin nodded.

"Mom and Dad think he ended up out there somewhere," Holden said indicating the ocean. "You know, caught in an undertow or something. You hang around here long enough, you find out everyone has an idea about what happened to him."

Austin picked up a small piece of driftwood, turning it around in his hands and pointed it at Holden.

"What's yours?"

"Called to the sea. That's what the crazy old fish lady said happened to him. I believed her. I was thirteen."

Holden turned and started back up toward the restaurant again.

"You sure I shouldn't just get the hell outta here?"

Holden didn't even turn back but continued his trudge up the pathway.

"Up to you, man. You got some place better to be?"

He reached the top of the path and shouted back over the surf.

"You should come up and get some dinner. And you'd better get off the beach before they freak out. Off limits to all family and friends, not just me."

Holden turned back and walked around the front of the restaurant. Austin shook his head in response and tossed the driftwood into the water. As he swung back and started up the path, he heard a sound intermingled faintly with the surf. He looked at the splashing waves, waiting to hear it again. It had been soft, almost musical as if something was calling from out in the water. The distant foghorn bellowed again and he continued his way up to get something to eat.

Once inside, he headed toward the family table in the back where he could see Aunt Meg setting bowls of food on the table. Two grizzled-looking men sat at the bar, deep in discussion. As he passed them, their words almost stopped him in his tracks. The older man was leaning in to the other using one hand to help him speak while the other one held a full mug of dark rich beer that was in danger of splashing overboard onto the floor.

"In Moby Dick, Herman Melville wrote that all men are called to the sea." he said adamantly. "He said there is magic in the ocean and that is why, in any city with a shore, or any town near a body of water, you will see men, women, and children gathered there. Staring out. Called to the water."

The other man laughed. "We're made up of mostly water, you old coot. It just seems like the sea is calling us home." He pointed at his friend's beer. "Drink many more of those and you'll be sleeping with the fish."

They both laughed and Austin moved on to eat with the family.

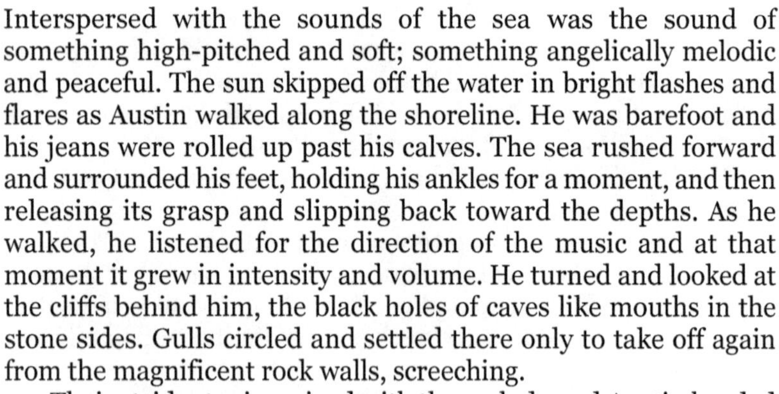

Interspersed with the sounds of the sea was the sound of something high-pitched and soft; something angelically melodic and peaceful. The sun skipped off the water in bright flashes and flares as Austin walked along the shoreline. He was barefoot and his jeans were rolled up past his calves. The sea rushed forward and surrounded his feet, holding his ankles for a moment, and then releasing its grasp and slipping back toward the depths. As he walked, he listened for the direction of the music and at that moment it grew in intensity and volume. He turned and looked at the cliffs behind him, the black holes of caves like mouths in the stone sides. Gulls circled and settled there only to take off again from the magnificent rock walls, screeching.

Their strident cries mixed with the melody and Austin headed off to find his music.

Mike stood at the bar of the Blue Fish. In one hand, he held a towel which was wadded up except for one corner that flapped about as he tried to explain the situation to his son. He spoke as much with his hands as he did his mouth and Meg stood to one side, mesmerized by the white corner of material flapping back and forth.

"He has a family," Mike said and indicated with his hands the direction of Austin's car in the parking lot.

Holden was frustrated and working hard to convince both of his parents to let Austin stay.

He walked back and forth, appealing first to his father and then his mother. He finally threw up his hands in frustration.

"No, he doesn't. I know she's your sister, Mom," he said and turned back to Meg. "But you know what Austin told me last night when we talked? He told me he'd rather be dead than live there with his mom and her new boyfriend."

Meg opened her mouth to object, but Mike plowed right on ahead overriding her.

"He could get a job! He could move out! He could have a life if he decided to grow up and have one. He's twenty-nine years old for Christ's sake!"

Meg shoved a shoulder in between them just to break them up and be able to speak.

"He's never treated you like a friend or family, honey. I don't know why you pretend he ever has."

Holden waved his arms like a referee calling for a time-out.

"Whoa, whoa. All right, just everyone wait one second."

Mike put his hands on his son's shoulders.

"This is a really bad time for him to show up here," he said.

Holden looked up at his father.

"Why?"

The question hung in the air like a dirty, transparent film between them. The parents exchanged glances.

"Tell me," Holden insisted.

Mike looked down at the floor in a non-answer. Holden waited a moment to see if either would cave and then stormed off toward his room. Meg watched him leave, making no attempt to stop him. She turned, pretending to get back to the restaurant work.

"I know what you're thinking," Mike said urgently.

Meg stopped, still facing away from Mike, while in a hushed voice he added, "And it's wrong. It is very wrong."

She turned and looked at her husband. Tears welled up in her eyes, but she knew he was right. She drew a deep breath and walked away.

～～

The song was louder as Austin approached the mammoth opening of a cave that resembled a rough-hewn tunnel of love at an amusement park. It looked like the water, at high tide, made its way into the base of the rock and smoothed out the sand into a hard flat surface. No footprints, animal or human, had marred its perfect surface since the last tide change. Now, as low tide pulled the water backwards toward the ocean, the mouth was completely accessible and Austin leaned up against the side of the opening peering into the hole.

The sound came again, strong, clear, beckoning, and Austin took a couple of steps inside. He moved slowly, staring into the darkness after the blinding sunlight outside. In the depths of the cave, he could see a speck of white among the massive universe of shadows. He ran his hands along the shell-embedded walls using the feel of their surface as a safety net for his bearings with each cautious step. A couple of gulls yelled out directly behind him, which made him jump.

Then they were gone and the musical humming slipped over him once more like a wave.

Austin took another step inside and now, being closer, he could see the speck of white had taken form. It was a woman, an old hag, and he ducked back to keep from being seen. When he peeked back out, he instead saw a beautiful young girl and quickly realized that the cave had been playing a trick on him as he'd come in from the sun. Long hair cascaded over her naked shoulders as her head dropped backwards, as if in a trance, and another strange, lilting tone rose from her. It all drowned out the sound of the rumbling sea behind him.

Doubting his own eyes, he couldn't believe this unique vocalizing was coming from her and he stumbled forward to get a better look. Hunkered down behind an outcropping, he tried to hide his approach. But he was drawn toward her and had to see all of her beauty for himself. He began to maneuver like a soldier on reconnaissance and crawled on his belly to the top of the last small rise in the floor of the cave. He felt she must have seen him, but if she had, she had given no indication of it.

Austin pushed himself up on his arms and peeked over the top of the rise. She was there, naked to the waist, with long hair that fell past the curve of her breasts. She wore some sort of silky white fabric or dress gathered in folds on her lap. As Austin stared, she closed her eyes and dropped her head back again. Something eloquent, full of longing mixed with the distant sound of the sea behind him grew high and strong from deep within her slender throat, carrying itself in an ethereal echoing off the walls of the cave. The sound was almost too much to bear and at the same time, it wrapped itself around Austin. He realized that it was two gently blended tones. He began to cry with emotional abandon as he heard the words she was singing.

"HOLD. . .DEN. . ."

She held the notes for what seemed like an eternity, gathered another breath, and let them escape from her beautiful throat for another time. There, with that second release of her musical bombardment, Austin realized she was singing the name of his cousin.

"HOLD. . .DEN. . ."

Shocked, he lost his footing. Loose rocks skittered from beneath him, echoing in the cavern.

The sharp scraping noises stopped her in mid-release and she turned to look at Austin with incredibly piercing grey eyes. He ducked back down behind the rise, but could still feel those eyes slicing right through the boulder, right through him, and it filled him with gentle confusion and fascination. Slowly, he lifted himself back up. She stared at him, making no effort to cover herself. A smile spread across her porcelain face, a smile that crept up from the corners of her mouth and drew Austin forward.

Mesmerized, he slowly walked up to where she was sitting. His body ached, empty and hurting, with the desire to touch her. Her face was tipped up towards his and her eyes had fallen shut, almost in mock embarrassment. Behind him, the surf cracked loudly. Barely believing his good fortune, Austin bent down and met her lips with his. Her hands started at the buttons of his shirt and he pulled away holding her with his hands on her shoulders to get a good, studied look at her.

Was this a dream?

For a flash, the old woman's face looked back at him. He blinked and the young girl smiled that slow smile again and Austin wanted her more than he'd ever desired anyone.

———

The Blue Fish Restaurant has never been able to completely rid itself of the smell of old drinks and seafood. The wood seemed to soak it in and absorb it like a polish. Now, it was embedded in the very grain of the worn countertop and the hardwood floors. It was all part of the atmosphere, like the smell of the ocean salt water and the sun baking off the packed gravel parking lot. It was always another day in seafood paradise there.

Holden sat a couple of drinks down in front of a young couple making eyes at each other and had just turned away when Austin burst in through the front door. His shirt was unbuttoned and he was breathing like he'd just run a marathon. Holden looked at him and laughed.

"We have a no shirt, no service policy here, but at least you have one on, even if it's wide open."

Austin rushed over to his cousin and whispered in his ear.

"You've still got a shower behind the restaurant?"

"Down in the back to rinse off the salt water," Holden said, confused. "Why?"

"I don't want your folks to hear me taking one. Thanks, buddy,"

He slapped Holden on the arm and ran back out the front door. Holden watched the door swing shut and laughed to himself as a patron signaled for service. After he waited on the patron, Holden grabbed a towel and walked out to the shower where Austin was washing off. Austin turned off the water and grabbed the towel from him.

"Tell me, right now, that you do not have a girl out here."

Holden looked at Austin confused.

"Do you have a girl or not?"

Holden, still trying to figure out what was going on, shook his head.

"You know all the girls out here?' Austin asked.

"Most of 'em."

"You know a girl who likes to sing topless down the beach a bit in the big cave?"

"Whoa, do I what?"

Austin shook his head.

"I don't even know where to begin, man."

"Topless in a cave is a good start," Holden said.

Austin handed the towel back to him.

"You gotta tell me who she is."

"I don't know who the hell you're talking about. You met a girl on the beach?"

"Not on the beach, in a cave. "And I didn't just meet her, Holden," he grinned at his cousin. "We've been pounding it in the sand for the last hour."

Holden stared at him; his mouth open. "And you don't know her name?"

"She wouldn't tell me. In fact, she wouldn't even talk to me. She just sang."

Austin began pulling his clothes back on.

"This is a girl you definitely know."

"Why do you say that?" Holden asked.

"Because she knows you. She was calling your name when I first heard her."

Austin began to give Holden his best impersonation of her singing.

"HO. . .DEN. . . Only now," he smiled. "I think she might be singing AUS. . TIN. . ."

He grinned at Holden, a great big shit-eating grin. He truly enjoyed his story telling and Holden was completely lost.

"Singing, man, that's what she was doing."

Holden took a step closer to his cousin and looked him in the eyes, checking his pupils.

"And what have you been doing?" he asked suspiciously.

"Nope. No, no, no. I haven't been smoking or drinking anything. Look at me. She was real."

"You know, I should be a little ticked off. I mean, she was calling my name and what did you do?"

Austin held his hands up in front of him, palms out. "You said you didn't have a girl."

"Yeah, but you didn't know that then."

"She looked at me and I looked at her and it was just going to happen, man." Austin pointed his finger at Holden. "You gotta tell me you're okay with it, though, you gotta."

Holden stared at him for a minute and then took a deep breath.

"You know, people see a lot of ghosts out there." He gestured toward the ocean. "Remember, this town is named after a shipwreck."

Austin gave him his best grin. "Well, she's not an apparition, but she is a vision."

"Yeah, maybe she's a mermaid. Look, I've got to get back inside before mom misses me."

Holden turned and headed back up towards the front door.

"Nope. She's not a mermaid," Austin hollered up to him. "I checked."

⌇⌇⌇

Austin was dressed and stood in the dark living room taking in all his aunt's and uncle's belongings. Noise from the restaurant filtered up from below. It felt good. It felt like a home here. Holden was a lucky boy. There was love inside these walls and Austin knew it. On top of a bookcase sat a collection of framed photos of boats, fishermen, and their catches and seascapes. Austin took down an old looking photo of a boy next to an old boat.

"That's Sammy," Aunt Meg said, startling him.

He turned to her, a little shamefaced being caught holding the photo. But she didn't seem to mind.

"That's from the summer he disappeared." She pointed to another photo near it. "There's Holden."

The boy in the photo appeared to be about ten years old and was displaying his fishing rod. The end of the rod was stuck in the sand and Holden's chest was puffed out with pride. Austin nodded and smiled and then gently set the photo of Sammy back into place.

"There's good fishing on the East Coast. Although, the best fish are all out west," he said.

"We need you to go, Austin."

Her voice was so soft that he wasn't quite sure he had heard her correctly. He looked at her quizzically.

There was pain in her eyes as she spoke. "You have no idea how hard that is to say but. . ."

"What is it?" His whisper matched hers.

As he looked at her, trying to decipher what her look meant, the voice wafted through the air like a scent and filled the room.

"AAUUUUUU...STIN..."

He turned toward the open window, not sure he'd heard what he thought he heard. He walked over to the double doors and threw them open. Twilight. Magic time. The waves crashed on the land below. Gulls cried out but other than that there was nothing. Aunt Meg was staring at him in pain when he turned back.

"Did you hear that?" he asked.

She stepped up to him and put her arm on his shoulders. They both stared out, listening.

"Holden told me that this town was named after a shipwreck. The Mariner was a ship?"

Aunt Meg nodded.

"It came in too close and was ripped apart on the rocks out in the cove."

That ethereal tone blended of a harmony of longing and desire breezed in the doors. Magnet-like, it caused Austin to take a step toward the balcony.

"AAUUUUU....STIN..."

"Austin," Aunt Meg stopped him with her tone. "Please tell me you didn't go down to the water today."

Her hushed whisper chilled him to the bone. She blanched and hurried away, her hands pressed to her face. Austin grabbed his coat off the rack and as he was leaving the room, he passed Holden on his way up the stairs.

"Where are you going?"

"Someone is singing my song," he said and headed down the stairs.

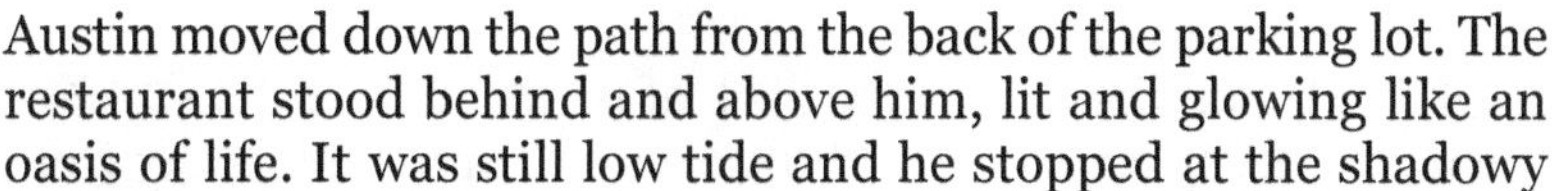

Austin moved down the path from the back of the parking lot. The restaurant stood behind and above him, lit and glowing like an oasis of life. It was still low tide and he stopped at the shadowy pilings to listen.

"AAUUUU...STIN..."

The sound was somehow brighter now and clearer. Austin began to move toward it, toward the cliffs. As he stepped away from the last piling, a hand grabbed him from behind and pulled his shoulder back. It held him from moving. Austin spun around and came face to face with Mike.

"Uncle Mike, you scared the crap out of me!"

"Get back up to the restaurant."

With the next blend of tune Uncle Mike looked down toward the cliffs. He raised his hand to silence Austin. For a moment, Mike was somewhere back in time. Then he turned and began to push Austin.

"Do it now, Austin!"

With the crash of the surf, she sang again.

"AAUUU. . .STIN. . ."

Both men turned toward the distant caves and saw the slender white silhouette as it moved towards them, picking its way along the rocks. The sea breeze wrapped and unfurled the silky material about the girl. Uncle Mike was transfixed.

"My God, it is true," he said.

As Austin tried to take another step toward her, Uncle Mike grabbed him by both shoulders and spun him around.

"You did go down to the beach today, didn't you?!"

Pale with fear, Uncle Mike spit the words into Austin's face. Austin could feel the fear behind the fury. The girl continued to move closer with her veiled silhouette alternately showing herself and then covering up in a move of enticement. She sputtered in and out of view, her entire silhouette changing like a television picture with a bad antenna. Her head dropped back again and that angel voice of beckoning released itself from her throat.

"AAUUU. . .STIN. . ."

Austin turned to look at her but was stopped by Uncle Mike who grabbed him by his chin and whipped his head around to face him. The veins in Mike's neck were bulging and his eyes were watery from a combination of the wind and his own fear. Through tight, clenched jaws he whispered to Austin.

"Oh my God. . ."

He grabbed the boy by the back of the pants and the scruff of his neck and marched him off towards the Blue Fish, away from his floating angel. They blasted through the doors to the kitchen and Uncle Mike threw Austin inside where he landed on the floor in a heap. Austin quickly spun around to face him.

"What the hell is wrong with you?"

Mike paid no attention to him, but slammed the door shut and latched the lock down tight.

"It won't work, Mike."

Aunt Meg stood next to Holden tearfully shaking her head. Austin was still on the floor disheveled and confused.

"Will somebody tell me what the hell is going on?"

Mike loomed over him and pointed a finger in his face.

"You care about what happens to you?"

He grabbed Austin by the back of his shirt collar and began to drag him, sliding across the floor, toward the front doors. Austin grabbed at Uncle Mike's hands.

"You get in that car and you get the fuck away from here! Now!"

"That has never worked." Everybody turned towards Aunt Meg. "Not if she has chosen him."

"Oh, she's chosen him alright," Mike said and released his grip. "She is currently down there in the seaweed calling his name.

The waitress entered the kitchen with a tray of dirty dishes. Aunt Meg pointed for her to set the tray down.

"Carrie, tell everyone in the kitchen to go home now."

Aunt Meg put up her hand to stop Carrie from inquiring any further.

"Tell them to stop what they are doing and to get out of here, now. No questions."

Carrie stared at the group, not moving.

"This instant, Carrie!"

Carrie ran back into the kitchen. Austin dropped his hands in frustration.

"Will somebody please tell me what the hell is going on?"

Meg nodded to Joe at the grill, who had been standing like a statue all this time. He dropped his apron on the counter and left. She moved into the dining room, but not before she looked back at her husband and gave him a small nod. Once in the dining room, she clapped her hands and the patrons stopped eating.

"Attention, everybody. We regret having to ask this so unexpectedly and please consider any dinner food or drink you've had tonight as complimentary, but we are going to have to ask you to leave for the evening."

～～

Upstairs in the bedroom Uncle Mike zipped up Austin's duffel bag while the boys looked at him dumbfounded. Austin shook his head in disbelief.

"Every seven years?"

"She chooses someone," Uncle Mike said as he stood up.

Austin threw a look at Holden and wondered if his cousin felt as foolish as he did with this ridiculous explanation. Uncle Mike continued his tale, disregarding the boy's bafflement.

"We only have the old story for any explanation as to how or why, but it's every seven years, it's always the month of August, and," He shot a look to Austin, "it's always someone who wanders out onto the rocks where the Mariner shipwrecked."

"This has been going on for two hundred years?" Austin said coolly.

Mike took a quick inventory of the room.

"What else do you have?" He asked.

Austin shook his head and smirked.

"You guys can't be serious about this. . ."

Uncle Mike turned to Holden, furious.

"Goddammit, what did we tell you about staying away from the water?"

Austin was shocked.

"Why? Because this girl is, what, some kind of sea creature who calls men to their deaths? That's almost laughable if it wasn't for the fact that I think you actually believe it."

Uncle Mike stared at Austin.

"I'm told her name was Elizabeth and she was either on the ship or was waiting for someone on it when it crashed into the cliffs."

Austin shook his head.

"Look, we inherited this, okay?" Mike said. "We don't fully understand it."

Aunt Meg burst into the room.

"Austin, get out of here!"

"I should have told you," Mike turned to his son. "Your mother and I, we were going to tell you this summer and just pray you wouldn't think we were crazy."

Aunt Meg screamed at Austin. "I said get out of here!"

Austin grabbed his duffle bag and the four of them left. Carefully they descended the stairs and opened the doors going into the shadowy empty dining room. As they stepped into the dining room, Aunt Meg motioned for them to be quiet and listen. The sea breeze rushed against the side of the building and the waves continued to fling themselves onto the shore. From down low and rising, there was a lonely, mournful howl and laced within its notes came that same angelic call.

"AAUUU. . .STIN. . ."

Everybody stopped, frozen in time. Austin stepped toward the front door only to be grabbed by Uncle Mike. Austin looked down at his uncle's hand on his arm.

"What is this, man? That's just a girl!"

Uncle Mike clenched tighter and whispered, "That is not anything you think it is."

"AAUUU. . .STIN. . ."

Austin turned to his cousin.

"You look me right in the eye and tell me you believe any of this!"

Holden stood by his father.

"He has no choice! How do you think we lost Sammy?"

The silence loomed in the room like a thick fog. Nobody dared to speak. Then sound slowly returned with the breeze and the sea could be heard below. Austin looked to Holden for a glimpse of sanity, but his cousin seemed paralyzed by what he'd just heard.

"There's a girl out there, you guys!" he said pointing to the ocean. "That's all!"

Austin pushed past Uncle Mike and charged to the front door.

"There's nothing to be afraid of!"

"Austin, don't you dare open that door," Aunt Meg screamed and reached out toward him.

Austin grabbed the doorknob, but suddenly stopped as he heard the sound of water rushing and looked down at the floor. Sea water had begun to leak in under the doors and up through the floorboards. Austin stared down, confused, and took a step back. The water was pooling and had now become deep enough to sustain little crabs and small sea life.

"AAUUU. . .STIN. . ."

Austin backed away from the doors as the pool of water continued to grow. A breeze picked up inside the restaurant which flung the fishing nets hanging on the walls from side to side and blew anything loose off of the tables. The wind continued to gain strength and from the water a pale, white hand began to emerge.

Everyone stepped back up against the wooden checkout counter. A second hand slowly rose from the wood and then the arms were both fully free from the forearms up. The palms slapped flat against the wooden slats and pushed as the head and entire upper body of the hag started to pull herself out of the floor. When she was halfway out, she stopped and looked up at Austin standing shell-shocked with the rest of the group. She dropped her head back and opened her mouth wider than seemed possible.

"AAUUU. . .SSTIN. . .!"

The strange, blended tones were more powerful within this enclosed space, much like they had been that day inside the cave. Aunt May covered her ears with her hands and Holden opened his mouth and screamed, but couldn't hear himself.

The woman pushed herself out of the floor and raised up tall in the center of the room. The wind whipped her flimsy dress about revealing herself totally nude to the group, a skin covered skeleton. Holden gawked at her as her arms reached out for Austin, moving her fingers, and beckoning him to her.

"AAUUU. . .SSSTIN. . .!"

The sound was massive and enveloped everybody in a cavern of song. The stench of dead fish flooded the air. Aunt May turned away as she tried to make the sound less painful. Drink glasses on the tables and bottles behind the bar exploded in a myriad of colored glass and liquid. Elizabeth held the notes, sustaining them high and loud, and then took a tentative step toward Austin. As if connected at the ankles, the group all shuffled backwards along the wall together as they attempted to stay out of reach of her advance.

"Austin, run! Now!"

Uncle Mike screamed at the top of his lungs, but Austin didn't move. He didn't run. His feet were glued to the dining room floor with the cement of fear as he stared straight ahead at her.

"I said run!" Uncle Mike screamed again.

Aunt Meg grabbed Mike by the arm.

"He can't, don't you see?"

Austin was caught in her deadly Medusa gaze. The thing moved toward him and the sound of her wet, bare feet could somehow be heard above all the other noise. Holden watched in horror from the side as he took in every repulsive detail. The train of her dress was wet with seaweed and mud in the back. It thrived with small eels and sand dabs and other minor creatures from the deep. As she moved forward, it dragged along behind her with something dark and rotten caught up in the fabric that rolled and bumped along with her steps. Finally, it broke loose, and Holden could see that it was a piece of ancient driftwood carved with the word MARINER.

"Dammit, Austin, move!"

Uncle Mike, desperate to do something to save his nephew, ran to the far wall and tore a fire axe from its moorings. With it raised above his head, he leaped between Austin and the girl.

"Michael!"

Aunt Meg's voice screeched from somewhere behind him.

He lunged at the oceanic nightmare and swung the axe. It sliced through Elizabeth, sloughing water across the room and splashing the others. He swung again and again like a madman. The melody of her cries gurgled and bubbled from where her mouth had been as she was systematically splattered to pieces. He turned the axe head sideways, using the flat of the head to take out larger chunks of water. He broke her into miscellaneous sprays and splintered her into splashes until she was nothing but puddled water on the floor. Exhausted, he dropped to his knees.

Two quick breaths and Uncle Mike jumped up, grabbed Austin in the same collar/crotch combination hold he had used before, and shoved him out the front door. He hauled him across the parking lot towards his little car with Austin's feet practically being dragged through the gravel; his arms flailing helplessly. The rest of the family followed behind in shock, saying nothing, not wanting to push Uncle Mike any further over the edge than he apparently already was. Mike looked down at Austin's face as he dragged him.

"Keys?"

Austin barely had time to nod before Uncle Mike yanked open the car door and shoved him in behind the wheel.

"Keep driving! Don't stop for anything! Drive away from the sea. Get off the coast as soon as you can and stay off it. Don't stop until you are home safe and sound and away from water!"

Austin, still dazed, tried to take one last look at Holden, but Uncle Mike stood between them.

He started the car up. The tires threw stones out of the parking lot. The sportscar's headlights swerved from side to side as it fishtailed through the gravel. They watched Austin speed back down the same highway he'd come up. Aunt Meg turned and looked at her husband.

"We had to try something, Meg. We couldn't just stand by and let it happen."

She laid her head on his chest.

"I know, Mike. I know."

In the distance came the sound of a car horn. It was one long blast like somebody was leaning on it. They looked down the road at the fleeting taillights of Austin's car. Suddenly, he crossed into the oncoming lane and came to an abrupt stop against the guard rail on the shoulder of the road. The horn stopped and the dust rushed around the taillights making them flicker red.

"Oh my God," Meg said, and they ran down the road.

The car sat at an angle where it had crossed the road and stopped against the metal guard rails facing the sea. They couldn't see anybody in the car as they approached, and Holden thought that maybe Austin was slumped over in front from the impact. Uncle Mike grabbed the door handle and tore it open. Sea water poured out of the car and small specimens of ocean life flapped and struggled on the ground. There was no sign of Austin.

In the days that followed, life slowly returned to normal. Police had investigated Austin's disappearance, assuming the impact from the accident had tossed him from the car and over the guard railing to the sea. His body was never recovered, but that didn't seem unusual after a fall from the steep cliffs into the pounding surf. The case was closed with the passage of time instead of a solution and there was little more that could be done.

It was a slow weekday afternoon some months after the incident as Holden sat alone at the kitchen table, staring off into space. Meg walked up to him and pulled an envelope from her apron and sat it on the table.

"Don't ever let your father see this."

Holden looked up at her quizzically.

"I found it in the bureau drawer where Austin had put some things."

Holden didn't look at it. Meg picked it back up, opened the letter and took it out. She pointed it at Holden.

"How long?" Getting no answer, she continued. "I said how long have you known?"

Holden continued staring straight ahead as he spoke.

"She'd been calling me, on the beach, in my dreams, in my room. I heard her everywhere."

"You knew it was your turn?"

Holden nodded at her.

"And that's why you invited him?"

Meg put the letter back into the envelope.

"He never cared about me," Holden said. "You said so yourself. He never treated me like a brother or even a friend. Not even after Sammy."

Meg closed her eyes and sighed.

"He said he'd rather be dead," Holden continued, "than living the way he does."

Meg opened her eyes and looked at her son in shock. Mike stepped into the room and seeing the two of them, he kept his distance in the doorway.

"Are we okay?" he said.

Meg turned to her husband.

"We're fine. Holden was just saying. . ." She couldn't finish and turned away. Mike looked at his son.

"I was just saying how much I'll miss Austin," Holden answered.

Mike nodded sadly and walked back out of the room. Meg took the letter in both hands and slowly started tearing it into pieces. She dropped the scraps on the table next to Holden and followed her husband out into the restaurant.

For this final short, and I mean short, I must openly admit I'm old and sometimes ornery. I saw a call for true stories for a book called Chicken Soup for the Grandparents Soul. *It was good pay for a little work if you had a tale to tell. No fiction was allowed. So, I decided to jump in.*

I wanted to close the collection with a little humor. What happens is a different take on the Tooth Fairy tale. If you were my granddaughter, you would understand just how dark this story is, especially to a child.

PAPA'S ARMS

A True Story

"White lies always introduce others of a darker complexion."
—William S. Paley

MY GRANDDAUGHTER, LILITH, had reached that scary but important age when her baby teeth were beginning to loosen and fall out. As one would expect, it frightened her. She would try to hide the fact that she had a loose tooth, not wanting anyone to touch it to see how loose it was or, even worse, attempt to pull it out. No amount of sweet talk about how it wouldn't hurt, or we just wanted to look at it to see how loose it was and definitely wouldn't pull it out would make her open her mouth to let us see. No stories concerning the beautiful Tooth Fairy coming by at night when she was asleep and exchanging teeth for money could get her to let us look. In the beginning, each loose tooth was a deeply traumatic experience for her.

Eventually she became used to the process, accepting it as a natural part of growing up from a toddler to a little girl and, in fact, began to look forward to both it and the coins that showed up beneath her pillow. She would proudly display the hole from each missing tooth like a badge of honor about how brave she had been pulling out a loosened tooth.

Half of the time they came out while she slept, brushed her teeth, or was chewing food. But that didn't stop her from showing friends and family alike the "massive" hole between her teeth and telling the story of the entire operation that had taken place to remove it. That segue, from childhood to grown-up, which this dropping of teeth represented, never left her mind.

One day, after she had pretty much passed through that childhood phase, we were standing next to each other, and I noticed her looking at my arm.

"You see how my arms are longer than yours?" I asked her.

"Yes," she said.

"That's because these are my grownup arms."

She looked down at her arms.

"Stick your arm out straight," I said, and she did.

I knelt down and stuck my arm out next to hers.

"See," I said. "Mine are longer."

I could see the wheels turning in her head. Little did I know that my wife had walked up behind us and was listening to this entire conversation. I stuck my other arm out straight.

"Do you know why mine are longer?"

"Because you're bigger," she said.

"You're right. I'm an adult and these are my adult arms."

Her big eyes looked from my hands to my shoulders, taking it all in.

"When you get a little bigger," I explained, "and your baby arms fall off, you'll grow adult arms like me."

She took one look at her own arm sticking out and ran off screaming. I laughed and turned around to see the scowling face of my wife.

"You're paying for the therapy," she admonished and went off shaking her head to comfort our granddaughter.

INTERVIEW WITH THE AUTHOR

Before we dive into the interview, tell us a bit about your upcoming release.

What Fresh Hell Is This? is a collection of my Dark Tales written and published in various venues up through 2023. I've had stories in other editors' anthologies, magazines, and even a Chicken Soup for the Soul book. But they have never been collected in one place before. So, in pulling them together I also added a couple of stories that had been written during that time period but never found a home.

Tell us about your backstory and your writing journey so far. How do you think your experiences affected your career?

That's a really interesting question. I have had so many. . .different life experiences, that I feel they must have affected what I write. Some of the real-life things in my life, and this is just scraping the surface, is that I'm the son of a Detroit cop who was the sergeant in command who raided an illegal gambling joint (a blind pig) in Detroit and gave birth to the Detroit riots in the late 1960s. I went to a private Christian college in Arkansas and ended up owning and operating Dark Delicacies, with my wife, Sue, the most famous Horror book and gift store in the United States. Something sure as hell affected me. My past is as good a guess as anything.

I went to journalism school in the Army. Years later I started writing and selling short stories, all of which had some dark angle. Later I started exploring longer forms, like novels.

INTERVIEW

Was there a moment where you thought about giving up, about leaving writing behind and pursuing another career instead?

It was never either/or. But sure, when the words aren't coming or when you are halfway through a piece and you hit that famous writer's plateau where you think everything stinks and nobody would be interested. You want to quit this useless endeavor that hardly pays. But then you have another beer or go to sleep on it and keep going.

How did you respond to your very first success as an author? Was it validating or underwhelming? Did it motivate you to achieve more or put your expectations into a different perspective?

I've had several of them—When I sold my first short story, When I sold my first non-fiction article, When Jeff Gelb told me he would love to co-edit the Dark Delicacies series of anthologies, and when Joshua Bilmes from Jabberwocky Literary Agency signed me on as a client.

Those moments are all motivating. I don't know how any of them could be underwhelming. As a writer you've worked so hard to have those moments. For me I have about 30 seconds of Sally Field, "You love me. You really love me!" Then I tell my wife. But none of it is as validating or comes close to comparing to when a total stranger comes up to you and says that they read your writing and they really liked it. The reader means more to me than anything. I connected. For a brief time, the reader and I were in the same head space and we both got it. That amazes me.

Which author most influenced your early career? And who still does?

Peter Straub, Richard Matheson, Thomas Tryon, Richard Laymon, Leonard Cohen, Richard Brautigan. Each one of them (and many others) for various and sundry reasons. I don't want to forget the songwriters, the lyricists like John Prine and, oh God, all of them that can tell a story of great poignancy in such a small space. I guess that means hats off to the early Twitter designer who made all of us learn brevity.

INTERVIEW

Which story are you the proudest of, a story that managed to capture a piece of who you are or was a singular accomplishment?
It's nothing of mine I'm most proud of but all those editors who forced me to write to an idea or theme if I wanted to be in their book. That was a big hurdle for me to jump. But it made me grow as a writer. In fact, everything I write makes me grow.

Somebody else said this first, but I liked it so I stole it. Somebody asked what my favorite book or story was, and I said, the one I just finished. Then they asked what my least favorite one was. I said the one I'm currently working on.

What is your greatest challenge as a writer? Do you struggle with dialogue, endings, or something else?
I hate writing the story. I'm very slow at it and fight it the entire time. But I love the rewriting/editing part. If I could begin at the end of the first draft, I would love writing. I've heard it said that you can't fix a blank page. So true. But, man, I hate creating the story.

What's the most difficult subject matter for you to write? Is there a topic, theme, sub-genre, etc. you shy away from? Why or why not?
Anything in English, which is the only language I know. But seriously the answer would be nothing. I tend to shy away from sexual scenes. But I think I get through them fairly well. I'm not a fan of science fiction because I'm not a fan of writing about technology. In those cases, where I'm working on a canvas that is too large for me to grasp, I remember to bring it back down to the characters—not the times or the scope. The people. I think you could set something in an alligator's ass filled with people and as long as you can make the reader care about the people you can bring them into the story.

It's a bit extreme but for me it's always about people in unique situations. The reader has to care about the people, or you've lost them.

INTERVIEW

What do you do for fun and relaxation? Is it difficult to turn off the writing muse?

I don't turn off the writing muse. You can ask my wife to verify that. The other morning, I woke up with an entire prologue in my head to the novel I'm currently working on. I wrote it down so as not to lose it. At this point it is still in the manuscript.

For fun and relaxation, I do about anything. Go out to eat with my wife. Stay home and prepare a meal with my wife. Listen to music alone. Go for a drive. It's weird, but I enjoy just being alive with my wife or even on my own. But the muse never stops.

Tell us about your research process for a book. Is it online and book focused or do you get out in the field with experts? If you do consult with people, are you still friends with some of them?

All of the above. When I was writing my novel The Survival of Margaret Thomas *I needed to learn more about little people in the old west. Did they have special saddles made for them? How did they mount their horses? The Net search wasn't yielding anything when I put in Short Person Horse Mounting. Well, it was, but not the sort of thing I was looking for. There was film with it, however. But we'll need to talk about that another time.*

So I got in touch with a saddle maker in Arizona who gave me some great information that ended up making a big difference in the book. Each book or story calls for a different approach. If it is only a Horror short story I can find a lot of what I need by looking in the mirror.

Outside of actual craft, what is the most useful skill you learned from being an author?

Patience. Trust in my own inner muse to come around and not to push. That has translated over to the rest of my life and removed a lot of the anxiety and stress that used to be a part of me.

How did being an author change you as a person?

Aside from the point I just mentioned above it made me look under appearances to find the real item, whether it is a person or a situation. I used to take things as I found them. Now it is easier for me to see that there is a lot more to everything.

INTERVIEW

Which response/comment from a reader has touched you the most throughout your career?
Director Kevin Tenney (Witchboard) and I were talking, and he had this same thing happen to him. When someone would give me a compliment, I really couldn't handle it so I usually came up with some smart ass retort, like you evidently don't read much or something just as stupid on my part. One time I could see the hurt in the person's face. Not because I made a smart-ass remark, people are used to that from me, but because I was invalidating what they felt and had to say. From that point on I learned to say Thank you.

What is your life-long goal as an author?
I wish you had asked me that when I was thirty. I'm seventy-one so there's not a lot to work with here. I want to know that I affected people when they read my work. If you create something—a painting, a novel, a movie, whatever it is and people have no reaction, you have failed. They can like it or hate it but I want to move the needle. I want their blood pressure to change. If two of them read it, I want them to discuss it between them. Otherwise, I may as well be writing the weekly grocery circular.

What legacy do you want to leave behind?
I'd like to stay in print as long as Stoker and Poe have. Now that's a legacy.

THE END?

Not if you want to dive into more of Crystal Lake Publishing's Tales from the Darkest Depths!

Check out our amazing website and online store
or download our latest catalog here.
https://geni.us/CLPCatalog

We always have great new projects and content on the website to dive into, as well as a newsletter, behind the scenes options, social media platforms, our own dark fiction shared-world series and our very own webstore. Our webstore even has categories specifically for KU books, non-fiction, anthologies, and of course more novels and novellas.

ABOUT THE AUTHOR

Del Howison is an author, journalist, actor (see IMDB), and the Bram Stoker Award-winning editor of the anthology *Dark Delicacies: Original Tales of Terror and the Macabre by the World's Greatest Horror Writers*. He has written articles for Fear.net, Cemetery Dance.com., and Writers Digest Magazine among others. His western short story *The Lost Herd* was turned into the premiere (and highest rated) episode, *The Sacrifice*, for the series *Fear Itself*.

His dark western novel *The Survival of Margaret Thomas* was shortlisted for the Peacemaker Award given out by the Western Fictioneers. He has been nominated for over half a dozen awards including the Shirley Jackson Award and the Black Quill. He is the cofounder and owner (with his wife, Sue) of Dark Delicacies, a book and gift store known as "The Home of Horror," located in Burbank, California. The store has won the "Il Posto Nero" award from Italy and been inducted into the Rondo Hatton Hall of Fame.

He continues to write and publish unsettling stories.

Readers . . .

Thank you for reading *What Fresh Hell is This?* We hope you enjoyed this collection.

If you have a moment, please review *What Fresh Hell is This?* at the store where you bought it.

Help other readers by telling them why you enjoyed this book. No need to write an in-depth discussion. Even a single sentence will be greatly appreciated. Reviews go a long way to helping a book sell, and is great for an author's career. It'll also help us to continue publishing quality books.

Thank you again for taking the time to journey with Crystal Lake Publishing.

Visit our Linktree page for a list of our social media platforms.
https://linktr.ee/CrystalLakePublishing

Follow us on Amazon:

MISSION STATEMENT:

Since its founding in August 2012, Crystal Lake has quickly become one of the world's leading publishers of Dark Fiction and Horror books. In 2023, Crystal Lake officially transitioned into an entertainment company, joining several other divisions, genres, and imprints, including Torrid Waters, Crystal Lake Comics, Crystal Lake Games, Crystal Lake Kids, and many more.

While we strive to present only the highest quality fiction and entertainment, we also endeavour to support authors along their writing journey. We offer our time and experience in non-fiction projects, as well as author mentoring and services, at competitive prices.

With several Bram Stoker Award wins and many other wins and nominations (including the HWA's Specialty Press Award), Crystal Lake Publishing puts integrity, honor, and respect at the forefront of our publishing operations.

We strive for each book and outreach program we spearhead to not only entertain and touch or comment on issues that affect our readers, but also to strengthen and support the Dark Fiction field and its authors.

Not only do we find and publish authors we believe are destined for greatness, but we strive to work with men and women who endeavour to be decent human beings who care more for others than themselves, while still being hard working, driven, and passionate artists and storytellers.

Crystal Lake Publishing is and will always be a beacon of what passion and dedication, combined with overwhelming teamwork and respect, can accomplish. We endeavour to know each and every one of our readers, while building personal relationships with our authors, reviewers, bloggers, podcasters, bookstores, and libraries.

We will be as trustworthy, forthright, and transparent as any business can be, while also keeping most of the headaches away from our authors, since it's our job to solve the problems so they can stay in a creative mind. Which of course also means paying our authors.

We do not just publish books, we present to you worlds within your world, doors within your mind, from talented authors who sacrifice so much for a moment of your time.

There are some amazing small presses out there, and through collaboration and open forums we will continue to support other presses in the goal of helping authors and showing the world what quality small presses are capable of accomplishing. No one wins when a small press goes down, so we will always be there to support hardworking, legitimate presses and their authors. We don't see Crystal Lake as the best press out there, but we will always strive to be the best, strive to be the most interactive and grateful, and even blessed press around. No matter what happens over time, we will also take our mission very seriously while appreciating where we are and enjoying the journey.

What do we offer our authors that they can't do for themselves through self-publishing?

We are big supporters of self-publishing (especially hybrid publishing), if done with care, patience, and planning. However, not every author has the time or inclination to do market research, advertise, and set up book launch strategies. Although a lot of authors are successful in doing it all, strong small presses will always be there for the authors who just want to do what they do best: write.

What we offer is experience, industry knowledge, contacts and trust built up over years. And due to our strong brand and trusting fanbase, every Crystal Lake Publishing book comes with weight of respect. In time our fans begin to trust our judgment and will try a new author purely based on our support of said author.

With each launch we strive to fine-tune our approach, learn from our mistakes, and increase our reach. We continue to assure our authors that we're here for them and that we'll carry the weight of the launch and dealing with third parties while they focus on their strengths—be it writing, interviews, blogs, signings, etc.

We also offer several mentoring packages to authors that include knowledge and skills they can use in both traditional and self-publishing endeavours.

We look forward to launching many new careers.

This is what we believe in. What we stand for. This will be our legacy.

Welcome to Crystal Lake Publishing—
Where stories come alive!